Harvest

SHARON BAYLISS

Published January 2020 by Animus Ferrum Publishing
Mishawaka, Indiana
http://www.animusferrum.com/

ANIMUS FERRUM
PUBLISHING

ISBN: 978-1-948661-75-1 - ebook
ISBN: 978-1-948661-76-8 – paperback

Once again and always, for my husband--my love for all seasons.

"and the enemy who sowed them is the devil, and the harvest is the end of the age; and the reapers are angels." – Matthew 13:39

CHAPTER ONE

September, The Night of the Harvest Moon

Elena slammed on her brakes, barely missing the encroaching red eyes of taillights on the car in front of her. Her cell phone flew off the center console and into the black hole between the seats.

"Crap!" She reached into the crevice, but her hand wouldn't fit.

"In 500 feet, turn left on George Bush Avenue." The muffled voice of the GPS app on her phone continued to boss her around from under the seat.

"Shut up," she yelled at the disembodied computer voice. "I don't need your help." At least, she shouldn't need help. A witch doesn't need GPS to find a wizard. But she couldn't stay focused on her goal. Random thoughts swirled through her mind, trying to pull her away from her target. *Am I supposed to have life insurance? Do all grown-ups have life insurance? I should*

1

probably get life insurance before I do this. Wait, what is *life insurance anyway?*

Her instincts wanted to lead her astray. To the nearest life insurance office. To go buy new underwear because she couldn't remember the last time she bought underwear.

How long do most people keep their underwear?

She shook her head as if she could literally shake out the unwanted thoughts. The computer lady gave more instructions from in between the seats, and she followed them without question, trying to think as little as possible.

As a general rule, she could find summer wizards as easily as she could find a wildfire pluming black smoke for hundreds of miles. If she placed herself within a mile of his location, she could follow his light and walk directly to him.

When the computer lady declared she had reached her destination, Elena had to squeeze through the clumsily parked cars clogging the narrow street. She hadn't attempted parallel parking since she her driving test and she cursed as her wheel hopped the curb. Carlos rarely let her drive, and even if he had, he would have made her get out and direct while he did the parallel parking. Because it went without saying that his little sister could not parallel park a car. Unfortunately, the evidence in front of her supported his theory. She could picture him smirking while he shook his head at her, relishing being right.

She had thought doing this alone would make her feel like a grown-up—free and in charge of her own life. But instead, she had the worst of both worlds. She had felt so alone and small on the dark country roads, like she hurtled toward a distant planet with the nearest human light years away. But at the same time, she wasn't alone at all. Carlos's presence hung in the air, and when she looked in the rearview mirror, for an instant she thought she saw his brown eyes watching her.

She left her errant wheel on the curb and examined her surroundings. College students wandered along the streets and in the yards, most with shiny silver beer cans or red plastic cups. She pulled down her visor mirror and examined her reflection. Even under the layers of smoky eyeliner and spidery mascara she looked like a terrified child. She had on far more make-up than she felt comfortable with, but she still added another coat of mauve lipstick to fill time. She examined her teeth and nostrils and poked at her stiff eyelashes for a while. She worried she had overdone the eyebrow pencil and looked like Frida Kahlo. She had a powerful urge to drive to the nearest Walgreens and douse her face in make-up remover. She put the keys back in the ignition, but pulled them out again and threw them into her large, crowded purse where they would become immediately lost.

Her mind wanted her to leave. Every instinct she had told her to leave. But Carlos had taught her to ignore false prophecy. As a witch, her fear had real power and it could plant false instincts and even prophecies in her mind. She shouldn't trust her gut. She had to stay the course.

She shoved her hand under the seat and wiggled her fingers until she grasped her phone and dropped it into her purse. Then she reached into the back seat and rifled through random shoes and discarded coffee cups to find the handgun she had wrapped in an old towel and tucked that into her purse as well. She thought about Carlos yet again. He would disapprove of the state of her car, her handling of her weapon, and most definitely, her shirt. She looked down at her cleavage to make sure her nipples didn't show. She may not have been as strong or as smart as Carlos, but she did have some common powers he did not. She could walk into the party without question… and most people wouldn't be looking at her face.

She stepped out of the car into the stifling air of a summer that had overstayed its welcome and walked down the sidewalk, trying to act confident. Her heels clicked too loudly, but except for a few leers, no one paid attention to her. The smell of Lone Star hung in the air. Most people on this block were on their sixth or seventh drink by this point. That should help too.

Without thinking about it, she glanced at the Harvest Moon looming large above the houses, and ignored by everyone on the street. The moon had followed her as she drove, remaining in her line of sight, taunting her.

She sensed the summer magic in the air. The warm magic wafted on the breeze like distant music. Of course, more than one wizard lived in College Station, and more than one summer wizard. Not a lot… but more than one. She could feel their pull and the faint flavor of their magic. But she searched for one specific wizard. Magic was like a fingerprint. A particular wizard touched time and the universe in a unique way. And this particular wizard not only touched the universe in a specific way, but also touched her life in a specific way, even though they'd never met. He would invade her life and destroy it. She could feel it coming for her.

She no longer needed to count the house numbers on fraternity row to find the right one. He emanated a bright, pulsating light, and might as well have worn a siren on his head. She stopped. The light now moved toward her.

He stood alone on the lawn outside of the house, staring at her. He should not have seen her coming. Despite the unexpected turn, she continued toward him across the lawn, kicking aside a few discarded plastic cups. As she grew closer, her face stung as if a nasty sunburn had blossomed on her cheeks. His yellow-green eyes appeared to glow in the dark like a cat's.

"Are you Lucas Prescott?" she asked.

"Who are you?" he countered. Unfortunately, her breasts didn't distract him. And if he was drunk, it didn't appear to muddle his senses. He looked her right in the eye and clenched his fists. He lowered his head and looked as if he might pounce.

"My name is Elena," she said.

"What do you want?"

"You are Lucas Prescott?" she asked again. She felt paralyzed. The way he had waited for her, he must have sensed her presence even before she sensed his. The realization sapped her confidence. Fall magic was far subtler than summer magic. She should have been the ghost of a shadow sneaking up on a burning star who couldn't see past his own light. She felt a quiver in her stomach. She didn't have the cunning of a hunter.

"Yes, I am. Why are you asking?"

She hadn't doubted his identity, but she needed him to confirm it. She released her dark half into the air around them. No one stood near, and in the chaos of several simultaneous parties on the street, no one paid them much attention. But a cloaking spell was prudent. The darkness seeped into the air around him, clouding the vision of everyone outside the bubble. The cloak wouldn't truly obscure them, but the brains of the people around them wouldn't register them. Lucas looked to the sky behind Elena. She knew what he saw. The cloaking spell would blot out the stars and turn the moon red.

Her hands shaking, she pulled the gun out of her purse and pointed it at Lucas.

He held his hands in front of him as if they would stop

bullets. He clenched his jaw and she could see the muscles in his neck tighten.

"I'm sorry," she croaked, wishing her voice sounded stronger. Despite all of her practice shooting targets, she didn't trust her shaking hands. She wanted only one kill shot. He didn't need to suffer.

"I haven't done anything wrong," he said. "And you know it."

She pursed her lips and shook her head at him. She wanted to say, *but you will.* However, her throat felt as frozen as the rest of her body.

"You won't kill me," he said. His words seeped into her skull and wriggled into her brain—a magical command. She held her breath and focused on keeping her hands firm on the gun. He could command her to turn the gun on herself, but she had to believe she had more power than he did.

Don't be distracted by the light. It's not real power.

"I'm sorry," she said again, trying to remember why she came here in the first place. If she could summon the power and importance of this act, she could do it. Carlos had told her once she pulled the trigger, she would feel the balance return to the world.

The gun felt hot in her hands and the warmth increased until it became pain. She had resisted his magical command, but the Mundane pain of burning hands became too much to handle. Blisters erupted on her palms, and she screamed and dropped the gun.

Lucas lunged for it, and Elena did too, managing to fling the gun out of his reach and into the heavy cloak she had created. He couldn't reach the gun, but he could reach her. He pinned her down with his knee pressing into her heart. She gasped for breath. Then his hands found her neck and wouldn't let go. She kicked and flailed as white spots popped in her vision. Her lungs burned with pain, desperate for one more breath. She said a prayer and focused all of her energy on one thought... *gun in hand... gun in hand.*

The gun found its way back to her. She felt the hot metal searing into her already burned skin. She grasped the gun, and without thinking, she pointed it at Lucas's head and squeezed the trigger. The force of the shot shook her whole body and caused ripples of pain to shoot down her arm. The sound pierced the air, much louder than she had expected. It echoed in her ears, and she became afraid the cloak wouldn't hold. The dark cloud she created closed in on her.

She didn't move. She kept her eyes closed. Lucas had fallen on top of her, and she felt his warm weight, hoping she had missed, but knowing she hadn't. As long as his body remained warm, maybe it hadn't happened. Maybe he would gasp and take another breath.

She felt warmth pooling around her heart and running down her waist. Lucas's blood. She pushed him off of her and he made a wheezing sound. He lay on his back next to her, pawing at a bullet wound on the side of his neck. He wheezed again and coughed a splatter of blood.

"Oh, no," she said. "I'm sorry." She considered shooting him again between the eyes, but she couldn't. She could save him some pain, but she never wanted to fire the gun again.

She pulled his head onto her lap and stroked his sandy blond hair. "Dormirse," she said. Then realizing she spoke in Spanish, repeated herself in English. "Go to sleep."

She tried to think of why she had killed him, but that felt selfish. She had no right to feel comfort. So, instead of thinking of the evil he would commit, she thought of the good he would never do. He may not have been a good man, but he was loved. He would have had children who would now not exist. And as she stroked his hair, all that went away. His children. His life. Every moment of beauty he would have ever known. Gone at her hands.

It took him too long to die, and her face burned with tears. She heard a scream. In her grief, she had let the cloaking spell fall. She heard shouting and dropped Lucas's head back on the ground.

Her phone trilled in her pocket. She glanced at it long enough to see a photo flash on the screen, announcing the caller. The selfie she had taken with a reluctant, but smiling, Patrick on the 4th of July. She silenced his call and ran.

Emmy watched Nathan flatten the burgers on the grill with his spatula. He hummed to himself, not aware of the habit. When he caught her watching him, he smiled.

"Hungry?" he asked.

"Very." They had spent the Saturday at a primitive campsite away from the rest of the world. She sat in the camping chair in her bathing suit, waiting for the lake water to dry in the hot air. The summer had mellowed enough to remind them fall would come, but Emmy didn't feel it. Her body still felt warm and summery from Nathan's touch.

As she watched him, she tried to bottle the moment, like her mother could do with memories. She wanted to keep everything—the smell of the charcoal fire and the lake water, the gentle orange light of the setting sun, the warmth of the sunlight still radiating from her shoulders. If Heaven were like this, she wouldn't be disappointed.

The phone rang, shattering her reverie. She had almost

forgotten other people existed. They should have found a campsite farther from cell phone towers. Both their phones sat on the picnic table. Emmy had lied to her aunt and uncle about her weekend plans. She fabricated some Mundane friends and said they were going to Six Flags. Carson and Jess didn't care much about what Emmy did. They never put much work into investigating her actual whereabouts, but if evidence of her lies fell right into their lap—like if one of her cousins told on her—they would feel obligated to act. But Nathan picked up his phone.

"It's my mom," he said with a tinge of annoyance, replacing his spatula with the phone.

Not surprising. Nathan's mother called him a lot, and Nathan always picked up when she did. In the same year Emmy had lost both of her parents, Nathan's mother, Thea, had lost two of her children. Shortly after, her husband left her. And when Nathan's younger brother headed to college a few weeks ago, she really fell off the rails, drinking more and constantly needing something from Nathan.

Emmy couldn't hear Thea's words, but she could hear the agony. Although no more than an indiscernible whisper, her pain filled the entire canyon. Their paradise had gone, and Emmy automatically reached for a towel to cover herself.

Nathan looked at Emmy with his bright green eyes. He locked his gaze on her as if he grasped at the edge of a cliff. Although his face had frozen, she could see everything in his eyes. She had seen that look many times before. Someone had died.

CHAPTER TWO

September

Patrick blew his whistle at a kid who had pushed his friend into the pool, causing him to crash into a toddler, pushing her under. The toddler didn't drown, but Patrick had to jump in after her and then fill out lots of paperwork.

"I didn't do anything," the kid shouted back.

Patrick returned to the present. The other kid he would have pushed now jumped in the pool of his own accord, landing well away from the girl paddling along in pink arm floats.

"You would have," Patrick said.

The boy scrunched his nose and cocked his head and then cannonballed into the pool. Thank God the pool would close soon. The smell of chlorine and wet feet lingered in his nose, following him home. The scent found its way into his sheets and clothes, and could outlive a trip to the laundry room.

He blew his whistle again to admonish the same little girl with the floaties the moment she began to break into a run.

"Walk!"

The alarm in the girl's eyes triggered the vision. A familiar wave of panic started at his heart and settled in his stomach. His breath felt too shallow, as if the chlorine suffocated him. He took a deep breath and reminded himself he had no reason to feel terror. Although, the responsibility for twenty or so kids jammed into the tiny pool invoked some degree of terror, this fear came from elsewhere.

The smell of blood settled in the back of his throat. *Not real,* he reminded himself, although the knowledge didn't dull the panic. For the past few months, a powerful vision had plagued him—one that baffled him as much as it upset him. It came without warning and consumed all of his senses.

He saw a princess doll with auburn hair—Princess Sophia from the Disney Channel. The doll lay on a tile floor with specks of blood on her plastic cheeks.

He knew that tile. His mother had picked that tile for the master bathroom in the house she had been building with Patrick's father. She ordered the tile before she died, and for the last two years the tile has sat, wrapped in plastic, outside the unfinished house. But in the vision, the tile covered the master bathroom floor in the finished home.

The vision rolled through his head as if someone else worked the projector.

He parks his Camry in the finished brick driveway of his parents' home. He has a duffle bag with him, so he must be home from college for summer or a holiday. He opens his duffle bag and pulls out a semiautomatic pistol. He leaves the bag and walks in with nothing but the pistol. He doesn't even close the door of his car. He uses his key to enter the house without knocking or announcing himself. A bearded dragon greets him at the front door. It's Evangeline's pet, Annabel Lee. She sticks her tongue out at him and taps her claws against the tile.

His father comes in from the kitchen and smiles at Patrick. He opens his mouth to say something, but Patrick doesn't give him the chance. He shoots him. The bullet pierces the side of his ribs and he falls to the ground, still alive. He stares at Patrick with wide eyes, and Patrick shoots him again at closer range, this time straight through the heart.

He hears his sister scream, and he turns to shoot Emmy, this time hitting his mark in one try with a bullet between the eyes. Xavier appears at the top of the stairs and Patrick takes him down too. He falls down the stairs, leaving a trail of blood in his wake. He has to go upstairs for Evangeline. She's waiting for him in the hall and floods him with a wave of death that almost knocks him down, but it's not enough. Even her powerful winter magic can't match a gun. He shoots her in the neck, and then again in the head to make sure she dies quickly.

He waits, but his mother does not appear, so he steps over Evangeline's body and walks into the master bedroom. He finds his mother waiting for him. She doesn't hide or cower. She stands and looks him in the eye. He shoots her in the heart and she crumbles, reaching her hand to him as she dies.

Patrick senses another living presence in the room, one who emanates powerful magic. He sees movement under the bed and a tuft of red hair. He kneels and looks under the bed. The red hair belongs to the Princess Sophia doll, clutched by a blonde little girl, who looks about three-years-old.

"Hi," Patrick says to the girl.

"Hi," she says back.

"Close your eyes," he says.

She closes her eyes and he presses the barrel of the gun against her small head and pulls the trigger.

"Watch out," a voice said. "Someone is about to jump out

from behind you and push you into the pool."

Elena's voice broke the vision. The smell; chlorine, sunscreen, and the familiar tropical scent of Elena's shampoo replaced the rusty scent of blood. The vision usually left a stain on him for hours, lingering like a foul odor. But at the sight of Elena, the fear ebbed. She smiled, looking much like she had when he first saw her. She had her thick, dark hair pulled into a ponytail, except for one errant strand tucked behind her ear. She wore a thin white button-down shirt as a wrap, and he could see the silhouette of her black bikini underneath. Her long, tanned legs glowed in the sunlight.

"If you were going to push me in, I would have foreseen it. You don't have the guts," he teased.

"Oh, really?" She pressed her hands into his chest in a feigned attempt to push him.

"Nope." Patrick grabbed her arms behind her back while she giggled. Then he released her arms so he could kiss her. "What are you doing here? You know I can't focus while you're hanging out at the pool in a bikini."

She giggled.

"Not kidding. This is very serious. Children will die."

Patrick blew his whistle at the same punk kid who would have pushed his friend. "Get off the lane line," he shouted.

"Ouch. That was right in my ear." Elena's voice surprised him. Even though she stood right next to him, when he turned to blow the whistle, he forgot she was there—for only a second, but it disoriented him.

"Sorry," Patrick said. "How is your grandmother?"

"What?"

"Your grandmother. Isn't that who you went to see yesterday?"

"Right. Yeah, she's fine."

"What's wrong?"

She arranged her face into a glowing smile and shook her head. He reached for her hand, hoping to read her better if he touched her, but she pulled away.

"Why do you think something's wrong?" she asked.

"You have a tell."

"I do?"

"You go invisible. You really did sneak up on me. I can't feel your presence. And unless I'm looking right at you, I forget you're there. Even with the bikini… "

"I'm sorry," Elena said, offering no further explanation. Patrick felt his anxiety edging back, but now he had a reason. *She is going to break up with me.*

"I'm not going to break up with you," Elena said.

"Please don't read my mind."

"Don't be so easy to read. Seriously, don't worry about it. Just family stuff."

"Can I help?"

"No."

Patrick didn't push her. He didn't want to talk about his own weird family stuff either. He knew her better than he'd ever known anyone, but at the same time, he didn't know her at all. Since they had met and started dating two months ago, he hadn't asked the questions about her life he should have asked. He didn't want her to say, *and what about you?*

He knew her grandmother raised her in South Texas. He knew she idolized her older brother, but he sounded like a real dick. He knew she had a niece she loved very much. And he knew her niece loved unicorns because he had gone with Elena to buy her a stuffed one for her birthday. That was about it.

Elena knew Patrick's parents had died, but he never shared many details. She knew he had siblings who lived in Houston and had an older brother in jail, although he hadn't shared many details about that either.

He saw her for the first time while working on 4th of July weekend. He had taken a shift at a different city pool to help cover the holiday. If he hadn't taken the shift, he would have never crossed paths with Elena. But of course, with fall wizards, fate may not tell the whole story. Perhaps he chose that shift specifically so he would find her, even though his conscious mind didn't understand why. Or maybe she found him.

He noticed her as soon as she walked in and stared at her as she walked down the stairs and around the large pool. He could tell she was a witch, and as she got closer, he could even tell she was a fall witch. Seeing Santa Claus riding a dragon seemed more likely than seeing a beautiful fall witch walking right toward him. As far as he knew, the only other fall wizards he had ever met were his aunt and cousin.

Although he had never seen her before, the sense of familiarity overwhelmed him. The feeling of déjà vu felt so powerful, he worried that during his darker times, his freshman year when he'd had too much to drink, he might have met her, humiliated himself somehow, and didn't remember it. But no matter how much he had to drink, he would have remembered her.

She came alone, which made her different. Most girls her age ran in terrifying half-naked packs around the pool, lining up in long rows to bake the youth and beauty out of their skin. She walked right by his stand and smiled at him like she knew him too, even as if they had agreed to meet. She didn't stop to talk though. She laid her towel on the ground near his post and pulled out a book.

Asking a girl out, especially a barely clothed, beautiful fall witch, would usually lead to a panic attack. For Mundanes, it wasn't worth the hassle. But by some strange miracle, he wasn't nervous. On his break, he went right up to her and introduced himself. He asked if he could sit with her and she said yes. After they had talked for a few minutes, he asked her if she wanted to go watch the fireworks with him that night. She said yes. Asking her out was so much easier than he ever would have imagined. Perhaps he *knew* she would say yes. As if she had walked into his life right then with the sole purpose of saying yes.

Their date had been almost too amazing to be real. Of course, the literal fireworks helped. Everything he said had been the perfect thing to say. Every joke got a laugh. Her dark eyes never left him, and her smile went on and on. The only moment not Hallmark card perfect was when he leaned in to kiss her for the first time. He didn't know which one of them had fumbled it, but they both stopped mid-lean. He could feel her warm breath and he saw her glance at his lips, but she wouldn't budge.

Throughout their date, he had yet to actually touch her. Not a hand on the shoulder, or an accidental grazing of the arms. Fall wizards could read people, especially when touching. What would happen when they touched? Would she know everything about him and not like him anymore? Did she worry the same thing about herself? Did she have thoughts she didn't want him to see?

She leaned back, the entire night lost in a fog of awkwardness. He could see the future splitting in a direction that might not include Elena and he changed track. He lunged back toward her and kissed her before he could change his mind. He hoped it seemed passionate, and not like a surprise attack.

He had no reason to worry, because when their lips met, he couldn't sense her thoughts, nor did he seem to have any of his own. Nothing existed but her, and the warmth of her lips, and the feel of her thick hair twining through his fingers. He had never had a kiss so devoid of thought, self-consciousness, or fear. He could live there forever, in a place without a past or a future. With no memories or prophecies.

When he pulled away, he did it much more slowly. He could feel the kiss rippling through his body. She had her eyes closed and mouth parted as if she didn't want it to end either. He didn't need magic or visions to know Elena would be in his future.

CHAPTER THREE

October

Emmy crawled into bed and completed the last step of her bedtime routine. She grabbed a tube of SPF 50 sunscreen off her nightstand and rubbed it on her chest and neck.

"I'm sorry no one ever explained this to you… but you can't get a sunburn inside… at night," Lacie said.

Emmy had thought her cousin was asleep, but lately, she didn't know if she ever slept. Lacie peeked out at Emmy from inside a cocoon of blankets. Her long, auburn hair obscured her blue eyes, but Emmy could still see her bemused expression.

"One day, you'll wake up with a sunburn, and you won't be laughing."

Lacie smiled and rolled the one brown eye Emmy could see and turned away, nestling back in for sleep. Emmy applied a new layer of Aveeno and inhaled. Her mother had had the ability to record her own memories and kept a mental store of all of her happiest moments. Whenever she wanted, she could pull one out and relive it again, and she could even invite others to join her. And the experience felt so real. To demonstrate the skill, one day her mother had taken her back in time to their trip to Disneyland. When she saw the castle, she felt the same pure joy and excitement she had experienced as a six-year-old. She had forgotten how simple and happy things could feel as a child, but it came back with perfect clarity. And she could feel her father's hand in hers, and she could smell freshly baked waffle cones.

Emmy also had this skill, but unlike her mother, she sucked at it. She had saved the memory from the weekend at Canyon Lake with Nathan. They had sat by the campfire, watching the crackling flames, and he just held her. The light of the fire and the stars seemed like the only light in the world. And no sounds except the crackling fire, the crickets, and Nathan's gentle breathing.

She had thought she had put that memory in a perfect capsule in her mind, so she could dive back in, like throwing herself into the warm lake itself. But it didn't work right. She couldn't sustain the immersion for more than a few seconds, and even then, it skipped and distorted like the memory was buffering. She only fully experienced the memory when her uncle Carson had grilled burgers in the backyard. The smell had worked like a turbo boost to her magic and she fell right into the memory like walking through a door.

Thus began her ritual of sunscreen at bedtime. She had worn the same sunscreen at Canyon Lake. She inhaled again and tried to conjure another memory from that weekend. Her body had felt warm and her heart pumped from a jump off a small cliff and the swim back to shore. Rocks and exposed roots covered the shore and Emmy kept stumbling. Then Nathan took her hands and pulled her up to him. She stood on tiptoes on a root and they kissed. Something about that particular kiss thrived in her memory. It had felt like happiness itself come to life in one perfect moment. She would find flickers of the memory. The smell of lake water. The warmth of sunburned skin. But she couldn't stay long enough to get to the kiss.

She glanced at her phone and read her last unanswered text to Nathan. *Wish you were here. Love you.*

Lucas's murder had gone unsolved, despite an entire party of witnesses. Some people said they had seen a girl kneeling beside him with blood on her. When asked about height, weight, race, hair color, and any other defining characteristic, they came up blank. By the end of the conversation, they would doubt whether they had seen her at all. Emmy suspected a spell, however, knowing a wizard had killed him didn't narrow the suspect pool much. Wizard or Mundane, no one had reason to murder Lucas.

Nathan's mother, alone in their big, empty house, spiraled quickly. She quit her job because she couldn't go to work. She couldn't pay the mortgage, so she moved into Nathan's apartment, where she mostly slept and drank herself to death. He had to deal with that every single day, on top of working a part-time job, and going to medical school. He didn't have much space left over for Emmy, in his home or his life. Emmy had trouble imagining a future without Nathan, but as their time apart spanned longer and longer periods, the possibility felt real.

Emmy gave up on conjuring her memory. She curled up under her covers and had made it to the edge of dreams when a sound cracked her sleep. She could see the crack as a lightning strike at the back of her eyelids—the last vestige of a dream before a sound dragged her back into reality by the toes. She sat up, wide-awake, as if hit with an electric current.

The sound that had woken her came again. Lacie had sat up in bed. Her eyes stared without seeing... or seeing something Emmy couldn't. And she screamed. Lacie's scream wasn't the shallow scream one might let loose on a roller coaster or haunted house. It came from her core; rough, dark, and unnaturally loud. Emmy's ear drums vibrated and strained. Her muscles had wound like iron coils of rope, and she wouldn't fall asleep again anytime soon.

Lacie thrashed her arms and scratched at her neck as if an invisible noose cinched around it. Her nails left red marks across her neck and chest. Emmy got out of bed and grabbed Lacie's arms to stop her. In this state, she was preternaturally loud, and also preternaturally strong. Lacie got an arm free and raked her nails across Emmy's face. Emmy winced, but wasn't deterred. Lacie was strong, but blind, continuing to stare with dead eyes. Emmy got behind her and grabbed her arms again, digging her knee into her back. She pulled her off the bed and she fell with a thump. She might have to add bruises to the unexplained scratches she'd have to deal with tomorrow. She kicked her leg and it hit the nightstand, causing her chandelier lamp to fall in a crash. They made so much noise.

As Emmy dragged Lacie into the hallway, she could feel Lacie's muscles soften, which meant she was waking. Now partially conscious, Emmy took Lacie by the hand and led her down the hallway. As she did, Emmy used her free hand to bang the walls in a tribal rhythm.

When they got to Emmy's aunt and uncle's room, she slapped her hands against the door at a frantic pace, and then finished it off with a few more traditional knocks with the side of her fist. Then she added the hardest kick she could manage with bare feet. She tried to turn the knob, but it wouldn't budge.

Lacie continued looking through Emmy and not at her. Sweat soaked her shirt and hair as if Emmy had pulled her through a rainstorm. She trembled in the over-air-conditioned air, and finally sank to the ground with her back against the wall, letting her legs fold under her. She continued to shake, but now more deliberately, undulating her body back and forth as if moving to trance music Emmy couldn't hear. Emmy knocked one more time on her aunt and uncle's bedroom door and then left. She slammed her door so hard, Lacie's soccer trophies fell on top of each other in a domino effect.

Emmy crawled back into bed and pulled the comforter over her head, but sleep didn't come. She felt like she had taken an injection of caffeine in the jugular and her heart fluttered like a hummingbird. She waited, listening for a door to open. But she knew from experience, the sound wouldn't come.

After a few minutes, Emmy threw the covers off again and got out of bed, flying back out of her room and into the hall. Lacie remained curled in a ball, trembling and drenched in sweat, but her eyes had changed. She didn't look at Emmy, but she had resumed blinking. Now she wouldn't look Emmy in the eye because of humiliation, not oblivion. She cowered in the dark as if locked in a dungeon hundreds of feet underground. But she wasn't in a dungeon. She sat outside her parents' door. They slept less than ten feet away. And her older sister, Ashlynn, slept even closer, right against the wall where Lacie leaned. Her younger brother and sister only a few doors down.

Emmy hated this part of the night more than the screaming. She dreaded the deadly, empty quiet. So still. So wrong. The moment that meant her siblings and parents either couldn't hear her, or chose to ignore her. However, Emmy had deduced the former. She didn't know about Jess and Carson, but her youngest cousin, Caden, proved the "can't hear," theory. He looked for any reason to pop out of bed, and could not ignore such a clear invitation to wake up. The only explanation was that he didn't hear anything.

Lacie's arm felt cold and wet as Emmy led her back into her room. Emmy imagined she had dreamt about drowning. Paralyzed under the water, unable to move, unable to save herself, knowing death would come… the way Emmy's father had died. But of course, she could have dreamt anything. The wet came from sweat, not phantom floodwater.

Emmy led Lacie back into bed and draped the covers over her as Lacie shivered in the AC-manufactured winter of their home.

"What were you dreaming about?" Emmy asked.

Lacie didn't look at Emmy. "I don't remember."

She lied. This was the game they played. Emmy asked. Lacie lied. Emmy asked again.

"Are you sure? Do you remember any images or sounds? Even a feeling?"

"No. I don't remember."

And Lacie lied again.

"It doesn't matter," Lacie said. "It's just night terrors. It's a parasomnia—a sleep disorder." Lacie defined parasomnia for Emmy, even though she had thrown around that fancy medical term for years, and of course Emmy knew the meaning by now. Lacie's know-it-all tendencies reminded Emmy of Patrick. It must be a fall wizard thing.

A doctor had diagnosed Lacie with parasomnia at four years old. Now, twelve years later, that single doctor's appointment provided enough explanation for the family. The doctor said it was normal and nothing to worry about. Night terrors were upsetting, but not dangerous. She would grow out of it.

But she did not grow out of it. For the two years Emmy had shared a room with her, the terrors had become more frequent and intense. And over the past month, they had come *every single night*. At this rate, they would both go mad from sleep deprivation.

"They've gotten so much worse though," Emmy said.

Lacie shrugged, but her voice grew softer. "I don't know."

"I know why you have night terrors. And it's not because of parasomnia."

"You do?"

"Yes." Emmy gave an exaggerated nod. Another part of their dance. "It's probably because you're a witch. A fall witch. You see visions of things that are to come."

Lacie stared at Emmy with her eyes unfocused. After a brief silence, she said, "No... that's not it."

Emmy picked up the glass of water from Lacie's bed stand and held it up for her to see. She traced her finger through the condensation along the side, summoning a painful cold from near her elbow. She used her finger to trace the words, "I AM A WITCH," in ice along the side of the glass.

Lacie watched her politely, as if Emmy performed a practiced card trick with a toy magic kit she had bought at Walmart.

"I'm tired," Lacie said. "I'm going back to sleep. I'm sorry I woke you up."

Emmy climbed onto a chair and held the glass high over

her head to get the most force of gravity possible. As she let the glass slip from her fingers, she envisioned what she wanted. She let her mind and her inherent magic work together, allowing her will to manifest in ways she could not fully understand.

The glass hit the hardwood floor with a shatter. Instead of the glass spilling into haphazard pieces throughout the room, the shards fell in the shape of a butterfly, sparkling an iridescent pink under the soft glow of the lamp. Emmy smiled to herself, satisfied with her creation.

"What is the matter with you?" Lacie asked, with her brow furrowed. "You could have woken up the whole house."

Emmy didn't bother pointing out the ridiculousness of this claim. If they didn't wake from Lacie's inhumanly shrill screams, the sound of one breaking glass wouldn't wake them either. Lacie looked at the butterfly and her eyelids fluttered. A drop of blood slid out of her nose.

"I'm sorry," Emmy said. She grabbed the trashcan and dragged it into her butterfly, scattering the pieces.

Lacie touched her face and looked at the blood on her fingertips.

"I'll clean this up. I'm sorry," Emmy said. "Go clean yourself up."

Lacie wandered into the bathroom as instructed. Emmy ran into the hallway closet to find a dustpan so she could sweep up the glass before Lacie came back. It wouldn't take much for Lacie to forget what had happened.

When Emmy first discovered her cousins could not perceive magic, it made her crazy. Now, she expected it. Jess— she suspected Jess—had done something to her children. A spell kept them from seeing magic. Emmy envisioned it as a repellant for the brain, clogging up any holes that would allow magical knowledge to enter. It bounced right off, like water grazing off a well-sealed deck.

At first, she had fun with it. She didn't have to hide her spells. She could do as she pleased without questions. But it had become less and less fun with time. Now it felt lonely. Like that same deep dungeon Lacie lived in during her night terrors. She had lived away from her brothers and sister for too long. And Nathan. No one saw her magic anymore.

She even had moments when she wondered if she had gone crazy. Maybe the glass didn't make a butterfly. The butterfly had only existed in her mind. No ice on the side of the glass, just Emmy's fingers tracing the smooth edge, imagining she had done something she hadn't.

When she thought about all the things she had suffered because of magic, she could explain everything that had happened to her family without magic. At the end of the day, her family's problems could not have been more human. Abuse. Adultery. Rape. Drowning. Murder. Anything stranger could be explained away as mental illness or PTSD. What if she was just insane? Doing exactly what the social worker had first accused Evangeline of—creating a magical narrative to make her trauma more bearable, to add intrigue and wonder to an otherwise broken world, and to give it all a reason better than—life just sucks.

Oddly enough, sometimes she shared her feelings with Lacie. She would listen and nod, with that eerie blank stare and nonsensical responses, but she could talk to her. Emmy worried if she kept bombarding Lacie with things her brain couldn't digest, she might break her brain. But it might be good breaking—that good destruction her mother had once explained to her.

CHAPTER FOUR

November, Thanksgiving Day, Afternoon

Patrick sat in standstill traffic on 290 heading into Houston. He hadn't used the accelerator pedal in a while. He only inched forward by releasing the break. Cars boxed him in from all angles and he felt trapped. Even if he abandoned his car and ran on foot, the steep concrete walls on either side of the highway would keep him confined on this interminable asphalt prison.

He took a deep breath and closed his eyes until the person behind him honked. Magic hadn't helped him avoid this traffic. He could sometimes follow his instincts to find a better route and avoid accidents before they occurred, but today, the only way was through. Every possible route was terrible. He thought if he waited until Thanksgiving morning to travel, he would avoid the worst of it. But that hadn't worked.

Although hurricane season had ended, the Gulf of Mexico

had one last treat for them before the holidays. Rain had flowed down his windshield for most of the drive. He didn't do well in the rain. Every time he saw even the smallest amount of water accumulating on the side of the road, his chest would seize. He would feel sure the water would rise any minute and swallow his car. He used to love the sound of rain, but now it drummed into his brain like nails. And his heart beat at the same frantic pace as the rain falling.

With his foot on the brake again, he checked his phone. He only saw his own unanswered text to Emmy. *Stuck in traffic, but yes, I am still coming. ETA 12:12 p.m.*

Patrick had recently made several promises to Emmy he had broken—or the same promise, on multiple occasions. He promised to come home on spring break, and he didn't. Then Memorial Day weekend. Then on the 4th of July. Now he promised to come home for Thanksgiving, and he actually had. But perhaps he had cried wolf too many times because she had ignored his texts and calls for a week.

He had his reasons for avoiding her, but he couldn't explain them to her. He had already caused the death of his parents. Even if his visions meant nothing—and even though he would never slaughter his family members—he thought it better to be safe than sorry. However, ignoring his family hadn't made his visions go away. They had only gotten worse.

His text to Xavier had also gone unanswered. *Coming to dinner?* he had asked. Xavier's relationship with the Oppenheimer family was… complicated. But he usually spent holidays there, if at least because that's where Patrick and Emmy would be. *Working tomorrow? If not, want to grab a beer?* Patrick added question two and three to his first unanswered question, then the traffic inched forward and he put his phone down. Patrick's relationship with Xavier was also…

complicated. He had never said it aloud, but Xavier blamed Patrick for their parents' death. Which was fair, because Patrick *had* been to blame. Since Xavier worked nights, he was probably asleep.

When the traffic flow froze again, he texted Elena.

Made it to Houston.

Unlike his siblings, her reply came back with supernatural promptness, as if she had already started the reply before she actually got the text.

*Have fun! Love you! *Kissy face emoticon**

A flash of lightning streaked across the sky in front of him and he clenched his jaw as if he expected it to strike him down. At the same moment the lightning flashed, an image of a red circle flashed in his mind, as clear and sudden as the lightning strike. The red lingered in his mind, and he thought he saw a few drops of blood hit his windshield along with the rain. The windshield wipers immediately pushed away the drop, leaving only a faint rusty streak.

Blood is not falling from the sky, he reminded himself. The odd red circle continued to hover behind his eyelids with every blink.

When Patrick pulled off the highway, he checked his phone again for any text replies, but the phone went dark when he touched it.

"Fuck," he muttered. He felt around for his car charger, but he couldn't find it in the center console where it belonged. He idly wondered if some light leaning wizards could charge their own phones. However, even if they could, Patrick's magic didn't work like that. He would probably make the phone deader.

Patrick watched the Oppenheimer's familiar neighborhood pop up around him. The grief hit him harder than he had expected. He had felt so much pain, grief, and guilt among these houses that it stayed here in a bubble around the neighborhood like a pain time capsule. He walked into the same crushing depression he remembered from the six months after his parents died. The visions had only provided an excuse. He didn't want to come home because he didn't want to feel this way again.

The Oppenheimers had an overtly ordinary home. In this neighborhood, about every third house had the exact same floor plan with only minor changes in outside coloring to trick the eye into thinking each house had some distinct character. Most people wouldn't feel anything looking at this house, but Patrick felt like he had walked through a portal into the darkest time in his life.

If anything, the reminder of his grief gave him some indication that he did feel better now. When he lived here, an invisible weight crushed him. He could barely lift his head. A sickening dread had accompanied this normal lawn, normal driveway, and normal young tree. He remembered seeing them on the way home from his parents' funeral and was unable to imagine any future after walking through the door. For a man preoccupied with the future, this felt like death. Life would stop. He would exist, but he wouldn't live.

He snapped out of it enough to apply to colleges and finish his senior year. But he never felt at home in his life. He had no home anymore. He wandered day to day through a mysterious reality that never should have been. In college, he had fewer reminders of his parents, and in time, life settled around him into something that felt real. But he never snapped out of it completely.

Until he met Elena. In a simple way, she changed his perspective. He could see a future with her—literally. He saw a life. A mostly happy one. The fact that he had a whole life ahead of him should have been obvious before he met her, but he hadn't seen it. She had made it real. She was a piece of his future he could hold and touch in the present.

When Patrick got out of his car, he could feel the wrongness before he could see it. He sensed a gaping absence surrounding the house. It didn't take a skilled wizard to notice this. Hell, even a Mundane could probably feel some energy radiating from the Oppenheimer home at one point. Powerful wizards filled home, and the repression of their magic made it even more glaring—a time bomb of pulsating magic.

Patrick heard a friendly meow and looked down. At least one family member would greet him. The Oppenheimers had an un-witch-like white cat with long hair. The girls had named her Elsa after the famous Disney character. They used to have Anna too, but she had disappeared. He scratched Elsa behind the ears, and she purred loudly, sending vibrations into his hands.

He walked around the bushes toward the front door, and Elsa nearly tripped him as she jumped in front of him, excited about the opportunity to go inside, as if he had just returned from a long vacation.

He stopped in his tracks at the end of the walkway to the door. The image blurred in his vision. He blinked rapidly to focus. He had recently seen phantom blood falling from the sky. He couldn't trust his eyes.

He reached for the door and touched it. When he pulled his hand away, he saw the red on his fingertips. Then he knew it was real. Someone had painted a red circle on the Oppenheimer's front door.

CHAPTER FIVE

October, The Hunter's Moon

The next night, Emmy woke with the same urgency as the night before. However, a scream hadn't woken her. Instead, the silence had roused her. That might not make sense, but that's how she felt. The silence seemed too loud.

Lacie's bed was empty.

Emmy left her room and tiptoed down the stairs. She prepared to open the front door as quietly as possible, then she remembered she didn't have to be quiet. Old habits died hard. She opened the heavy latches and pushed open the door with an unbridled creak.

About a month ago, the family noticed mud tracks up the stairs one morning. They blamed the cat, which only made sense if the cat could shape-shift and leave human footprints. Emmy followed Lacie on her nighttime "walks," whenever she could. Someone had to keep an eye on her.

The full moon bathed the front yard in cool blue light. The shadows stretched across the yard, creating grotesque mirrors of the lawn furniture. Emmy had a feeling of de ja vu. Emmy had followed Lacie out several times now. Had it always been the full moon? She remembered the shadows of the moonlight looking the same.

She rubbed goose bumps on her arms. Was Lacie a werewolf? She smiled at herself as soon as she thought it. Wizards were real, so werewolves could be real. But she had never seen Lacie sprout any extra hair or slaughter small animals on her nighttime escapades. But it couldn't be a coincidence.

Lacie stood in the middle of the cul-de-sac, barefoot and staring at the moon. The moonlight shimmered on her hair and turned her skin a cool blue. The moonlight also illuminated the sparkles of broken glass on the asphalt and Emmy winced, worried about Lacie's bare feet.

Then the light changed. The light glinting on the glass came from a lower angle. Headlights.

Shit.

One of the neighbors was coming home late. And if they came home at 2a.m., they weren't sober. Emmy suspected the fat asshole two doors down who washed his car shirtless three or four times a week.

Emmy dashed into the road, jumping over the glass like Indiana Jones avoiding traps. She grabbed Lacie's clammy hand at the same moment the headlights blinded them. The pick-up truck squealed to a stop. Emmy braced for impact, but it didn't come. Drunk or not, he slowed enough to stop before hitting them.

After an odd pause, Lacie screamed. The scream came too

long after the car stopped.

"Shh… " Emmy said, pulling her back toward the lawn.

"I don't want to," Lacie said. "I don't like it."

"What?" Emmy asked.

"What the hell are you girls doing?" asked the car-washing asshole Emmy had suspected. He had a slight slur to his question and gave them nothing more than a red-eyed glare before turning into his own driveway.

The next night, Emmy woke to the sound of frantic scratching. Lacie had stayed inside tonight, but she wasn't asleep. In the darkness, Emmy's vision took time to focus, and even then, what she saw didn't make sense.

Emmy turned on the light and Lacie shuddered, holding her hands up to shield the light from her eyes and practically hissed at her. *So… a werewolf or a vampire? Or some kind of combo?* A rusty red color covered her hands and Emmy's stomach flipped, thinking blood. But the "blood" shimmered. Bronzer? All over her hands and smudged on her arms and swiped across her face. She had created a giant rust colored circle on the wall. She turned away from Emmy and continued filling in the circle, rubbing and rubbing.

"Lacie?"

She ignored her.

"Lacie?"

"I'm almost done. Leave me alone."

Emmy watched her, transfixed. The circle had perfect proportions, and Lacie worked on any uneven edges, stepping back to check it for balance. Emmy felt unhappy butterflies flutter in her stomach. This felt wrong.

"Just go back to sleep," Lacie said, still working on her mural.

"Why?" Emmy asked, unable to articulate her many questions.

"It's cloudy."

"What?"

"I couldn't see the moon," Lacie said, as if she explained something painfully obvious. She used a ruddy finger to wipe a tear from her eye, leaving a strange streak of battle paint across her cheek.

"Okay," Emmy said evenly.

"I can't see without the moon. I can't see what's going to happen next."

She stopped and put both hands on her mural. Lacie had re-created the moon in her bedroom.

"I understand," Emmy said.

That wasn't strictly true. But she understood more than Lacie knew. She knew Lacie was a fall witch. She knew fall wizards could see the future... at least in a way. She didn't know what the moon had to do with it, but she understood what Lacie meant. Whether she knew she was a witch or not, she could see the future, and she knew it.

CHAPTER SIX

November

On the Saturday before Thanksgiving, Emmy wandered down the stairs after sleeping late. Her parents had not approved of her sleeping past ten. "You're sleeping your life away," her mother would say. But the Oppenheimers didn't care, or didn't notice. If Emmy was alive and accounted for, they had succeeded as her legal guardians for another day. She might have stayed in bed longer, but she had to eat something eventually.

When she reached the bottom step, she froze. She heard one of the most recognizable sounds of fall; a football game. She considered her options. If she used an obscuring spell, she could try to slip into the kitchen unnoticed. But if she did get caught, she would lose the rest of her day. She considered going back upstairs and scaling the side of the house to escape that way.

Even Mundane men believed they could impact the results of a football game. By wearing a lucky shirt. Watching or not watching the game. Having certain company. Wizards were worse. Emmy wasn't sure if Carson could actually impact the results of the Texas A&M v. Alabama game, but he thought it possible.

Last season, Carson decided watching the games caused the Aggies to lose, so he made Jess watch them while he hovered in the hallway demanding updates. Afraid to somehow break the spell, he shouted away anyone else who tried to pass through the area. Unless A&M happened to score when they walked by, in which case, Carson would confine them to that spot until the end of the game.

During a game, the air felt like it might crack from the strain of all the magic. Sometimes she could hear it, a straining cracking like ice under too much weight. Although, if he did use magic to impact the outcome of the game, why didn't it work? If he wanted them to win, wouldn't they just win? And then what would be the point of sports at all? Unless other wizards cast spells for Mississippi State, and the real game for wizards was to see which magical fans cast the better spells for their team.

Emmy risked the walk through the living room to the kitchen. She cast a shroud over herself and vowed not to make eye contact with anyone. However, although she kept her head down, she noticed an unexpected sight out of the corner of her vision.

The Aggie game played on the television, and anxious magic pulsed in the air, but Carson wasn't on the couch. He and Jess sat in the loveseat that faced away from the TV, huddled over the laptop. They looked like two teenagers watching porn and hoping to not get caught. Distracted,

Emmy must have let her shroud fall, because Carson looked up suddenly. When he saw her, he shut the laptop.

"Look who's up," he said. "Sleep well?"

"No," Emmy said.

"Hmmm," he replied. He got up with the laptop and Jess followed him.

"We had pancakes, but I've already put away the leftovers," Jess said, the buzzing intensity in her eyes a stark contrast to her easy tone. "They are wrapped in foil in the fridge. You'll just have to heat them back up."

"Okay," Emmy said.

Without any other explanation, they left the game on and went up the stairs. Forgetting about her hunger, Emmy paused a moment and then followed them up the stairs. She darted into the bathroom of the boys' room, only one wall away from Carson and Jess's bedroom. She sat next to an Iron Man action figure with his arms and legs ripped off and replaced with Legos attached with Play-Doh.

She had improved her focusing spell. At least that's how she thought of it. No one had taught her this spell or given it a name. She figured it out herself. She could obscure sound with a muffling spell, so she had worked on using the spell in the opposite way. Instead of adding invisible fuzz to the air, she stripped it away, while focusing on a single sound, gradually whittling away every other sound. Even her breathing and heartbeat. She felt like she died a little bit, even though she knew her heart continued to beat, she couldn't hear or feel it.

For a while, they didn't say anything, and Emmy wondered if she missed the conversation. Finally, she heard Jess sniff. Crying or allergies, she couldn't tell.

"If something bad was going to happen, you would know. We would have noticed," Carson said.

"You're not listening to me," Jess said. "This *is* happening. Now. It's already happening. It happened to Madeline Foster."

"It's an old, *old* ritual, Jess. People don't do that anymore."

"Come up with all of the excuses you want. This. Is. Happening."

"You don't know that for sure. I am not going to tear apart my life because of a wild guess."

"I never said I was guessing," Jess said with a wild shrill in her voice. "Sometimes I think this damn cloaking spell is working on you too. It's making you stupid." After a pause, Jess said more quietly, "I'm sorry. I don't think you're stupid. I know it's hard to accept that something this horrible could be real."

"I know it's real. That's why I live a lie every day of my life. And now you're telling me that not even that was enough."

"It's different now than when we were young. Worse. I don't know why."

"Well, you should know why. They are your people."

Jess didn't reply, but Emmy winced anyway. She had gotten a whiff of Jess's fury. "How dare you?" Jess finally said with a hint of a growl. "You and the kids are my people. The only people that matter to me."

A loud knock shook Emmy's concentration. She automatically glanced up at the bathroom door, but the knock had come from the other side of the wall, on Carson and Jess's door. Emmy heard Ashlynn's tinny voice in their room, but not clearly. The spell had broken.

Emmy ran back into her own bedroom and wiggled the mouse of the desktop computer until it flashed to life. She brought up Google and entered Madeline Foster. The first search didn't give her much, just Facebook and Linked In profiles for the many women in the world named Madeline Foster. She tried Madeline Foster Houston and the first few searches came up with the same news story on different outlets. A recent story, with a photo of a smiling little family in their Christmas card photo. The headline read, *Family of Four Brutally Murdered.*

CHAPTER SEVEN

November, Thanksgiving Day, Afternoon

Elsa meowed at Patrick impatiently while he stared at the red on his hand. Blood would look darker, especially after it had dried. He smelled it. Spray paint. But that didn't make it much less unnerving. Now he really accepted the house was empty. There were no wizards in this house. Or no *living* wizards in this house.

He skipped knocking or ringing the doorbell and pulled out his key to open the door.

"Hello?" His voice came out quiet and wheezy, so he tried again. "Hello?" he bellowed.

He waited for some response and none came.

He stood in the doorway and took in the house. He had expected the smell of roasted turkey and caramelized onions, but found only empty air. The house remained illuminated with lights on all over the house. The fan whirred in the living room, Legos cluttered the hallway, and a transformer stood sentinel on the stairway. Jess and Carson always made the kids clean up before they went anywhere. Always. The house felt cold too. If they had left, they would have turned down the air conditioner to save electricity.

Elsa meowed incessantly. Without knowing what else to do, Patrick obediently followed Elsa to the kitchen and filled her empty bowl with cat food. They wouldn't leave Elsa. Elsa munched while Patrick stood frozen in the kitchen.

He had the absurd idea he might have gotten the day wrong. He pulled out his phone, and then remembered he had no charge. He pulled out the phone charger from his bag and plugged his phone into the kitchen socket and then headed for the stairs.

He tried out various theories in his head. *They thought I wasn't coming and decided to go out of town for Thanksgiving break. They had so little faith I would arrive; they didn't think they needed to tell me.*

Walking up the stairs reminded him of his vision. He could see Xavier's image at the top. But of course, he wasn't there, and his vision hadn't taken place in this house. His legs felt heavy as he walked up the stairs.

He went into the room Emmy and Lacie shared. His heart jumped when he saw another red circle. Although, on second glance he saw this one appeared more orange than red and the middle had been filled in. It looked like a planet. Burnt orange fingerprints scattered the rest of the wall and doorframes. In the bathroom, orange tinted water puddled around the sink and on the hand towel.

Patrick went back into the bathroom and leaned over the toilet, thinking he might throw up. He didn't know what had happened, but that didn't stop it from feeling like his fault. He should have come home sooner.

He went back downstairs and grabbed his phone, now at ten percent power, and double-checked the date. Thursday, November 23rd, labeled with the descriptor *Thanksgiving Day (U.S.)*. The little green bubble for text messages continued to sit empty with no red notification of a missed text.

He didn't see much point in trying to call again, so he scrolled through his contacts until he found Heartsong Academy. He pressed call.

A man with a Chinese accent answered. "Cheng Dynasty. May I take your order?"

"My name is Patrick Vandergraff. I'm calling to speak with Evangeline Vandergraff. Code word sparrow."

"Hold please."

Patrick listened to the Chinese restaurant background music while on hold. Someone overhearing the conversation wouldn't make much sense of it. He didn't call Evangeline as much as he should, but he knew the drill. Heartsong Academy was a heavily guarded "school" for disturbed young wizards. Evangeline had lived there for two years. They touted their high security in the pretense of keeping the students safe, but it had far more to do with keeping the world safe from the students. One couldn't find the school unless they had been invited and arrived exactly at the scheduled time, and every time one called they heard a different greeting. Patrick had seen the bills the Oppenheimers paid to keep Evangeline far away from them, and they always came from something else. One month a car repair shop. Then a plastic surgeon. Later a catering bill. Only the amount and the account number stayed the same so the client could confirm where the bill came from.

A different woman without a Chinese accent came on the line.

"How can I help you?"

He repeated himself. "My name is Patrick Vandergraff. I'm calling to speak with Evangeline Vandergraff. Code word sparrow."

"I'm sorry sir, I cannot confirm or deny the existence of that resident."

"I'm her brother. I'm on the list. Patrick Vandergraff. Code word sparrow."

"Once again. I'm afraid that I can't confirm or deny the existence of that resident."

"I don't need you to confirm her existence. I know she exists. I just need to talk to her." At this point, he would have appreciated a simple confirmation of her existence. "Actually, I don't need to talk to her. I just want to confirm that she's there and she's safe."

"I'm sorry, sir. I cannot help you."

The woman hung up, and Patrick cursed under his breath. *What the hell?* He was on the goddamn list. He'd called before. Unless someone had removed his name.

He tried calling back and heard a different man's voice on the line this time. "You've reached Southern Star Wireless customer service. How can I make your day better?"

Patrick hung up. He didn't feel like talking in circles again.

CHAPTER EIGHT

The Cold Moon, two years ago

Emmy didn't know how it had started. A look. A few catty words. Maybe even less. An unspoken thought. A whiff of angry magic thrown in Evangeline's direction. It didn't matter. Evangeline had been like a dam full of cracks. A gentle breeze could have caused her to break.

Emmy didn't know what caused the final break. She only saw the breaking. Of all the dark memories she had, she hated this one the most. Not because anything bad had actually happened, but because she felt certain she would die. Perhaps she did. In any case, she touched death. Looked it right in the face. And she would do anything to avoid feeling that way again.

She had lay on the couch staring up at the fan. Perhaps it had mesmerized her somehow, because it took a while before she realized how disoriented she had become. The fan moved clockwise and counterclockwise at once. Then with every spin, the lights appeared to flicker. The darkness that seeped into the room was unlike normal darkness. As opposed to simply the absence of light, this darkness was its own entity.

She sat up quickly then, suddenly drenched in sweat. Her heart raced, thrumming at irregular rhythms. Her mouth tasted like rust.

She tried to stand, but the world seemed to lean. With a jab in the gut, she realized the world didn't *seem* to lean. It did lean. The flat screen TV keeled forward and hit the ground in slow motion. Then the ground shifted under her, causing her stomach to jump like a sudden drop in an elevator. She screamed. At least she thought she did. Her ears rang, and the sustained squeal muted all other sounds. Her eyes burned and watered. She wiped the moisture from her eyes, expecting blood, but found only tears.

The world lurched again and the light bulbs in the fan above her shattered, so completely the glass became dust. A gentle snowfall of glass dust fell into her hair and on her shoulders. The darkness thickened. She could only see brief pulses of light. Again, more than simply an absence of light, but a creature. A demon. She feared to breathe, lest the darkness be inside her.

She could only think of two explanations for why the brightly lit day would go dark. Either the sun was dying, or *she* was dying. Synapses popping out one by one until nothing remained but her and the darkness. Either way, she felt certain she would die. She had felt fear many times, but never with such urgency.

Clutching anything she could touch, she left her bedroom, and felt her way down the hallway. Between pulses of dark, she saw the drywall splitting in long cracks as if the whole house would cleave in two. Drywall dust filled the air, obscuring even the fading moments of light.

Ashlynn and her younger brother stood in the hallway. She would have expected them to cry or scream. Or cower. But they didn't. They stood motionless, their eyes pale blue orbs, seeing nothing. Emmy screamed again, her lungs burning from the effort. They didn't move. She saw Ashlynn's eyelids flutter. Then a thin line of blood fell from one of her nostrils.

"Ashlynn," Emmy said. She touched her arm and then dropped it. Her arms felt clammy, like eels rubbing against her legs in the deep ocean.

"Xavier," Emmy yelled. She didn't know why she had chosen his name to scream. Somehow in her panic, Xavier meant safety.

No one came.

She moved further through the gloom. She scratched at her arms, certain her skin had peeled away. Her breaths grew too shallow. Time was up. She was dying.

Then the darkness emerged from the end of the hallway. Death, here to take her. It moved toward her and Emmy thrust herself into the wall. Anything to avoid the dark cloud. But the cloud didn't come for her, it passed her, moving down the stairs. When the cloud passed, Emmy saw that the darkness was her sister, Evangeline.

Jess followed the cloud. She said something to Emmy, maybe, "Go back to your room." But the raspy words caught and shuddered on every other syllable, as if Jess were a demon too.

The darkness lifted and Emmy couldn't remember why she had expected to die only moments ago. However, she couldn't find relief. The darkness could come back any time. And she would do anything to stop it; a thought that continued to haunt her.

As the terror ebbed, she heard Xavier's voice, and her panic spiked again. "Help me," he shouted.

Emmy ran towards his voice and found him kneeling over Lacie. Her eyes had turned white and she convulsed on the ground, her arms and legs thrashing. Her leg swung into the edge of the table and Emmy thought she could hear a bone crack. Xavier managed to grab her arm, but it didn't do much to help. Blood trickled from Lacie's ear and it splattered on her neck as she thrashed.

As terrible as the scene before her was, the world refocused into normalcy. But the damage remained. Cracks in the walls. Shattered glass. Water sprayed from a broken faucet in the bathroom. If the sun didn't shine so brightly through the windows, she might have thought tornado. Earthquake maybe. But in Texas? Even Evangeline couldn't be this powerful. But maybe Emmy didn't understand what dark magic could do. Destruction, sure. But this?

Carson appeared behind Emmy and shoved Xavier aside. "Don't touch her," he growled.

"He's just trying to help," Emmy said.

"Call 9-1-1," Carson said as he tried to use his weight to calm his daughter's flailing limbs.

CHAPTER NINE

November, Thanksgiving Day, Afternoon

Patrick wouldn't be able to relax until he talked to another wizard. Any other wizard. Or at least, confirm someone he knew still existed. He thought of Elena first, but he wasn't ready to bring her into this… whatever this was. And she couldn't help. The second person he thought of might actually know something useful.

"Patrick?"

He nearly dropped the phone at the sound of her voice. After all of the dead air he had heard recently, he hadn't expected to hear a voice on the other line.

"Samantha?"

"Why do you sound so surprised? You're the one who called me." She laughed. "Did you butt dial me?"

A man said something in the background.

"I'm sorry. No, I called you on purpose."

49

"What's up?"

Her voice sounded light and carefree. He should hang up now before he found a way to poison her life again.

"I'm not sure, really," he said. "It's just… everyone is gone. You're the first person who was not gone."

That probably hadn't made sense. Samantha stayed silent on the line for a few seconds. "I don't understand. Are you okay?"

"I came home from school to visit Emmy and Xavier, and they're not here. Neither are my aunt and uncle or cousins. It's like they all disappeared."

"What do you mean?"

"As far as I can tell, they took nothing with them and drove away. And there was a red circle on their door."

Patrick held the phone away from his ear as a loud clattering noise reverberated through the phone. When Samantha came back on the line she said, "I dropped the phone."

In the background, he heard the man ask, "What's wrong?"

"Just give me a minute, please," she said to the man. "I'll tell you when I'm off the phone." She spoke back into the receiver. "Hang on."

A door closed. He could hear her breathing on the other line.

"Did you say there was a red circle on their door?" she asked in a whisper.

"Yes. What does that mean?" His heart pummeled.

"I don't know. They never knew."

"What?"

"When Imogene was alive, she never talked to me about what happened to her family, but I looked into it after she died."

Patrick thought about Imogene often, but her name still seemed to fall from the sky. What could she have to do with this? God or fate or magic had delivered their punishment. It was over.

Please God, let it be over.

"I don't know if you ever knew this, but Imogene's family was murdered. That's how she ended up in care. Her parents and both of her brothers. Someone broke into their house one night and shot them. They just took them down one by one. Even the fucking baby. Imogene's younger brother was still in a crib when he was shot."

Patrick's throat felt frozen and he thought he might not manage to talk even if he had any idea what to say. The horrible image was too similar to his vision. He reminded himself again. *I would never kill my family. Or anyone's family. I would never kill a baby.* He didn't like how often he had to remind himself of that.

"Why… why are you telling me this?"

"The killer—or killers—didn't take anything, and they didn't leave anything. Except for a red circle on their door."

CHAPTER TEN

November, Thanksgiving Day, Morning

In the wee hours of the morning, Emmy woke again, but not in the usual way. Lacie woke her on purpose.

"Emmy. Emmy." She had grabbed her chin and wiggled it from side to side to wake her while she repeated her name over and over. Emmy blinked. All the lights were on. She rolled over to look at her phone. 3:47am.

"You have to get up," Lacie said. Lacie dropped an empty duffle bag on top of Emmy. "Dad said we're leaving in fifteen minutes, so just pack what you can."

"What?"

Emmy crawled out of bed. She sat and stared for a moment.

"Come on!" Lacie said, tugging on Emmy's arm. "We're running late."

"Late for what?"

"Don't you remember? We've got to catch a flight."

"I—"

Lacie emptied her underwear drawer into a reusable grocery bag. Ashlynn ran into the room holding one sandal.

"Where the fuck is my other shoe?" she screamed. "Lacie!"

"I don't have your shoe! Get out!" Lacie screamed back.

"You're a lying little cunt," Ashlynn replied. "I know you have it."

"Five minutes!" Carson yelled from the hallway.

Ashlynn groaned and stomped out of the room again.

Emmy stood up and tried to digest her surroundings. She felt like Scrooge in A Christmas Carol, watching a scene from her life unfold without participating. It had to be a scene from the past or future. It didn't feel like the present.

Emmy grabbed Lacie's arm. She hardly noticed, dragging Emmy along as she moved back toward her closet. "How long have you known about this vacation?" Emmy asked.

Lacie didn't reply.

Emmy's younger cousin, Madison, peeked into the room. "I can't find Elsa," she moaned.

"I'm sure Mom and Dad already took her to the kennel," Lacie said.

Madison nodded and wandered off back out into the hall wearing only one sock.

"Where are we going?" Emmy asked. She squeezed Lacie's arm harder.

"Ouch," Lacie said, shaking her off.

"Where are we going on vacation? What airline are we flying? What time is the flight? IBA or Hobby? Will it be cold or hot? Should I bring a swimsuit or ski goggles?"

Lacie paused for a moment and narrowed her eyes. Her

face turned grayish and Emmy thought she might throw up or pass out. But the look passed. She shook her head at Emmy and chuckled. "Quit being weird. Just pack."

"If you don't know the answers to my questions, that's not normal. Ask yourself why you don't know. *Think* for once."

"Emmy."

Carson had said her name calmly, but had somehow managed to infuse the single word with a flood of emotions that flowed out of him and into Emmy. Fear. Grief. Rage. Emmy released Lacie's arm.

Emmy felt her eyes grow wet. She could feel the darkness coming again. She had worked so hard to feel okay, but all the anger, and hurt, and grief stayed right at the surface. One little prick and it would all flood out.

"Come here, please," Carson said to Emmy, his voice flat and firm, the kind of simple command no one could deny. Despite all of the rage hovering around him, his voice remained calm. He had feverish, over-bright eyes and kept touching Emmy's elbow.

Emmy followed him into the hallway and into his bedroom. He closed the door behind her. He stared at his own hand on the doorknob. His shoulders looked too heavy for his body and he appeared ten years older than he had yesterday. He had somehow gone from blonde to gray in one night. Emmy didn't know if he planned to say anything or if he wanted to lock her in this room to get her out of the way.

As if he had heard some silent cue, Carson let go of the doorknob. He placed his hand on the door gingerly as if checking to see if the paint had dried. He had placed a spell on the door.

"Mark and Jenny are dead," Carson said, without looking at Emmy.

The names sounded familiar, but Emmy couldn't place them.

Carson looked at her. "My cousin and his wife," he explained hotly. "We went to their house for the 4th of July."

"Yeah, I know," Emmy lied. "They're... dead? How?"

When he spoke again, his voice shook. "And Brock... and Ava."

Emmy's throat constricted. Brock and Ava, her second cousins, were around four and six. At the 4th of July party, Brock had brought Emmy toy after toy, asking her to play. Finally, she agreed to blow bubbles for him, and he and his sister had chased the bubbles around the backyard, seeming like they had too much energy to ever sleep again.

At Emmy's parents' funeral, Ava had been only two. She had screamed and Jenny had taken her out of the sanctuary. Later, Emmy had seen her running back and forth in the foyer, playing chase with her older brother. She had bright, blonde hair tied into unruly pigtails. The frizzy effect made her head looked like it glowed with a halo.

"Car accident?" Emmy asked, although she knew better. Something much darker had come for them.

Carson shook his head. "Murder."

"Why?" Her pain and outrage couldn't fit into one word, but it felt like the best word. Children shouldn't die. And they certainly shouldn't be killed.

She didn't know them well, but that monster of grief lurking right below the surface threatened to consume her. She felt like darkness crept into the edges of her vision and she flew backwards, further away from her uncle's shadowed blue eyes.

"Liv," Emmy said, a sudden missing piece falling into her fading vision. "Mark and Jenny have three kids," Emmy said, remembering. "The older one is named Liv."

"She's fine," Carson said. "She's with Aunt JoJo."

"How did she get away?" Emmy asked.

"She didn't. They just didn't kill her."

"Why?"

"I don't know."

Emmy felt like he *did* know, but that wasn't the most important detail right now. She had lived.

"And you think we'll be next," Emmy said. "That's why we're running."

Carson nodded, a small jerk of his head like a muscle spasm. "I'm asking you… I'm *begging* you, don't make this difficult. This isn't the time to try to poke holes in Jess's spell. I just need to get them all out of the house and hidden as soon as possible. There is no time to explain magic to them and there is no lie I can tell that will make sense. Whatever I say, they'll argue and ask questions. We don't have time for that. Do you understand?"

"If you want my help, you have to tell me what's happening. If you can't figure out how to mind control me, you're going to have to use your words."

"It's the reaping," Carson said, so quiet it sounded like hissing. He stopped without further explanation.

"You know full well that I was raised without magic. I don't know what that means."

"The reaping is an ancient ritual. When the Harvest Moon is a Blood Moon, fall wizards practice human sacrifice. They think that if the Harvest Moon is red, the gods are asking for blood… and they think it's their duty to deliver."

"That sounds crazy," Emmy said.

"Of course it's fucking crazy," Carson said. She couldn't remember the last time she had heard him curse. If ever. "Fall wizards are fucking crazy."

Emmy didn't remind Carson he had married one.

"But the thing is… fall wizards don't do that anymore," he said. "This is old, old magic. There are always some fringe groups that still practice the reaping, but it's never… like this. Wizards have been being slaughtered all across the south ever since the Harvest Moon. And it doesn't seem to be stopping. Jess thinks it might go on until the Cold Moon in December, but as far as she knows, it's supposed to only last one night, the night of the Harvest Moon. So, I can't explain what's going on, Emmy. I just know wizards are being murdered. First the Fosters, and now… Mark and Jenny." His voice broke on their names. "And we've been watching the news. Murders are happening everywhere. We can't say for sure if they've all been wizards, but all of these murders are really similar. Whole families of people being killed for no apparent reason."

"It tastes like blood," Lacie said. "Why am I green?"

Carson went pale and looked behind Emmy. Lacie had not only opened the door, but also come inside, and stood right behind Emmy. Lacie had not only broken through her father's spell, but also created one of her own, walking right into her father's line of sight but remaining invisible.

Lacie collapsed. She didn't crumble; she turned rigid and fell hard like a tree trunk against the wood floor. Then she began to convulse.

"Damn it," Carson said. He went to her and got down on his knees to hold his daughter still. He glared at Emmy as if this was her fault.

No, this is your fault. She's too smart for your spells. Too powerful.

CHAPTER ELEVEN

November, Thanksgiving Day, Afternoon

Samantha put the phone on the table and did her best to swallow her fear. She couldn't accept the truth. She was far too busy being happy—blissfully, perfectly, happy. But perhaps nothing that perfect could be real. One part of her happiness—the biggest part—was a lie. She wasn't really a mother.

Samantha reached down to tussle Sophie's tender blond curls. She loved the feeling of her hair and her skin, all so soft and new. Sophie lay on her stomach in a purple dress, kicking her little bare feet. She ignored Samantha playing with her hair, too concerned with the Doc McStuffins puzzle to pay attention to her mother. *Not* her mother.

"What is it?" Zander eyed her from across the room.

"Daddy, will you help me?" Sophie asked, even though Samantha knew she didn't need help with the puzzle she had completed hundreds of times. *Not* her father.

No, he was, because he chose to be. And he was far, far better than her real father. Sophie was lucky. Samantha was lucky.

"Not now, sweetie," Zander said. "Who was that?"

Something had shifted. Something had started that would tear apart their make-believe family. But Samantha wasn't ready. She loved their simple little life. They didn't have to worry about money because of Zander's inheritance. So he went to school at LSU and Samantha got to focus on the only thing that had ever made sense in her life— being a mom—and not just anyone's mom, Sophie's mom. Her life used to feel so small, so flat. Nothing more than survival. Sophie opened it up in exponential ways she couldn't even describe. She had been colorblind, and loving Sophie had been seeing color for the first time.

They had a small house outside of Baton Rouge with big windows that filled the rooms with light. The kitchen table and chairs were also white, as were the tiles and the walls. Nothing to get in the way of sunlight. And with the help of some magic with essential oils, the kitchen always smelled like freshly peeled oranges. The house was small, but on a large lot with an expansive garden. Gardening came easily. The power of Zander's spring equinox magic made everything bloom. She couldn't kill a plant if she wanted to. Everything lived. Everything flourished.

She and Sophie spent their days in the garden. Sophie loved to eat berries right off the plant. Samantha would catch her with purple-stained lips and light scratches on her arms from the thorns and Sophie would swear she had absolutely not eaten any berries. So Samantha would chase her with the water hose while she giggled. And it was happiness.

"It was Patrick, actually."

"Patrick Vandergraff?" His eyes flicked to Sophie. "What did he want?"

"Nothing. He was looking for Emmy. Obviously, I couldn't help him."

"Is everything okay?"

"I'm sure she's fine."

Zander kneeled down next to Sophie and she handed him a puzzle piece. He pretended not to know where it went.

"Here, Daddy," she said, taking the piece back.

"You're so much better at this than I am," he said.

Samantha turned back to the onions and herbs she had been chopping. Moments ago, she had been humming to herself and looking forward to cooking her first Thanksgiving meal for her family. They were having stuffed peppers instead of stuffed turkey, but the kitchen was as warm and filled as any meat eater.

"Do you have any idea yet… what she might be?" Samantha asked, trying to sound casual.

Zander glanced up at her from his spot on the floor, now more helpfully putting together an edge piece.

"You were the one who told me you can't determine a child's magical season. At least not until they are around eleven or twelve," he said, bringing his gaze back down to the puzzle. "But it doesn't matter… right?" he asked.

"Sometimes you can tell earlier if the child is really powerful or if they are near a solstice or equinox."

"Can I have juice?" Sophie asked.

"No, you just had some," Samantha said.

"Daddy, can I have juice?" Sophie asked.

Zander gave her a playful glare and she giggled in anticipation before he tickled her side. "You heard your mother. Now you get tickled.”

She laughed, squealing and rolling around the carpet until Zander stopped.

“You know I don’t care what she is,” Samantha said, not ready to drop the subject. *But other people might.*

“What am I, Mommy?” Sophie asked, her blue eyes now focused on Samantha.

She kept forgetting Sophie was old enough now that they couldn’t talk about her right in front of her and expect her to not understand.

“You are Mommy’s beautiful little fairy princess.”

Sophie had yet to do anything magical. Magical skills grew at the same rate of other human skills. Babies can’t walk and talk and do fractions, and they can’t do magic either. They pick it up gradually as they go along. Wizards got stronger with age until they plateaued at peak abilities in early adulthood.

Sophie’s mother was fall and her father was winter. Just like anything else written in your DNA, the child follows the parents. She could be fall or winter, or somewhere in between. But even that wasn’t certain. Caroline came from a summer family, so she could have recessive summer traits she might pass on to her daughter. Spring would be the least likely, nearly impossible.

“Fall would make the most sense. She’s probably fall,” Samantha said.

“Probably, but it doesn’t matter,” Zander said with finality.

He didn’t understand. Samantha would love her no matter what the season. If she wanted a child just like her, she would have waited to have her own. But she wanted Sophie, now and forever.

But she needed to know. She needed to know if her daughter would be hunted.

CHAPTER TWELVE

November, Thanksgiving Day, Morning

Lacie's seizure had passed and she regained consciousness. However, her eyes remained unfocused and she didn't speak. Carson scooped her up in his arms like a seven-year-old who had fallen asleep in the car on the way home. He carried her up to her room and kissed her on the head. He told her he loved her in a way that seemed too potent, as if he thought he might be saying it for the last time.

Jess had pulled Emmy into the hallway. "I need to stay with the others. I need to protect them." Jess looked off to the side, her eyes turning red. "Lacie doesn't need me like the others do. She'll be okay. In fact, she's safer without being close to such a large group of winter wizards. But I don't want her to be alone. And you… you won't attract them. You're not marked."

"Marked for what?"

"For death. Marked for death, Emmy. I'm sorry I haven't told you sooner. But it's never been this bad. The Blood Moon comes and goes. We stay inside. We keep to ourselves. We don't practice magic. And that's good enough for them. Not this year."

"Who?"

"Los Segadores."

"What?"

"Emmy, I need to ask you to do something else. Something that will be difficult for you."

"I… "

"Don't speak to Patrick. Don't try to contact him. Don't answer his phone calls. It's only for a few weeks. Just wait until after December 3rd."

"Can you explain that?"

"I know you think we don't pay attention to him, but we do. Even though he's a legal adult, we're still responsible for him. We've been watching. And he has some… dark associates. Please trust me. Just tell me you'll keep your distance. Please."

Emmy watched the Oppenheimers drive away in their Suburban. Her chest felt hot. She had begun to think of them as her family and a home she could always go back to. Of course, they never cared for her as they did their real children. Why would they? But she thought they loved her more than this. All that warm feeling of family and belonging so easily broken. And not just for Emmy, but for their real daughter, Lacie. They discarded her as soon as things became too difficult. She should have expected that, because it happened to Evangeline, and then Xavier. It might have happened to Patrick too if he hadn't moved out to go to college. Why did she think she was different?

She had been so angry with her mother for hiding magic from them, but her mother would have never chosen fear over her family. When her shield broke, she let it fall. She didn't run. She didn't abandon anyone, even though her father probably deserved it. Jess and Carson were cowards.

Lacie sat on her bed with her legs folded against her body. Emmy sat on her own bed. Jess had removed her spell from Lacie. Keeping the spell intact had become more dangerous than the alternative, but that meant Lacie needed to be removed from the family to keep her from infecting the others. Jess would keep her other children in their bubble as long as she could.

Emmy didn't know how this would work. Would the spell take time to wear off? It would be nice if Lacie suddenly knew all about magic, but Emmy doubted it would work that way. Emmy would have to explain it to her. Lacie touched a scrape on her forehead and then examined the blood on her fingers.

"Oh, I forgot you hit your head too. Do you need ice?" Emmy got off her bed and leaned over to examine her forehead. "I think you were lucky. If you had been a few inches closer to the dresser, you would probably have a dent in your skull. You went down hard." Emmy got up and went to get a wet towel to wipe off the blood. "Hang on," Emmy said. "You stepped back right after you started talking nonsense. Did you know? Did you see yourself fall?"

Lacie said nothing and continued to stare at her with her dulled blue eyes while Emmy dabbed at her wound.

"I think you're okay," Emmy said. "It's just a scratch."

"I don't feel good," Lacie said.

"Maybe I should take you to the hospital."

"Where are Mom and Dad?"

Emmy swallowed. "They left. Scared of something called Lo Sega Door… or something."

"What is that?"

"I don't really know. But your mom seems to think they won't come for us."

Lacie trembled. Emmy pulled the wet washcloth away, in case the cold made it worse.

"You're safe," Emmy said. "It's okay… I'm not going anywhere," she added, although everyone who had ever said that to her had lied. "But… when you feel better, I'd like you to go with me someplace. If what your mom and dad said is true, I'm worried about Xavier and Evangeline. I'm going to call him and see if he'll take us to Heartsong to pick up Evangeline. At least until all of this is over. Although if I'm on my own now, maybe she can just live with me. I don't know… I mean, I guess they'll come back. Your family."

"Xavier?" Lacie asked in a weak voice.

"Yeah. Is that okay?"

Lacie nodded. Lacie's question about being green had sounded absurd, but she did now look green. Emmy feared she would seize up again.

"How are you feeling now?" Emmy asked.

"Scrambled."

Emmy picked up her phone and called Xavier. The phone went right to voicemail. "He's probably asleep."

Emmy began to pack a bag of her own. "We'll drive to his apartment. If he's not there. I have a key."

CHAPTER THIRTEEN

November, Thanksgiving Day, Evening

Patrick drove to Xavier's apartment. He ran up the stairs and let out a long breath when he saw the door. Nothing. No red circle. He squeezed his shaking hands together. He had run too fast and now felt dizzy. He banged on the door. He waited a while and banged again. Then he stepped out on the railing to look for Xavier's car. He stared at the assortment of cars parked below, then remembered he didn't know what car Xavier drove. If he even had a car. He had put off driving lessons for a long time.

This trip had been a waste of time. Most people wouldn't have felt that way. Checking on his brother next made sense. However, Patrick had *known* he wouldn't be here. He had seen himself banging on the door and getting no response. But he had done it anyway.

Patrick had to calm down and start thinking rationally. If

he paid attention, he would see how all the pieces fit together, and how they would fit together in the future. If he looked any further than the end of his nose, he would see something. At least, that's what Elena liked to say. She chided him often for thinking like a Mundane. She believed since he was a fall equinox wizard, he should know more than anyone else about the future and the present. She believed if he really paid attention, he would see it. But right now, nothing came to him. The people he cared about most had vanished and he had no idea why or where they might be.

He got back in his car and drove again without even thinking about it. He had no "home" to go to. So he went to the closest thing he had. Technically, it *was* his home. The deed was in his name.

Every time he returned to Houston, he returned to the house, because his parents lived there. They sat on the back porch drinking beer and grilling steaks. They asked him about college, complain about how he looked too thin, and give unsolicited advice. His mom would wash his clothes for him. His dad would check the oil in his car. And they'd take care of him, even though he was grown. No matter how old he got, he could go back home and his parents would take care of him and love him without condition. As he ventured off into the wild world, home would be his anchor. Always there. Never changing. Ready whenever he needed it.

Of course, that was all a fantasy. But he had discovered an obscene streak of stubbornness in himself. His parents built a house to live in and grow old in. And he stuck with that truth, even though they had died. He had never told anyone about his fantasy and his siblings didn't know he came here. This was the first time he hoped Xavier or Emmy might interrupt him. Maybe they came here too sometimes. But he doubted it.

Xavier went out of his way to avoid emotion and Emmy swam in it. She would be a blubbering mess before the house was even in view. Patrick, on the other hand, had the perverse need to punish himself with his grief. They died for him, after all.

As soon as he heard the crackle of gravel under his tires, his stomach lurched with a familiar wave of grief. He passed the finished stone mailbox with the letter "V" emblazoned in gold, and up the gravel path they would have paved one day. Eventually, he would have to do something about it. The gravel washed away, dried up streams exposing the red clay soil beneath.

He remembered when they first came here in the spring and flowers and buzzing insects filled the land. Today, the sky was an empty shade of white. The evergreen cedars around the house would not change colors with the fall. Instead they looked gray, heavy with dust. The smell of them made his throat burn. He remembered fighting these trees with his father to clear the land. They would go home covered in sap and scratches. That rich, syrupy smell of cedar would forever make him think of his father.

The house loomed above him as it always did—protected by a bubble of repulsive magic Patrick had created. No one would crash in or vandalize the house. Not if the perpetrators wanted to avoid bleeding from the eyes.

The plastic sheet covering the unfinished section hovered in a ghostly way, partially detached. Patrick could keep people away, but nature was an entirely different beast. The plastic sheeting required frequent replacing.

Patrick unlocked the front door of the house—even though he could have walked through a wall if he wanted to. But his parents would greet him at the front. His father would shake his hand and then pull him into a hug. His mother would give him a too aggressive squeeze that would leave him feeling slightly strangled. His dad would offer him a beer, acting scandalous about allowing his underage son to drink, even though every college student drinks every weekend. But he would do it to show he now treated him like a man, like an equal, and Patrick would appreciate that more than he would let on. His mother would ask lots of impertinent questions about his life. Asking question after question about his classes and his roommate, and the girl he was dating.

Eventually, we would bring Elena through these doors as well. She would be nervous, and he would be nervous, and his parents would act weird and embarrassing, but he would be so proud all the time. He would be thrilled to get to see that amazing woman sitting at the table where they would eat Thanksgiving dinner.

If he walked in the house at this time of year, air warm from cooking and fragrant of roasting turkey would greet him. Instead, the air felt empty, devoid of any smell that might mark a living, breathing home. The house had lost the chemical odor of wood and paint that comes with a house under construction. Now it had the same cedar scent as the outside air. But what could one expect with large unfinished holes in the house? The living room was nothing more than a bare slab of concrete he had furnished with a camping chair and card table.

He threw his keys on the table and went through the kitchen to try to fix the plastic sheeting. The kitchen was the second-best part of the house. There were no appliances, but otherwise, the room was finished. The ceilings were high and the entire back wall was a window. The ceilings were planked like a ski lodge.

There was no electricity, so this was the room with the

best light. And the granite counter tops sparkled with orange fire during the sunset. His mom would have cooked dinner. She would have offered him food as soon as he walked in. Unlike in his bare apartment fridge, there would always be food here, magically filling the fridge and pantry.

The best place in the house was his parents' master bedroom, although the room was not much more than a cement plank. The stairs to the second floor had been finished, so he could go upstairs, however, the entire western side of the house was largely unfinished. The master bath was a large room with holes in the floor where the toilet and shower would have been. The bedroom was nothing but a concrete slab, but a concrete slab with a hell of a view. The room faced west, so they could watch the sunset. He could stare out at the rolling hills and big Texas sky his parents would have seen every morning when they woke.

Jess and Carson wanted to continue the construction his parents had planned. Then they would sell it. Patrick vetoed this. Later they tried to convince him to continue the construction so he could live in it one day. He didn't allow this either. To this day, he had trouble explaining his opposition. His parents would have preferred that option. Leaving something undone for all eternity would have driven his parents crazy, especially his father, who prided himself on completing construction projects on time.

If he hadn't died, he could have completed it himself. But he did die, so he had to leave it unfinished. That's the deal. They left everything else unfinished and abandoned. The house was no different. He didn't care if his choice made no sense. He would do—or not do—whatever he wanted with his own house.

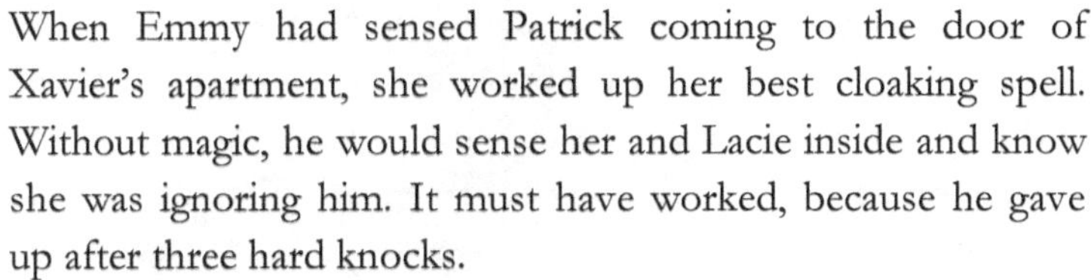

When Emmy had sensed Patrick coming to the door of Xavier's apartment, she worked up her best cloaking spell. Without magic, he would sense her and Lacie inside and know she was ignoring him. It must have worked, because he gave up after three hard knocks.

When they arrived, Xavier hadn't been in his apartment and his car was gone. And in classic Xavier style, he had left his cell phone on the counter, of no use to anyone. To Emmy, Xavier had always felt like a shell person. Like the real Xavier had died long ago, but his body managed to walk around. A shadow pretending to be a real person. As time passed, that didn't change. That shadow just got better at pretending. When the shadow was kicked out of the Oppenheimer's house, it knew it should get a job and an apartment. It should eat and sleep and shower. But other than those basic components of a life, there wasn't much else. His small apartment was devoid of all decoration, with only the things he needed to live. And even though he only worked as a night stocker at HEB, he didn't lack money. Their parents had left them enough in a trust. The only nice things Xavier chose to buy were his television and computer, both of which cost more than everything else he owned times ten.

As far as she knew, he went to work at ten at night to move bread and mangoes and things from the stockroom to the shelves at the grocery store. He must have talked to co-workers and managers sometimes, but she imagined he had little human contact. Then he went home and slept during the day like a vampire. Then woke up and played video games until he had to work again. She wasn't aware of him having any ambitions at all, and he would continue doing this for sixty years.

Sometimes Emmy would imagine he was a secret agent. Or a superhero. Or maybe doing something scandalous like dealing magical drugs. But Emmy knew he was just a shadow, and that was all he would ever be.

Emmy stared at the login screen of Xavier's Netflix account.

"What would your cousin use as his password?" Emmy mused aloud. "Because I have absolutely no idea."

"He's not my cousin," Lacie said.

"I guess not technically." Emmy said, with a clenched jaw. She didn't appreciate Lacie's determination to exclude him from her family. She should have known how it felt to be disowned.

Emmy tossed the remote at Lacie. "I'm going to bed. We'll go to Heartsong tomorrow, with or without him."

CHAPTER FOURTEEN

November, Thanksgiving Day, Evening

After they ate, Samantha sat on her porch watching Sophie run back and forth across the lawn in her bare feet, playing some imaginary game beyond Samantha's understanding. Zander had gone out to grab some things from the grocery store and she'd used the time to call her aunt and ask her about the red circle. She had said nothing reassuring.

Samantha watched leaves fall from the trees across the street. Their patch of eternal spring stayed green all year. The flowers blossomed. The fruits ripened. The only hint of fall was the brown maple leaves that blew from the nearby trees, adding a hint of red and yellow to the rich green of their lawn.

As Zander came through the front gate with shopping bags, the grass turned a shade greener. Sophie careened into his legs. "Daddy!"

"Hey, little bug," he said, putting his hand on her head.

"I found a spider."

"Really? Was it a nice spider?"

"His name is Carl," she said and bounded back toward the little pile of leaves blown in from other yards, enjoying the crunch under her feet.

"I need to tell you something," Samantha said. She should have started with "hello."

"Okay," he said cautiously.

Samantha herded Sophie back inside, not taking the time to wipe the mud off her legs. Zander started munching on red grapes while he unpacked the groceries.

"Maybe you should sit down," Samantha said.

Sophie ran through the front door, her timing impeccable as always. "Can I have a snack?"

"We just ate a huge meal. And then you went outside and ate every tomato off my plants," Samantha said. "How is there still room in your little belly?"

"Here," Zander said. He put his grapes in a bowl and led her into the living room and turned on the first kids' show he found.

"I can watch TV?" she cried, as if she'd just won a fabulous prize. "Thank you, Daddy. I love you."

Zander came back in and sat back down. "Sorry. I know you don't like her watching."

"It's fine."

"What is it? What's wrong?"

"It's about Imogene."

His face went pale. They hadn't mentioned her in a while. It hurt too much. The one girl they would both love more than they would ever love each other.

"It's about how her family died," she continued.

Dora the Explorer asked questions from the living room and

Sophie shouted something back.

"Yeah?"

"You know that after she died, I looked more into her family's case. At least what I could find on the Internet. It was like getting to know her better, even after she was gone."

He nodded.

"You know that everyone in her family was murdered, except for her. Her parents, and her older brother, and her baby brother, who was murdered in his crib."

Zander cringed at the image. Some things never lose their shock value.

"They never solved the case. It's one of the ones that those true crime creeps like to analyze on message boards. Anyway, there is still a lot about the case on the Internet. And a while back, I found this picture."

Samantha handed him her phone, with the photo she had pulled up on the screen ready to show him.

"It's a picture of the crime scene."

"I don't want to see that," Zander said, turning his face away from the screen like he smelled something rotten.

"No, it's not of a body or anything. It's just the front of their house. Look at the front door."

Zander tapped on the phone to relight the screen and he looked at the photo.

"Can I play Bubbles?" Sophie said, appearing at Zander's side and reaching for the phone.

"No," he said, more sharply than usual, pulling the phone out of her reach. "Go watch your show."

She scowled for a moment and then arranged her face into an impressive pout and then stomped back into the living room.

"It's like she knows," Zander said.

"Do you see it? On the door?"

"It's a red circle," Zander said. He pushed the phone back toward her and looked up at her with his shining dark eyes. "What does it mean?"

"So, you don't know? You've never seen it before?"

"No. If it's a wizard thing, you know I don't know. I wasn't raised with magic."

"I didn't know either, and I didn't worry about it until Patrick called me the other day. He said that the same symbol had appeared on his aunt and uncle's front door. The house where Emmy lives."

"That's what Patrick told you when he called? Why did you lie?"

"I just… I don't know."

"I know this is going to sound heartless… but what does this have to do with us? Warn Emmy. Tell her to hide, but leave it at that."

"She is hiding. At least we hope so. Patrick doesn't know where she is."

"I know it must be boring being at home here with Sophie all the time. You don't have to do that. We can get someone to watch her during the day so you can go to school… they're not going to know. They're not going to ask questions."

Zander had started school this fall and had chosen to study social work, which Samantha didn't understand. They had both spent enough time with social workers in their lives, and if she ever went to college, she would want nothing to do with it. But Zander had said the best people he had known growing up had been social workers. She thought he would fit right in. One of the best people. That described him perfectly.

"Why are you bringing this up right now? I'm happy here with Sophie. I'm so happy."

"Then why are you looking for trouble?"

"Are you guys fighting?" Sophie poked her little blond head around the corner.

"No, sweetie. Just boring grown-up stuff," Samantha said. "Give her the phone," she said to Zander.

Zander pulled up the game she liked to play and handed her the phone. She widened her eyes and formed her mouth into a little "O." "Thank you, Daddy!"

"You know, I'm the one who said you could have it," Samantha said, shaking her head.

Zander moved his chair to sit closer to her and leaned in so she could feel his crackling spring magic. She felt less afraid with him close.

"I'm just saying that our first priority should be keeping Sophie safe," Zander said in a near whisper. "And if we want to keep her safe, and if we want to *keep* her, we need to stay far away from the Vandergraffs... and the Prescotts."

"Just listen to what I'm trying to tell you. I'm not done explaining." She reached out and squeezed his hand.

"Okay."

"I know who killed Imogene's family. And I know why. And I know why she was the only one spared."

"You do?" he asked with wide eyes.

She nodded. "There's a reason why the Mundanes could never solve the crime. They didn't die for Mundane reasons. They died for magical reasons."

Zander glanced into the living room, and Samantha followed his eyes to see Sophie's blond head looking down at the phone.

"I had suspected it had something to do with magic, but I didn't know what. This morning I called my aunt—the one I lived with for a while—and I asked her what the red circle meant."

"And?"

"At first, she didn't want to say. She asked me if I had seen one, and I said no, not in real life. She said I shouldn't worry about it. That it had nothing to do with spring wizards and that if I knew what was good for me, I would stay far away from any markings like that."

"Sounds like good advice."

"If it was just us, I would. But we're not *all* spring wizards, are we?" Samantha glanced at their daughter again.

"Okay," he said.

"I told her that I really needed to know, and so she told me. She said that she didn't know that much about it, but that the red circle is the sign of Los Segadores."

"Who?"

"They're vigilantes. They kill bad wizards to keep them from hurting anyone."

"Doesn't sound like a terrible idea. Like some kind of wizard police?"

"No. It's not like that. There are no laws. No trials. No juries. They just claim to know who deserves to die. And it's always solstice wizards. They kill winter and summer."

"But just the bad ones right," he said with a childlike innocence. In some ways, he did seem like a child. Always fresh, always new. Like the first day of spring every day.

"That's what they think, but how can a baby be bad? They haven't had a chance to be bad or good."

"What baby?"

"Imogene's little brother. That's what the red mark was. Los Segadores had marked them for death. Imogene came from a family of winter wizards. All of them were winter wizards, except for her. That's why she is the only one they spared."

"I don't understand. I don't know what Imogene's parents were like, and she barely did either. She was so young when they died. But what could her brothers have done? They were children."

"That's what I'm saying, Zander. It's not about what they had done. It's about what they would have done. That's how fall wizards think. That's what Los Segadores does. They don't punish crime. They prevent crime."

"You can't be serious. That's too horrible."

"They don't think so. They think they're doing something noble."

"But a child. There is no virtue in killing a child."

"Of course, I agree with you. But do you understand now, why I think this might concern us?"

Zander hadn't put the pieces together until Samantha had spelled it out for him. But now he understood. She could tell by the way his face turned gray and he glanced again at Sophie's curls spilling over the top of the couch.

CHAPTER FIFTEEN

November, The Day After Thanksgiving

While Patrick sat in the waiting area at the state prison in Livingston, he regretted his choice. The room had the faint smell of cigarettes and powerful antiseptics, and one of the florescent lights kept flickering, giving the room the feel of a cheap haunted house. He sat in a cracked plastic chair that seemed to bite him when he moved. Two other people sat in the room. An older woman wearing a pink turban and a boy who looked about five, kneeling in front of his chair and rolling a small die cast car along the seat. He wondered if the woman in the turban was bald because of chemotherapy. She made him think of his mother and the cancer she survived, only to be murdered months later.

He had never visited his brother in prison. He had no reason to. He only visited people he cared about and wanted to see… and often not even then. Although, since he had driven the hour to sit in this most depressing of rooms, perhaps he cared more than he had thought. Of course, caring about someone didn't always mean warm and fuzzy feelings. He did care about his brother and what happened to him. He cared a lot about what happened to him. He wanted him punished for his crimes, and there weren't many things he cared about more than that.

He had last seen his brother in the courtroom when Jude had been found guilty of two counts of murder in the first degree—the murders of his wife and his mother. Patrick didn't know how murder trials usually went, but he assumed this one had been stranger than most. The outcome had little to do with law or justice—but on which brother could wield a stronger magical influence over the judge, jury, and lawyers. Patrick won. Jude may not have committed the murders that led to his conviction, but that didn't bother Patrick. He had committed crimes that should be punished. And now Jude served a sentence delivered by Patrick himself—twenty-five years for his crimes of rape, accessory to child abduction, and unlawful imprisonment.

Patrick had come here for confirmation that Jude hadn't disappeared into thin air like his other siblings. And he had gotten that when the squat, red-nosed woman at reception had looked up his name in the system and approved a visit. If Jude were dead or missing, he assumed she would have said so.

Patrick had already stood up to leave when a guard came into the room and called his name. Patrick had come this far— he might as well confirm Jude's continued existence with his own eyes. The fear that Jude might find some way to escape prison using magic lingered in Patrick's brain at all times. It would be comforting to know the prison had held him. Jude certainly wasn't the first wizard to be in prison, and perhaps wizards worked on the other side of the bars too.

The guard took him through another metal detector and into another room where he scanned Patrick with a wand and had him touch some special paper to check for drug residue. While he worked, the guard recited various laws and warnings regarding what Patrick could and could not do during his visit.

"If you wish, you can have one hug on arrival and departure," the guard explained.

"That won't be necessary," Patrick said.

"Other than that, no touching," the guard continued. "Keep your hands visible on the table. Don't attempt to pass anything to the inmate and don't accept anything from him."

"Yeah, fine."

Patrick already had butterflies in his stomach before all of this fanfare, and now he had a full swarm. What had he been thinking coming here? He could have searched for Jude's name on the prison website to confirm his location.

Patrick walked into a third room, a small room with white walls and white floors. It seemed too small to fit both of them. Jude sat at a folding table wearing a tan prison jumpsuit that said *Property of the State of Texas*. Jude stared at the table, tapping his fingers, like he sat in algebra class.

Patrick sat in the chair on the other side of the table. The sound of the chair legs scraping on the floor seemed deafening. He didn't expect to feel so terrified. Caroline's torture had stayed with Patrick, a ghost pain that tingled in his back and arms when he tried to sleep. It had gotten better over the years, but returned now, as if Caroline's magic continued to live under his skin and knew he was close to Jude. Patrick tried to keep his breathing even, but he knew Jude could sense his fear no matter how well he masked it.

"Patrick," Jude said, now looking at him with his pale gray

eyes, more of a statement than a greeting.

Patrick couldn't say anything in response, not that he knew what to say. He didn't know if Jude had cursed him, or if it came from blind terror, but his throat felt frozen. He couldn't swallow and might start slobbering any minute.

Jude returned his silent stare for what seemed like hours. Patrick felt stuck on pause, unable to break out of the moment. He felt so trapped inside his own fear he couldn't use magic, either offensively or defensively. The only magic in the room flowed in one direction, from Jude into Patrick.

Finally, Jude leaned forward, putting his elbows on the table.

"Where is she?" Jude asked.

Patrick didn't understand the question. He wondered if he had blacked out for the first part of their conversation and had only now surfaced.

"Who?" Patrick asked, his throat burning from the effort of breaking out of the deep freeze.

Jude slammed his fist into the table and Patrick startled. Jude glanced off to the side, as if checking to see if the fist slam had got him in trouble.

"I got what I came for," Patrick said. "You're still here."

"Of course I'm still here," he hissed.

Patrick got up to leave.

"Sit down," Jude said.

He felt as if he had broken the trance and could now leave and never see Jude's face again until Patrick saw something out of the corner of his eye that made him pause.

Jude had slapped at the table again, causing his sleeve to pull up high enough for Patrick to spot an angry red mark. He only saw it for a moment, but it seemed deliberate and symmetrical. Maybe a tattoo. But something about it seemed sickeningly familiar.

"What is that?"

"What?"

"On the inside of your wrist."

Jude pulled up his sleeve and Patrick's stomach seized. A red circle. The same circle he saw on the Oppenheimer's door, but the red came not from paint, but from blood sucked to the surface of the skin. For a moment, he forgot whom the circle was branded to and reached to touch it. However, at the last minute, the guard's incessant 'no touching' warning echoed in this mind. Good advice, although the Mundane guard did not truly understand why.

"What is it?" Now, instead of feeling frozen, Patrick's body felt too hot.

Jude narrowed his eyes at Patrick, but he didn't look at the mark.

"What do you think it is?" Jude asked.

"Tell me."

Jude stared at him, his gaze preternaturally penetrating. He probably enjoyed the opportunity to withhold information Patrick wanted. Patrick should have left, but he found himself sitting back down.

"Emmy is missing," Patrick said. He didn't bother mentioning Xavier and Evangeline. Jude wouldn't care. But at one time, Evangeline had believed Emmy was Jude's talisman, a person with magical protective powers. After everything that had passed, he wasn't sure anymore. He didn't know if he believed in talismans at all. But maybe Jude did. In any case, if he still cared about anyone, it would be Emmy.

"Missing," Jude repeated. His face remained impassive. The betrayal hit Patrick like a punch to the gut. Jude's lack of reaction bothered him more than he had expected. Their last connection had broken.

"I came home for Thanksgiving and she was gone. Along with the rest of the Oppenheimers. That circle…" He pointed to his arm. "… was on their door. That's why I need to know what it means."

Jude leaned forward again, and Patrick leaned back. Last time he leaned like that, Patrick had felt paralyzed. Patrick could sense Jude's magic coming from him, like invisible tendrils invaded him. He shook his head in a way that probably appeared insane. He couldn't really shake off Jude's magic.

Where is my daughter?

Jude hadn't asked the question aloud. He had invaded Patrick's mind. It felt as if he lay in bed, thinking he was alone, and someone whispered in his ear.

"Stop," Patrick said, hating how pathetic he sounded. He continued to shake his head, like a horse ridding himself of a fly.

"Where is she?" Jude asked again, now aloud. "I can't find her." His tone now sounded alarmed, and too human. He didn't make sense. Whoever this person was, Jude wouldn't find her in prison. But Jude meant he hadn't found her in Patrick's mind.

Patrick stomach dropped, as if he had left on a trip and forgotten something critical. Really critical. Like a child. He could picture her in his mind, with wispy blonde curls and chubby toddler legs. He felt like he had memories of her transposed on top of a life with no memories of her, as if he had lived both lives simultaneously.

What the hell?

"You have a daughter?" If he had a niece out there somewhere, he needed to know about it. The strange turn of the conversation distracted him from the strange mark on

Jude's arm.

Although his question had been genuine, Jude seemed to think Patrick was fucking with him. He jumped to his feet so quickly Patrick nearly toppled backwards in his chair. The motherfucker made him cower and he hated it.

Patrick stood up too, grabbing his chair, ready to use it as a weapon, but two guards had already come in and slammed Jude's head into the table and snapped on handcuffs.

"Where is she? Where is she? Where is she?" Jude continued to bark as they led him away. In the last moment, his eyes softened and he looked at Patrick with disarmingly human pain. "Just tell me she's okay," he said.

Even if Patrick had a response, he wouldn't have had the chance to share it. Jude disappeared behind the swinging door, and another guard already led him out the other way.

When Patrick exited the final gate, the season's first wintery gust greeted him. The pleasant cool provided a brief distraction from the unease he felt, but it didn't last. He thought he would feel better if he saw his oldest brother alive and well. But he didn't feel better because his oldest brother wasn't alive and well. He died a long time ago. This man wore his brother's skin—skin with an ugly red mark on the wrist. And now, he had more questions than answers.

"Mr. Vandergraff?"

Although now a legal adult, people rarely called him 'Mr. Vandergraff.' He didn't like the sound of it.

A young woman with red hair and freckles dotting her nose approached him as if she had waited for him. She appeared ten or fifteen years older than him, but her short stature and smattering of freckles gave her the appearance of a little girl wearing her mother's pantsuit.

She reached out to shake his hand, but Patrick didn't return the gesture. "How do you know me?" he asked, narrowing his brow.

She scrunched her pert little nose at him. "I admit, I have a contact here who had promised to call me if Jude Vandergraff had any visitors. I've been trying to contact his family members for months now, but no luck." She smiled again with that little nose scrunch. He didn't know if she meant the scrunch to be cute, but he found it creepy.

"What do you want?" Perhaps he shouldn't be so rude, but the woman unsettled him. She was a Mundane, but he sensed something off about her energy, like she might have the smallest flicker of magic less powerful wizards might not have sensed—like a pea under a tower of mattresses. Most wizards believe one was either a wizard or a Mundane. Black or white. But Patrick doubted that. It made sense there would be some kind of spectrum. Wizards usually mated with other wizards, but not always. If one was part wizard, would they be part magical? He made a mental note to ask Elena.

"My name is Carrie Anne Carr from the Innocence Force. I'm representing your brother in his upcoming appeal hearing."

She tried putting her hand out for a shake again, but Patrick ignored it. Despite her smile, her words made it clear they weren't on the same side.

"What appeal?"

"I was hoping I could ask you some questions about the night your mother died."

"He was ruled guilty and sentenced to twenty-five years without parole," Patrick said.

"The verdict can be overturned in certain situations, and I believe your brother is innocent."

"No."

Carrie Anne opened a file she was holding, even though she must have known what the file contained without having to make a big show of looking at it.

"In my years of practicing law, I've never seen such a pathetic defense. The incompetence is staggering. They didn't even attempt to corroborate his story. It took me about fifteen minutes to find the evidence I needed to re-open the case."

Crap. He had worked hard to warp and confuse the brain of Jude's defense attorney, the judge, and the jury. He had never considered he might have to continue the job after the ruling.

But it might not be too late. He concentrated and tried to reach into her mind and poison her with new ideas and images that supported Jude's guilt, but the magic didn't. Her brain seemed slimy, like trying to get a footing on slippery rocks in a lake.

Apparently unperturbed by Patrick sliding into her brain and right back out again, she took a photo out of her file and held it up. The photo showed Jude leaning against a car, staring at his phone while he pumped gas. "This is security footage from a gas station in Highland Park. Do you know when this was taken?"

"Who hired you?" Patrick asked. "Or do you just hang around jails looking for dangerous people to spring?"

She scrunched her nose again and gave him a tight-lipped smile. "I'm not able to share that."

She held the photo back up. "This was taken at the exact same time the fire department arrived at your brother's house. Do you know what that means?"

She didn't wait for Patrick to answer her question. "It means your brother couldn't have murdered his wife and mother. At least, he couldn't have set the fire. And the forensic evidence doesn't support the prosecution's case either. Naturally, your brother's fingerprints were around the house, but not on the knife that killed your mother. Only Caroline's fingerprints were on the knife. And her death was very strange. Cause of death was officially determined to be smoke inhalation, but that doesn't explain why or how her skin was ripped to shreds. And the cause of the fire was never investigated at all. I've seen plenty of cases where incompetence has led to the incarceration of an innocent man, but this… " She shook her head, unable to find the words.

Patrick sucked on his teeth. "He's not innocent."

"I'm telling you your brother didn't kill your mother. You'd think that might be good news for you… unless of course *you* did it."

She smiled her tight-lipped smile again and laughed in a way that sounded like a high-pitched hiccup.

Patrick didn't understand the laugh. Was she making a joke or was that an evil cackle of triumph?

"You can't possibly think I killed my mother," Patrick said.

"Actually, no. I don't. The timing doesn't work for that either. When your mother was killed, you were being pulled out of a flooded river."

Patrick tried again to invade her mind, and once again, he couldn't grab hold. Her mind seemed to be filled with actual slime. He had to resort to trying to convince her in the usual way.

"Jude is a bad person," Patrick said. "If you get him released, he will hurt more people. And that blood will be on your hands."

"Well, that's not how the justice system works. If he didn't commit this crime, he's been falsely imprisoned. You can't lock someone up because you don't like them, or because you think they might do something bad."

"He raped someone. Helped kidnap someone else."

"Then he should be convicted for that." She raised her eyebrows at him. "It seems to me that you know he's innocent. Is that right, Mr. Vandergraff?"

"No." Now he wondered if she was recording him. Crap. Did he say anything he shouldn't have? "I'm not saying that," he said loudly. "He killed my mother and his wife."

"And what about the baby?"

He once again felt the sudden falling feeling of having forgotten something critical. He couldn't grab hold of this woman's thoughts. What other memories—or entire people— had fallen out of his mind?

Patrick shook his head.

"The house was full of baby things," the lawyer continued. "But they never found the remains of a child."

Patrick's throat felt dry. "I… I can't explain that."

"I assume the child was Caroline's. There is no record of her having a child, but her autopsy showed that she had given birth to a child at some point. So, if that child didn't die in the fire, where is it?"

"I don't think she had a child," Patrick said, although he was no longer convinced. But he hated thinking he had a niece somewhere, not only abandoned, but also forgotten. This had to be a trick, although he didn't understand the purpose, if not to fuck with him.

"I also noticed your father died the very same evening. Is that right?"

She said it so matter-of-factly it felt cruel. She might as

well have swiped her nails across his cheek.

"So tragic," she said. "And such an *incredible* coincidence."

"What are you saying? You think I somehow killed him too? That's a neat trick." His voice shook and he vowed to shut up. She would never guess how the deaths were related, or how he was guilty, but she was close enough to the truth it felt like she was yanking him by the entrails.

"A *trick*, yes. That's what it would take," she said. "A magic trick."

Carrie Anne pulled a business card out of her jacket and handed it to Patrick.

"Call me if you decide to be helpful."

"Wait," Patrick said. "When is the appeal hearing?"

"Monday," she said.

"*This* Monday?"

"As I said, I've been trying to contact you for some time."

"That's not enough time."

"Not enough time for what, Mr. Vandergraff?"

Patrick didn't reply.

"Have a good day," she said.

She turned and awkwardly walked across the gravel in her square heels. He headed to his car at a swift pace, wanting to get far away from her. He rationalized with himself to calm down. Okay, so she seemed to be a Mundane who either knew Patrick used magic to frame his brother, or suspected it. That was strange, but not impossible. Maybe she was part magic and knew about magic but couldn't practice. Or maybe a wizard told her about magic. It didn't matter. She was a Mundane, so she couldn't hurt him in a magical way. And she couldn't explain her theory to other Mundanes. She might, however, win her appeal, since she happened to be right. But Patrick could wreck the appeal like he wrecked the original case.

He stopped and reached for his pocket. He sensed his phone would ring and he held it in his palm. When the phone rang, he saw Emmy's face flash across the screen and his heart jumped.

"Thank God," Patrick said aloud. "Emmy," he said into the phone.

"Hi." Her voice was quiet on the other line.

"Where are you? What is going on?"

"I got all your messages. I'm sorry I haven't called back." Her voice sounded distant, as if he imagined it.

"Damn right you're sorry. I've been freaking out. Why the hell have you been ignoring me?"

"I know. It's just… I'm not supposed to be talking to you. But I wanted to tell you I'm okay. We're all okay. Please stop looking for us."

"What? Why? Where are you?"

"I can't tell you. But we're fine."

"So, you're with Xavier and Evangeline too?"

"They're fine. Please, just don't worry about it."

"Don't worry about it?"

"I'll call you later. Okay? I love you."

She hung up the phone.

"Emmy?" he asked. "Dammit."

His hands shook as he crawled back into the driver's seat. Knowing his siblings were okay but had cut him out of their lives for some reason, was better than them being dead… but felt like shit in a whole other way.

With his hands shaking as he pressed send, he called Elena.

"Hey there!" she said, her voice the exact opposite of Emmy's. It sounded close and real, and most of all, happy to hear from him.

"Hey."

"You told me you would text."

"I'm sorry. I've been preoccupied."

"Is everything okay?"

"Yeah. Hey, is it too late to accept your invitation to spend Thanksgiving with your family?"

Elena gasped, and he could hear her smiling through the phone.

CHAPTER SIXTEEN

Fall hit east Texas suddenly. Emmy wondered if it had been coming gradually all along, and she hadn't noticed, or if the trees did turn red and gold overnight like God took a brush to canvas while she slept. The sky had turned pale gray, and the air had grown colder. She opened the window a crack to feel the crisp air fill the stuffy car. Emmy could smell a hint of saltwater on the air too. They must be close.

"It's cold," Lacie said.

"Sorry," Emmy said, closing the window.

Lacie rubbed her arms. She looked pale and Emmy kept stealing glances at her. "Are you feeling okay?"

"Sure," Lacie said. "How much farther?"

"I don't know. You can't find the place with a GPS, but I think it's close. This all looks familiar."

"What happened to the trees?"

The gold and red tinged trees had fallen away, leaving open plains with scatterings of dead trees. When she saw the battered state of a billboard advertising a gentlemen's club, she figured it out.

"A hurricane," Emmy said. "Ike or Rita. Or both. I'm not sure. They all seem to hit land here. That's why there is nothing around here. As soon as it's built, it falls down again."

"So why build a school here?"

"To be away from the Mundanes, I guess." Emmy wondered though. Did they choose this place because of the hurricanes? Or did hurricanes choose this place because of Heartsong Academy? Wizards were deeply connected to the seasons and the climate. And if one put a whole bunch of powerful, troubled wizards from all four seasons in one place, could they cause storms? If anyone could, it would be Evangeline. Emmy had the fleeting image of her standing on the beach raising her hands to call up a towering tsunami.

"Mundanes?" Lacie asked.

"People who aren't wizards."

"Oh." Lacie pressed her fingers against her temples as if she was pained.

"Does it hurt you? When I talk about magic?"

"Yes, but it's getting better. At least I can actually hear you now." She paused and pressed her hand against the glass, and then examined her fogged handprint. "It still feels like a weird dream."

"I understand."

"Is Xavier a wizard?"

"Yeah. Of course. Everyone in your family is."

"He's not in my family. He's not related to me."

"Oh crap," Emmy said suddenly.

"What?"

"We just passed the turn off. They don't make it very easy to see. But it's the sign for Seaspray Marina."

With no cars anywhere in sight, Emmy did a wide U-Turn across the highway, and then turned onto the nearly invisible road by the battered sign for the marina, which didn't exist. The car bumped on the uneven road.

"Are you sure this is the right place?" Lacie asked.

"It's a wizard school. Are you expecting a big neon sign?"

Despite her show of certainty, this road always felt like the wrong place. It looked different each time and she had the nagging desire to turn around. But it was intentional and due to a spell. Mundanes couldn't get this close. They would realize they had made a wrong turn and would turn around. Wizards could resist the repulsion spell, but they still felt it.

"This really doesn't seem right," Lacie said. She looked out the window uneasily.

"Trust me."

Emmy let out a quiet sigh when she saw the gate looming ahead. When she had visited last spring, the gate had been draped in honeysuckle, and the sweet fragrance had permeated the closed car doors. Now the gates were flanked with milkweed flowers, each one with a flittering orange flower. On second look, she saw they weren't flowers, but a jumble of monarch butterflies, stopping on their migration to Mexico. Above the gates loomed a massive maple tree with a gorgeous display of multicolored leaves that blended outwards toward the branches with an ombre effect. Fall. The gateway had personified spring before and now it personified fall.

"It's pretty," Lacie said. "Is this it?"

"Yeah," Emmy said, gaping at the colorful tree above. She stopped to examine a cluster of monarchs and smiled as she watched them dance from flower to flower, folding and unfolding their wings.

Emmy went to the call box to announce herself, but

stopped in her tracks, so distracted by the fall display, she hadn't noticed. The gate was unlatched and hanging open.

Emmy felt a quiver in her stomach. Security here was tight. It was hard to get in, and even harder to get out. They would not leave the gate open. Emmy envied the wizards in movies who had a wand to brandish. Or even the Mundanes who used guns for the same thing. Right now she felt like she needed a weapon greater than her own blood and bones.

She heard the gentle rumble of a car behind her and turned, her senses now heightened like a frightened cat. A release of tension nearly toppled her over when she saw Nathan's truck peek through the brush. When he stepped out of the cab, she could only muster a bizarre squeaking sound.

"Thank God," Nathan said.

Emmy ran at him so fast that when they collided, she felt a shock as their contrary magical forces smacked together. If they had been more powerful, she could imagine they would have created a clap of thunder above them. Nathan held her face in his hands, running his fingers along her cheeks and neck as if checking to make sure everything was still in the right place. Then he embraced her, so hard she could barely breathe with her face pressed into his chest. She was filled with warmth that had nothing to do with magic.

"I'm sorry I didn't get here faster. You should have waited for me."

Emmy remembered how furious she was with him and wiggled out of his grasp. Before she could tell him off, he continued. "It's my mother. She's just... she wouldn't let me leave."

Emmy wanted to know how a middle-aged woman a foot shorter than him could have kept him so contained, but there were many ways to imprison someone that didn't involve brute strength. And she could tell by the pauses in his statements and the wild look in his eyes, he wasn't ready to share the details.

"I'm just glad you're okay."

"She's scared," he continued. "I'm all she has left."

"What about Leona?" Emmy asked. Emmy had only met Nathan's sister Leona once, but she knew how poorly her summer family treated her. They didn't treat her *badly*; they treated her like a non-person, like she didn't count. Nathan had come here to be with Emmy, and his little sister residing at this school was pure coincidence.

"Leona is not in danger," Nathan said matter-of-factly, providing a subtle confirmation that what Jess had said had been true.

"Hi. It's Lacie, right?" Nathan asked.

Emmy had briefly forgotten about the presence of her cousin. Lacie had her arms wrapped around herself and she stared at the ground uncomfortably.

Lacie smiled weakly. "Hi."

Nathan turned his back to Lacie and leaned in closer to Emmy. "Why is she here?"

"Her mom broke the spell. She knows she's a witch. She's still acting weird though. I think the spell is still messing with her brain."

"I can hear you, you know," Lacie said.

"Sorry," Emmy said.

"He is one too, isn't he?" Lacie walked closer to Nathan. "And he's different."

"A summer wizard, yeah."

"Have you pushed the call button?" Nathan asked.

"No, the gate is open."

"What do you mean?"

"I mean what I said. The gate is open."

Not taking her at her word, Nathan gently pushed the heavy gate, making a shrill squeaking sound. Nathan stood like stag listening for a hunter.

"We should go," he said. "Now." He took Emmy's hand and she pulled away.

"No," Emmy said.

"If the gate is open, then something has gone wrong. Maybe the Los Segadores are already here."

"So what? That's even more reason for us to go in there. The whole point of coming here was to make sure my sister was safe. And I thought you might want to check on your sister too."

"You don't know Evangeline is still in there."

"If she had left, she would have tried to find me."

"You don't know that."

"If you don't want to go in now, you're just being a coward."

"Maybe," he said calmly. He paused for a long time. "I've lost too much."

He didn't elaborate, but Emmy understood what he meant. His life had been marked with grief the last few years. He had lost even more than she had.

"I know," Emmy said. "I just... don't want to lose Evangeline. Please."

He nodded and they embraced again. Out of the corner of her eye, Emmy saw an uncomfortable Lacie staring at the multicolored tree. But as Emmy felt little tickles of something falling on her arm, she realized Lacie may not have been staring away simply out of awkwardness. The tree above them sloughed leaves. Not in the gentle way of autumn, but a sudden and dramatic waterfall of leaves. The green leaves in the middle quickly turned blood red and fell too. Time seemed to have sped up.

What made trees turn bare? Winter. "Evangeline," Emmy whispered.

Emmy broke her connection with Nathan and walked through the gate. The gate made another high-pitched squeal as she walked through.

"Emmy, hang on," Nathan said. But he followed without trying to stop her.

"Evangeline?" Emmy asked, scanning the scene.

"I have to say, this isn't what I expected," Lacie said who had also appeared at her side. "I'm not sure what I expected. But not this."

When Emmy had first arrived at the school, she had a similar feeling. She had expected, or hoped, for something more Hogwarts-esque. At least, she expected a school. And although she hadn't hoped for it, she might understand if it looked like an institution or jail. But it didn't look like any of those things.

"Is it… invisible?" Lacie asked tentatively.

"No, that's it. That's the main office."

"It looks abandoned."

The main office sat inside a house on stilts. The stilts were twice as high as most of the other houses in the area. Emmy didn't know much about construction magic, but she assumed something magical had been in play. The stilts may have saved the house from flooding, but hurricane-force winds would surely wipe it away. Maybe they did. Maybe they rebuilt it every time. But the small house on top of the long, thin legs looked like a spider.

A thick blanket of dead leaves covered the open area in front of them. A few other trees inside the grounds had experienced the same exodus of leaves. Emmy saw that the empty trees followed along a path, one that ended right behind them. She must be close. At least, somebody was close.

"Evangeline?" she called again. "Anybody there?"

"It's not Evangeline," Lacie said.

"How do you know?"

"I'm not sure."

Nathan clutched Emmy's arm and she didn't know if he realized he was doing it. He continued to look around, scanning the area, just short of spinning his head in a full circle like the demon girl on *The Exorcist*.

Emmy tried to reach out her fingers of magic to feel the area. She felt surrounded by cold winter magic, but then the wind would shift, and it would feel like summer, or fall. It felt like everything all at once. The air was thick with magic; so much it made her ears ring and her nose burn.

"I don't understand," Lacie said. "Where do the students live? There isn't room for many people in that one house."

"They keep them apart. They live alone in cabins all over the property."

The staff called them "cabins," but they were really more like towers. As if in a fairy tale, they lived alone in locked towers.

"Like that one," Emmy said. She pointed to a small house on the horizon. The spindly stilts were barely visible, so the house appeared to hover.

"I thought that was a hunting blind," Lacie said.

"Emmy," Nathan whispered.

He pointed toward the gate where a little boy stood. Emmy startled at the sight of him. He had pale white skin and black hair. His coloring was so stark he appeared to have walked out of a black and white movie into the warm autumn scene. The only hint of color was a rust-colored smear of blood on his cheek, which she assumed was blood. Or perhaps red mud? He faded in and out of the scene like a hologram. He radiated fear. Emmy could feel it in her throat like a burning cold.

He ducked behind a tree, and the leaves cascaded down in an urgent fall. The wind picked up as he did so, and the leaves swirled and tossed in agitation.

"Hello," Emmy said, but her voice caught in the wind. "What is your name?"

Emmy did her best to not be afraid. He was just a child. Just like Evangeline and Leona. Except he was much younger. Torn away from his parents at seven or eight.

"My name is Emmy. I'm Evangeline's sister. Do you know her?"

The boy crouched down like a cat about to pounce, and Emmy was careful not to make any sudden movements, while still trying to treat this child like a child, and not a monster. However, unlike a cat about to pounce, the boy didn't have Emmy in his sights. His eyes were directed to her side.

"This is Nathan," Emmy continued. "He's Leona's brother."

The boy pointed at Lacie. Lacie stood a few feet behind her and Nathan.

"That's my cousin, Lacie," Emmy said.

The explanation didn't calm the young boy. He crouched down lower and then jerked suddenly, causing the gravel on the ground to fly up toward them. As Emmy and Nathan scattered to the side, covering their faces with their hands, the barrage continued. Everything on the ground in the vicinity shot toward Lacie with a hurricane-like gust. Lacie screamed and fell to the ground, covering her face with her arms.

"Stop that," Emmy shouted, but he didn't stop.

Slowly, the barrage stopped. Emmy sensed enough quiet around her to risk opening her eyes. It had not been Emmy's command that made the boy stop.

Evangeline stood on the roof of the spider house, perched like a gargoyle in blue jeans and bare feet. Apparently, she no longer noticed or cared about the dangers of gravity. Emmy gasped as Evangeline jumped from her perch and slowly moved through the air before landing easily on the ground. Emmy blinked. She couldn't have seen that. Maybe the roof wasn't as high as it looked. The little boy ran back into the brush.

Nathan and Emmy went to Lacie and pulled her out of the pile. Her face and arms were covered in small scratches, but she looked okay. Lacie stared into empty air absently, and Emmy helped her knock the leaves out of her hair.

"You're okay," Emmy said. She hoped the boy had only sent things flying and not actually hit Lacie with dark magic. Emmy knew how that felt, and Lacie wouldn't recover quickly. Sometimes they never recovered.

With Evangeline, sudden and intense physical contact could be dangerous, but Emmy didn't care. She ran at Evangeline and hugged her, hardly believing the warm, soft person in her arms was actually her sister. Emmy always felt surprised to find that Evangeline was a real person, and not some cold, dark cloud she could see but not touch. She was warm and smelled like spiced orange peels. Evangeline stepped back slightly, but eventually wrapped her arms around Emmy too.

"You're okay," Emmy said, mirroring the same statement she had used for Lacie. Remembering Lacie, Emmy pulled back to scan the area for that creepy little boy.

"He's gone," Evangeline said. "And he's harmless."

"I doubt that," Emmy said.

"You shouldn't be here," Evangeline said. "Neither should you," she said to Nathan. She looked at Lacie but said nothing.

"Where is Leona? Is she okay?" Nathan asked.

"Yes, she's here. And she's fine," Evangeline said. "I believe she's in her cabin."

"What's going on here?" Emmy said. "Something's not right."

"The gate was open. No one checked our ID," Nathan added.

"It's good to see you, but you should leave," Evangeline said.

Emmy wanted to shove her. She had this terrible smugness only event wizards could manage. Event wizards, with magical dates on the two equinoxes or two solstices, were the most powerful wizards, and even more potent when they worked together. Fortunately, event wizards from the different seasons struggled to work together well. Evangeline, a winter solstice witch, looked at her warmly, but with complete condescension, like Emmy was a lost little puppy who needed to head back home to her owner.

"Do you know about the Los Segadores?" Nathan asked.

"Yes," Evangeline said. "Turns out, the headmistress and most of her staff are members. They had us penned in here like lambs for slaughter."

"Oh my God," Emmy said.

"But the thing is… we aren't lambs."

That coldness in her voice seeped into Emmy's backbone. Something bad had happened here. Emmy's breaths felt shallow. They were surrounded. Children and teenagers now flanked them on all sides. There were probably about twenty-five or thirty, and all of them could probably melt her skin off her face if they felt like it. However, aside from all being between the ages of about ten and eighteen, they weren't the same, in looks or in magic. The bizarre blend of agitated magic made her want to vomit. She could feel waves of hot and cold and the wild, poisonous taste of spring magic. However, she didn't sense any of the tepid balance of fall.

They all had their eyes on Lacie. Emmy knew it would happen before it did. Not a premonition like Patrick would have, just a gut feeling.

Lacie wheezed and her face turned purple. She grasped at her neck, scratching at her skin, trying to remove some invisible obstruction.

"Stop," Emmy yelled at no one in particular. Lacie fell to the ground with a crunch in the leaves and Emmy followed her, kneeling next to her.

"Help me," Emmy said to Nathan. He kneeled next to her and placed his hands over Lacie's neck, but Emmy could tell he had no idea what to do.

Her face turned blue and blood vessels popped in her eyes. "Stop," Emmy screamed, now looking at Evangeline, who stared at her with disinterested green eyes.

With a new gasp of horror, Emmy watched the skin on Lacie's arms split and bleed. Red seeped through her shirt. Red circles were engraving themselves all over her body.

"Stop," Evangeline said, calmly but firmly.

Lacie took in a frantic gasp and then coughed and wheezed again in alternation. Emmy rubbed her back helplessly. At least Lacie could breathe now. Sort of. The red circles on her arms and neck shined with blood, but not too deep.

"If you could stop that so easily, why didn't you do it sooner?" Emmy spat at Evangeline. "She's not a member of the Los Segadores," Emmy shouted to the group at large. "She just barely found out she was even a witch. For fuck's sake."

Emmy stood up to face Evangeline. "You're right. Clearly, coming down here to make sure you were okay was a waste of time. You and your army of little demons are doing just fine. We're leaving."

Lacie's wheezy breaths had become slightly more even. The whites of her eyes were specked with red, but she had regained a more normal color.

"Where is Xavier?" Evangeline asked.

Lacie started to say something, but she erupted into a fit of coughing.

"Maybe we should take her to the ER," Nathan said.

"Put her in the garden shed with the others," a boy said, appearing at Evangeline's side. He had dark brown hair that looked like it had never been properly combed, and brown eyes that darted around so quickly, Emmy couldn't imagine he could see anything properly. He tapped his fingers against the side of his blue jeans and the dry leaves by his feet smoldered. Evangeline stomped them out with her foot, casually, like this was a common occurrence.

"Emmy is right, she probably isn't a member of the Los Segadores," Evangeline said. "But we can't take the chance."

"Wait. What is happening?" Emmy asked.

"We'll take her away from here," Nathan said. "You won't have to worry about her."

"She could be a spy," Evangeline said. "I don't want her running off to join her clan."

"She is not a spy," Emmy shouted in exasperation. "Just last week, her biggest concern was a calculus test."

"I failed that test," Lacie said flatly.

"The Los Segadores must already know where you are

anyway," Nathan said. "You as good as said so. They've already been here."

"It's not that simple. *Here* is not always the same place. You only got in because I let you in."

The fire starter boy grabbed Lacie's arm. She pulled back, but then suddenly made a whimper of pain, trying to pry his hand off with the other hand. He was burning her.

"Stop that," Nathan said. Emmy felt a rush of heat next to her. The air around Nathan rippled with heat. The rippling air moved away from him and toward the fire starter boy. Emmy turned her face away, feeling her mascara melting her eyelashes together.

When the heat passed, she saw the fire starter boy was grinning, the rippling air gently hovering around his silhouette like clear flame. Lacie however now looked badly and Emmy could faintly smell burning hair. Lacie swayed and fire starter boy caught her, leading her away by the shoulders.

"Nathan, don't cast spells in her direction unless you can aim better," Emmy said. "She's already been hit with enough."

"Well, what am I supposed to do? Nothing?" he said, wiping sweat from his reddened face. He also smelled faintly of burning plastic and she wondered if he had managed to melt his own clothes or shoes.

Emmy followed the fire starter boy with Lacie, and Nathan followed her. Lacie stumbled like she was drunk.

"She's going. Don't push her," Emmy said.

The stairs up to the spider house didn't go back and forth like most stairwells. The building had one long stairway that appeared to hover in the air. The steep cascade of steps reminded her of the stairs up a Mayan temple. Apparently uninterested in helping Lacie walk up the stairs, the fire starter boy slung her over his shoulder. She flopped there and did not resist.

At least he didn't drag her up the stairs. Emmy followed, trying to keep up, but fire starter boy moved oddly quickly. The wind had picked up and Emmy felt like any gust might push her over the edge.

"You okay?" Nathan asked, as he placed his hand on her back.

Emmy had stopped. A faint smell had bothered her before her mind had fully registered it. A metallic bite in the air. Emmy saw dark smudges on the stairs.

"I'm fine," Emmy said, and she continued up the stairs, the salty air whipping her hair in every direction.

The rushing wind nearly covered the sound of a scream at the top of the stairs, but Emmy heard Lacie's wail before the gust sucked it away. Her heart pounding, she rushed up the last few steps and through the door left ajar.

Lacie sat in a small chair in what looked like the lobby of a small hotel. She had managed to look pale and bright pink from sunburn at the same time, covered in splotches and smears of her own blood. She didn't look at Emmy, but had her green eyes fixed unblinkingly on a dead hand peeking out from behind the counter.

CHAPTER SEVENTEEN

November

Elena jumped out the car. With the enthusiastic slam of the door, Patrick thought she might be angry. She ran at him fast enough he had to take a step back when he caught her in his arms. He inhaled her smell and relished her warmth, realizing how much he had missed her. He kissed her long and hard, intermingling his fingers into her thick hair, not noticing she had company until he heard an awkward cough.

Patrick ended the kiss and took his eyes off of Elena long enough to get a better look at the person with her. Once he did look at him, he had to force himself not to stare. The man was tall, thin, and Albino. He had white skin patched with over-large freckles, nearly translucent hair, and eyes that had a tinge of red. He wore an old-fashioned brimmed hat that contrasted with his otherwise normal outfit of jeans and T-shirt. He leaned against the driver side door of an ancient station wagon.

Patrick couldn't tell if the car was rust-colored, or actually covered in rust.

"Hello," Patrick said hesitantly.

The man nodded without smiling.

"That's Pike," Elena said, with no further explanation. "I'm mad at you," she said, although she continued to smile at him and look flushed from their kiss.

"Why?"

"Because you waited this long to call me." She had her hands interlocked in his and she gave him a nail-digging hand squeeze. "You went home to see your family for Thanksgiving, and they weren't there. I think that's worth a call."

"I knew you were with your family," he said vaguely. "I didn't want to wreck your Thanksgiving if there wasn't anything you could do about it." He didn't know if that was the truth. He couldn't explain why he hadn't told Elena about his family's unexplained disappearance. It just hadn't felt right for some reason. And wizards shouldn't ignore those niggling feelings. It meant something, even if he couldn't put it into words. He worried it meant he put Elena in danger by bringing her into his problems.

She hugged him again, and as she spoke, he could feel her breath on his neck. "I can help you. We'll find them together. Even better, we'll ask my brother. He knows everything. Literally everything."

He suppressed an eye roll.

"*We'll* figure this out," she said. "You're not alone." Her big brown eyes sparkled, and he felt guilty for being immensely happy she was there. At that moment, he wanted to be selfish. He wanted her by his side, no matter the danger.

"Besides," Elena continued. "You're a great wizard. You probably already know exactly where they are and have known all this time."

"That's not helpful."

"I'm serious." She grabbed his head with her hand playfully. "You can't focus. You would know everything there ever was to know if you could clear your mind from all the noise. I'll help you."

She interlocked her arm with his. "Come on. Get in."

Patrick eyed Pike. "I have a car. I can drive."

"Your car won't make it through the repulsion spell, and it takes a long time to do all the spell work to allow it through. Let's go back to camp and we'll come back for your car later."

"Camp?"

"Yeah. What did you think, my family lived in a house?"

"Um… yes?"

She laughed and tugged his arm. "Come on. It's not far from here."

Patrick got in the back of the car old enough to legally vote, and it smelled like weed. He smiled at her awkwardly; trying to dispel any thoughts that might come off as judgmental, in case she tried to probe his mind.

They headed out from the prison and went west. He should have insisted on taking his car. He could have followed Pike and parked it somewhere outside of the enchantment. She pulled him in the car so fast he didn't have time to think. He didn't have anything with him except his wallet and phone, and his phone had only a few hours before it went dead.

"How far are we going?" he asked.

"It's not much farther," Elena said.

She smiled at him and giggled.

"What?"

"You're nervous," she said. "It's cute."

"I'm not nervous." Not nervous, but maybe mildly

terrified. However, the terror of meeting his girlfriend's family for the first time was a boring, normal-person terror that felt comforting in its predictability.

"They're just my family. They're just *people*. Just normal, nice people. Okay, maybe not normal… and not that nice. But they *are* people. I'm sure you'll fit right in."

"Because I'm also a person?"

"You're not just *any* person."

"This is all very helpful," he said, now also laughing. She had a contagious laugh. "Very reassuring."

The car turned suddenly, and Patrick grabbed onto the door.

"What the hell?"

Pike had turned off the road and directly into the piney wood. Patrick braced for an impact that never came. The man found a perfect hidden space between the trees just big enough for the car. He drove forward at a speed only slightly lower than the one they enjoyed on the highway, speeding inches away from branches and scattered boulders until they came to a larger clearing filled with other cars and motorcycles.

Elena got out of the car and Patrick followed her. He was met with the welcoming smells of burning charcoal and roasting meat and corn, and something sweet, maybe sweet potatoes or roasted nuts. She hadn't been kidding when she said 'camp.' Further along in the clearing, there were six or seven tents and a handful of small trailers. Patrick had no idea itinerant people like this actually existed, at least in present day Texas. Were they gypsies? Was that still a thing?

As they walked through the makeshift campground, everyone had a smile for Elena. Patrick's reception was cooler, neutral glances and curt nods. No one seemed surprised to see the new visitor. But how surprised did fall wizards ever really get? From the gentle balance of even magic in the camp, he sensed the vast majority were fall wizards. The most he'd ever seen in one place by far.

They were also the most mismatched group he had ever seen. Some dressed like they walked out of a renaissance fair, some dressed liked they walked out of a Gap ad. Except for a few children with their parents, no one appeared related. It's like they were all plucked from completely different families in completely different places. Which, maybe they had been. From the few wizard families he knew, it seemed normal for wizard families of other seasons to have one fall wizard. That was the way it happened with him, Lacie, and Caroline. Perhaps fall was a recessive gene that only showed up occasionally like red hair and green eyes.

Elena went straight to a large tent where a little girl, maybe about six years old, walked back and forth along a log, humming to herself. She looked like a miniature Elena and wore a Princess Belle outfit with red rain boots. Her face lit up and she ran to them. To Patrick's great surprise, she went straight to him and hugged his legs like she knew him.

She took him so off-guard he almost pushed her off as if a little gremlin had attacked him. Instead, he patted her head. "Hello," he said.

"This is my niece, Isabella." Elena smiled and tugged on the girl's ponytail. "Dejalo, mija."

Isabella released Patrick's legs and turned to Elena. "Look at my dress," she said, now turning to Elena. "Daddy got it for me."

"Que bonita!" Elena said.

Isabella looked at Patrick expectantly.

"Oh yes, very nice," he said. "You look like a princess."

"I *am* a princess," she clarified.

"And this… is my Abi," Elena said, her eyes gleaming.

Patrick hadn't noticed the woman at first and might have mistaken her for a pile of clothes. Elena had talked about her "Abi," often. Patrick knew Abi was short for abuela, the Spanish word for grandmother. He also knew Abi had raised Elena from a baby. Therefore, he had expected someone younger, as in a normal grandmother age, like sixty or seventy. Abi was the oldest person he had ever seen. Patrick had a great-great aunt on his mother's side in her nineties. And this woman could have been her mother.

She was the epitome of the media's view of a witch. Her deeply hunched shoulders were covered in multiple shawls, and she had a bandana wrapped around her deeply crumpled face. She sat at a card table rifling through—believe it or not—tarot cards with bony fingers and unsettlingly long nails. The old woman eyed Patrick with cloudy white eyes and gummed something at him with a toothless mouth.

"La Muerte," she said, holding up a card with a skeleton draped in a black robe.

"Don't worry," Elena said quickly. "She shows everyone the death card."

"Hello," Patrick said.

"She doesn't speak English."

"She's your grandmother?" Patrick asked, lifting his eyebrows.

"Yes. Well, no, she's my tatarabuela. I'm not sure what the English word is for that. I call her my Abi, but she is actually my grandmother's grandmother."

"That translation can't be right. Your great, great grandmother can't still be alive."

"She is, and she's right there."

"How… "

"She is only one hundred and eight."

"Shouldn't she be inside or something?"

"No," Elena said simply.

His neck tightened as he heard the crunching of leaves behind him. He turned and saw a man with tattooed arms and black eyes walking toward him. The man smiled and held out his hand, but his smile didn't extend to his eyes.

"This is my brother, Carlos," Elena said. "This is Patrick," she said, now addressing Carlos.

Patrick shook his hand and as soon as their hands touched, a clear truth filled his mind.

This man is going to kill me.

They released hands and Carlos stopped smiling. He focused his eyes on Patrick.

He knows I saw something when we touched.

Carlos smiled again when he looked at Elena, but again the smile seemed wrong, like skin stretched too tight.

"Welcome," he said, glancing back at Patrick. The word had a shadowy quality, as if he really meant the opposite. He didn't want Patrick here. When would he kill him? Now? Tonight? In a year? In any case, he wanted Patrick dead.

"Vanessa." Carlos whistled gently, like he was calling a dog. A woman, who must have been Vanessa, answered his call, putting down the dishes she was washing with a hose. She had long black hair, which she managed to swing in the right ways to keep her face hidden. But of what he could see of her, she was beautiful—willowy and graceful with perfect, creamy skin. She also felt different. Her magic was brighter and lighter. A spring witch. He wondered what she was doing here. "Get Patrick something to drink. I need to talk to my sister."

Patrick's instinct was to refuse and not leave Elena alone with her brother, but that would not leave the best first impression. Elena squeezed his hand and whispered, "I'll be right back."

Vanessa peeked out of her hair briefly to give him a mild smile and then beckoned him to follow her.

He followed her to a different campsite. She had a large cast-iron pot over her campfire. She leaned over it and stirred gently, the tips of her long hair nearly falling into the pot. Much like Elena's Abi with the tarot cards, Vanessa leaning over to stir her cauldron was far more witch-like than what he ever saw from other witches in his life. She ladled some of the warm liquid into a coffee mug and handed it to Patrick.

He eyed the concoction dubiously. It appeared to flicker with its own internal light, which might have been a trick of the eye, just a reflection of the nearby fire. Or not...

"What is it?"

"Tea."

He decided to tempt fate, as to not offend. He inhaled, and the tea smelled like... moonlight. He knew moonlight didn't have a scent, but that's what the smell reminded him of, nonetheless.

He sipped it and it tasted like herbal tea. Something minty with a dusty aftertaste.

"This is good," Patrick said.

He didn't feel strange, other than warmer than he should from the tepid tea. He felt reassured when Vanessa ladled out a cup for herself but played it safe by sipping the least he could without being rude.

Isabella launched herself into the campsite and grabbed Vanessa by the skirt.

"Where is my Poppy doll?" Isabella asked.

"I don't know, mija. Look in the tent. Hang on." She held her back and rubbed dirt of off Isabella's cheek with her thumb. Isabella wriggled away and went for the tent.

"Is she your daughter?" Patrick asked.

"Yes."

"Oh, that makes sense then."

"What do you mean?"

"Oh… nothing. Just that you're a spring witch. You seem to be the only one who doesn't belong."

"I don't belong?" Her tone remained flat, but hearing his own words repeated back put him in his place. Clearly, *he* was the one who didn't belong. *She* was part of the family.

"I'm sorry. That didn't come out right. I just meant you're a spring witch with a whole bunch of fall wizards."

"You were raised Mundane, weren't you?" Vanessa used her hand to waft the scent of her tea toward her.

"Yes. Why?"

She shrugged and pulled a thin shawl over her slender shoulders. "It's not uncommon for fall wizards to keep a spring wizard in their clan. We bring good luck."

"What do you mean… like a lucky charm?"

When he said it, he felt like he'd gotten his foot in his mouth again. She was a person, not a rabbit's foot or children's breakfast cereal. However, she gave no indication of offense.

"Yes, exactly like that," she said.

Patrick paused for a moment and looked around. He saw eyes on him from a few other sites. Gap ad girl looked away and shut her Yeti cooler loudly. Another man wearing a turban, standing not at a campsite, but in the middle of the clearing for no apparent reason, smiled at him when he caught his eye. Patrick nodded slightly and turned back to Vanessa.

"Well, do you?"

"Do I what?" she asked.

"Bring good luck?"

She cocked her head to the side and showed her first hint of a smile. "Yes and no," she said enigmatically. "I thought you would know all about spring witches."

"Why?"

"Didn't you once love one?"

"What? No. Yes. I mean… I wasn't in *love* with her. How did you know about that?"

Her tiny smile disappeared, and her breath caught, almost imperceptibly.

"Just an educated guess," she said shaking her head, her pale cheeks showing a brief flash of a blush.

"I can't find it," Isabella moaned, falling out of the tent, and thankfully breaking the unexplained awkwardness that had passed between them.

"Well, if you left her in the van, we'll have to get her later."

Isabella groaned and threw up her hands in exaggerated outrage, then stomped back into the tent.

With Isabella gone again, Vanessa stared at Patrick as if waiting for him to say something. He found himself drinking more of the mystery tea than he had planned, just for something to do.

"So, are you and Carlos… married, or together?"

"What does that mean… together?"

"Um… " Patrick didn't know if she meant it rhetorically or if she really didn't understand the question. In any case, she stared back into the pot and stirred as if she had forgotten he was there.

The smell of the campfire intermixed with the cool November air was deeply nostalgic and it made him miss his family so much it created a thick pain in his torso and neck. He had smelled campfire in Caroline's perfect image of fall when he had broken into her enchantment to save his sister. The fall she created had come from him. His perfect fall. His perfect self. His perfect life.

Somehow, cooking s'mores and playing charades around the campfire with his family had become a symbol of the perfect moment. The perfect place. Where life was simple and happy, and the love was so thick in the air he could almost touch it.

Before he realized what was happening, he fell right into the perfect moment he had recalled. Leaves crunched behind him and he turned to see a six-year-old Emmy stomping the leaves. He nearly toppled off the cooler. His heart raced with the disorientation. Then he remembered what his mother had told him about her being able to save a memory and re-enter it. He must have done that without knowing it. He ached to return to the memory, but real feet in the present crunched toward him.

He saw no available flat surface, so he put his tea on the ground to avoid drinking more, just in case the tea had caused the sudden dive into the past.

Elena and Carlos had come to join them, with another man following. Elena leaned if as if she was about to kiss him, but stopped suddenly, settling for an awkward shoulder bump instead. Under Carlos's watchful eye, she had probably done the right thing.

The man with Carlos was dressed like he had just walked out of Cabela's in camo pants and a bucket hat. He had a rifle in one hand and something around his neck that might have been night vision goggles. He had a boyish grin with a light smattering of freckles and messy tips of blond hair poking out under his hat. However, Patrick guessed from the light wrinkling around his eyes he was in his thirties. Patrick may have imagined it, but he thought the man smelled faintly of blood.

"This is Harry," Carlos said. He watched Patrick and Harry carefully as they shook hands and then glanced at Harry after they released their grip.

"My name is Paul, actually," the man said. Patrick was surprised to hear a British accent. It sounded odd coming from the man who Patrick had presumed to be a full-blooded Southern redneck.

"Carlos calls him Harry because he's British," Elena said, rolling her eyes slightly. "You know… Harry Potter."

"Actually, I'm from South Africa," Paul corrected again, patiently.

"Good to meet you," Patrick said.

"Harry is my chess partner," Carlos said.

"I see," Patrick said, although he didn't see at all. Perhaps they really did enjoy playing chess together, but he suspected it meant something else.

"Perhaps not for much longer," Paul said testily. "Now that *you're* here."

"Why because I'm here?" Patrick asked.

"He's just cranky because I'm beating him so badly," Carlos said.

"That's because you cheat," Paul said.

"Hell no."

"You touch your pieces. And it's hard to argue otherwise in current company, wouldn't you say?"

Carlos held his hands up innocently and smirked. "It's not my move."

Patrick got the impression they were screwing with him, fully aware he knew less about wizards than they did, but he refused to take the bait.

"Paul, there is something I've always wondered," Patrick

said. "In South Africa, where the seasons are backwards, are you still a fall wizard?"

"Of course I am, mate. We have fall in South Africa."

"I know, I just meant… never mind."

"Welcome to the camp," Paul said.

Elena beamed at Patrick, completely oblivious to the simmering rage radiating from behind Carlos's forced smile.

CHAPTER EIGHTEEN

Samantha carefully folded Sophie's tiny pink shirts and dresses. By habit, she held each item up to her face to inhale the honeysuckle smell of fresh laundry before she put it away. She avoided the use of most chemicals, or as she liked to think of them, "potions for Mundanes." She crafted her own laundry detergent out of rainwater, vinegar, baking soda, and honeysuckle pollen. When she added a cleansing spell to the concoction, it could get out any stain.

"Mommy," Sophie said. "Mommy."

"Yes, baby," Samantha said, not looking from her carefully folded clothes.

"I need a Band-Aid."

"What for?" Sophie had a habit of asking for a Band-Aid for invisible injuries and they went through them way too quickly.

"I have a booboo."

Samantha put down a small purple sock to examine what

she assumed would be an invisible or nearly invisible affliction.

"No," she whispered, and then she screamed it. "No."

Sophie's blue eyes got wide and turned slightly red before they overflowed with tears.

"I'm sorry, honey. I didn't mean to scare you."

Samantha bent down and hugged Sophie before gently unfurling her little arm. Her pristine skin was marred with an ugly red circle.

"Does it hurt?" Samantha asked gently.

Sophie nodded her head, tears now dripping from her chin.

"I need a Band-Aid," Sophie said again.

"Okay, sweetie. Hang on."

With shaking hands, Samantha retrieved a box of purple Doc McStuffins Band-Aids from the bathroom cabinet. Sophie had followed her and was holding out her arm with her lip quivering. For Sophie, a Band-Aid could magically heal any injury. Out of sight, out of mind. But Samantha would not be able to cover the sand dollar sized circle with a Band-Aid.

"I need the ouchie cream too," Sophie said. "It hurts."

Samantha obediently grabbed the antiseptic cream and traced the clear ointment around the circle. As a spring witch, she had some healing powers, so she visualized the skin becoming smooth again, the pain lifting out of her child's arm and back out into the air. But there was no change. If anything, the mark darkened in opposition.

However, Sophie's tears turned to sniffling, so she hoped she had at least removed the pain.

"Can I give you a big girl Band-Aid?" Samantha asked, hoping she had a larger gauze pad to cover it.

"Will it make it go away?"

Samantha hesitated to answer the question. She didn't

want to lie and say yes, but she couldn't bear to say no either.

"You won't be able to see it," Samantha said. She kissed her forehead, in part to hide her face so Sophie wouldn't see her crying.

Vanessa served Patrick the best flank steak he had ever had, with a side of roasted corn that tasted like every fall festival from his childhood rolled into one bite. During the meal, he almost felt comfortable. He was on a camping trip enjoying a crackling fire, the rich aromas of smoked meats, and a sky full of stars hidden from him in the city. And on this trip, he also had Elena's head resting on his shoulder. He wished he could live in the present and 'savor the moment' as people say. This would have been a present he would have enjoyed if he didn't have his mind on what would happen next.

After eating, Patrick found a moment alone with Elena.

"Are we staying here tonight?" Patrick asked.

"Where else would we stay?"

"Well, I didn't know I would be camping. I don't have a tent or a sleeping bag or anything. And I'm not dressed."

He had his arms wrapped around her, in part to keep warm as the temperature dropped.

"Let me ask you something," Elena said. "Have you stopped blindly searching for your siblings long enough to actually *look* for them?"

Patrick didn't want to admit she was right. He worked hard to push away his powers. He didn't like seeing the future. And as his powers had grown, he knew less about the future, and not more. He once believed the future was one path and he could use his powers to part the fog and see that path. But as more of the fog parted, he saw that the future branched into an infinite number of paths. And even as a fall equinox wizard, he felt his limitations. He might have been able to see down some of the paths, but he knew there were others out of sight. And he couldn't always see all the way down the paths or how these paths impacted the greater world. The more he saw, the more he understood he didn't know which path to follow.

"Come here." She took his hand and pulled him up. She led him to the nearby fire where Vanessa and Paul, but thankfully not Carlos, had gathered.

Paul sat, idly staring into the fire as if entranced. The flickering light reflected in his eyes, strengthening the illusion. Vanessa sat nearby with Isabella asleep with her head in her lap.

Elena handed Patrick a long stick with a blackened tip. "Stir the fire."

"Seriously?"

"Yes," she replied indignantly.

"What am I supposed to be doing?"

"Cleromancy. You stir the fire and then the arrangement of the coals will tell you where they are."

He laughed uncomfortably and Elena's nostrils flared slightly in the firelight. He sobered up quickly.

"What's so funny?"

"It just sounds . . . " *Ridiculous? Stupid?* "Random," he finally said.

"Sometimes our Mundane bodies have trouble comprehending our magical spirits. And *you* are especially oblivious. This is just a way to turn the answers into something your Mundane eyes can see."

"That actually makes sense."

"Of course it makes sense," she said icily.

Patrick saw Paul smirking at him. Vanessa ignored him, and watched her daughter sleep, raking her fingers through her hair gently.

"I'll try it," Patrick said. "What else do I need to do?" He really hoped he didn't have to chant or something.

"It's just like anything else. Clear your mind. Focus on the question you want answered. I find it helpful to close my eyes so I'm not distracted. Then I just feel it click when the answer has revealed itself."

Patrick stood over the fire with the stick. The heat seeped into his jeans and he wondered how hot denim had to get before it combusted. He had to close his eyes in any case to keep the smoke out. The smoke burned his lungs and he had to focus to keep himself from coughing and turning away. He thought about how angry his father would have been if he had randomly stirred his carefully engineered campfire, and he smiled to himself.

He used the memory to conjure a gut feeling that meant "family." A mixture of love, belonging, and grief that defined everything they were. He closed his eyes and stirred the fire. He could feel a larger log dislodging and imagined sparks had scattered the ground. He resisted opening his eyes to check for embers on his shoes. He continued stirring until he felt the click Elena had described. He felt done. The resistance of the logs had disappeared because they had fallen into the right place.

He stepped back and released the cough his lungs had been craving. He enjoyed a deep breath of crisp air away from the fire before turning back around. His stirring had brought the fire down to a smolder and the scene had become much darker. Elena, Vanessa, and Paul stood over the ring looking inside. Their intense interest left him with a sense of disquiet.

Paul and Vanessa had appeared half asleep moments ago. He didn't like them seeing the results before him, like having someone else open his report card before he got to see it.

"What is it?" Patrick asked.

"The answer is for you, not us," Elena said. "You have to look."

He didn't know what he expected to see, but by the way they gawked at the fire, he expected something more dramatic. He only saw the expected pile of coals any Mundane could have created by stirring a fire.

However, like one of those magic eye pictures that looked like nothing at first, after he stared at the coals for a moment, the image jumped out at him. And then he couldn't un-see it.

Most of the coals remained in a meaningless heap in the middle. But the ones on the outside had arranged into a perfect circle, as if someone had reached in and meticulously sorted them. He had seen this same circle before.

"Oh," he said. "I know where they are." He chuckled to himself. "It's sort of obvious. I should have known without magic."

Even his Mundane self had thought it was the next best place to go. He didn't know which of the "emotionally disturbed" young wizards had the particular quirk, but someone at Evangeline's school spent a lot of time arranging rocks into circles on the beach near the school. As soon as he saw the circle of coals, the image of these rock circles jumped into his head. The three of them looked at him with bright eyes.

"Well?" Elena asked.

"Heartsong Academy," Patrick said. "They are all at Heartsong Academy. Or they will be. They're on their way."

CHAPTER NINETEEN

Xavier sat in a lumpy truck stop restaurant booth watching two men sitting across from each other. Xavier had been calling them the cowboy and the hipster in his mind. The cowboy looked like he'd walked right out of a Western wear shop in hat and boots and Wrangler jeans, and the hipster had a too-long beard and wore flip-flops and a Hawaiian shirt which appeared to be worn ironically. The cowboy ate steak and drank Dr. Pepper and the hipster picked at a BLT and sipped ice water with lemon with a look of distaste. They looked at their respective phones and ignored each other. Other than being fall wizards who believed winter wizards were sub-human, these two did not have much in common.

Xavier, on the other hand, had no food. He had been sitting in the booth for twenty minutes, but every waitress had ignored him. He hadn't even been given a menu. But he hadn't come to eat, so he didn't mind.

Extremely poor customer service was a downside of invisibility spells. He couldn't literally make himself invisible. But he excelled at repelling spells. People wouldn't look in his direction, and if they did see him, they'd forget him again within seconds. He had found a way to make himself so unremarkable that his presence was not registered.

He could easily slide under the radar of Mundanes, but Xavier had been following these two fall wizards since Beaumont, and they had yet to even sniff the air in concern about the proximity of a winter wizard. *Idiots.* But to their credit, he was damn good at this.

He used the quiet of being ignored to clear his mind and focus. He was out of his magical comfort zone. Xavier was a November wizard, near the cusp between fall and winter. The dark vacuum of his winter magic made it hard to see, but he could occasionally get glimpses of premonitions. Like a tiny sliver of light peeking over the horizon right before twilight.

He had to follow them, although he didn't understand why. A lot rode on his feeble semi-fall premonitions. Evangeline, Emmy, and Lacie were hundreds of miles in the other direction, much closer to the leader of Los Segadores. But that was often the difference between fall wizards and winter wizards. Winter wizards reacted and fall wizards planned. He wouldn't fall into the winter wizard trap.

Both of the men's phones chirped with discordant text alerts. Even their phone sounds didn't get along. They received their messages and looked at each other for the first time in their meal.

The one in the cowboy hat shook his head and chuckled darkly. The hipster sneered, also seeming to get the joke.

"Dumb ass flowers," Cowboy said. "How far?"

Hipster typed into his phone. "Not far. We can be there by

midnight."

"Good."

"I just wish they would behave like proper springs and sleep in the grass. That would be much easier."

"Eh, we'll figure something out. I'm thinking they're not the sharpest tools in the shed."

Nathan grabbed Emmy by the shoulders to pull her back. "Oh God," he whispered. She backed into his chest, not bothered by the vice-like grasp he had taken her in.

Put her with the others, Evangeline had said. Emmy hadn't thought much of the statement. She had assumed she referred to a place to stay. A place to rest. Where other people happened to be. But others meant… what? Other fall wizards? Was this the missing staff?

With Nathan and Emmy frozen in place, the fire starter boy walked past them. He went back out the front door and locked the door behind him.

With the door closed, the smell of blood overwhelmed her. Emmy wiggled out of Nathan's grasp. If she had to vomit, she'd rather not spew all over his hands. She kept her hand tightly attached to his though. Her head felt too light. She needed to breathe to keep from passing out, but that would mean inhaling the scent of blood. The scent was so thick in the air she could taste it. The blood coated her tongue and her throat.

"Bathroom," Emmy croaked.

Emmy headed to the hallway on the side of the counter. She felt sticky blood under her shoes like old soda on the floor of a movie theater. She saw three bodies piled behind the counter. Two men and a woman. She couldn't pinpoint how they had died, and she doubted a medical examiner would have been able to do much better. Their skin appeared burned and cut. The man's throat had been ripped out, with fleshy pieces of ligament sticking out of what was left of his neck. And the woman propped up on the wall had no eyes. She stared at Emmy with two dark, bloody holes.

Emmy keeled over and threw up on her shoes. When she opened her eyes, she saw and smelled the blood again, leading to another heaving. Nathan had his hand on her back, and he kept saying, "It's okay… you're okay," although Emmy couldn't imagine how any of this was okay.

When she finally stopped retching, he led her away from the bodies and back toward the door. Emmy caught a welcome whiff of salt air and saw Nathan had busted open one of the windows. Lacie also leaned on the sill, unbothered by the litter of glass dangerously close to her arms.

"Are you okay?" she asked.

"I don't think so," Emmy said.

Nathan kicked the doorknob. The cheap brass knob dangled, but Nathan couldn't get the door to budge.

"They used magic to lock us in," he said. "Don't worry. I'll figure it out."

"They're killers," Emmy whispered. "Do you think Evangeline did this?"

Nathan stopped staring at the frozen door and looked at Emmy. "I don't know," he said, his face grave. "Not necessarily. You saw what those other kids could do." He turned to Lacie. "How are you feeling?" he asked.

Lacie didn't respond. Her eyes had glazed over. She stared out of the broken window at the distant Gulf, transfixed by the crash of the small waves.

"If those three are Los Segadores," Nathan said quietly, as if the dead people could hear him. "They were probably killed in self-defense."

"If they could do… *that*, they probably also could have cast spells to paralyze or banish them. The way they died… " Emmy didn't finish her thought, unable to find words to adequately describe the image now burned into her mind for the rest of her life.

Nathan brushed the glass from the window off the pane with his jacket and stuck his head outside. He grunted and cursed.

"It's a long way down, and there doesn't seem to be a way to climb over to the walkway, at least not safely."

Emmy remembered when she had jumped off her own roof to test her magic when she was thirteen years old. Where was that fearlessness? Back then she hadn't truly understood fear. She thought fear was all scary movies and haunted houses. Since then, she had learned she was wrong. There was so much to fear in the world. Perhaps it had something to do with losing her talisman. Her parents and Evangeline had thought that would be a terrible thing. And it had been terrible, but it didn't kill her. However, it changed the color of the world, immutably and permanently.

And now that she had a future with Nathan, her fear had increased a hundred-fold. Now she had something to lose. Something good and real and beautiful, but fragile.

As she looked out the window at the ground below, her hands started to shake. Nathan took her hand and squeezed it, as if he understood everything she had been thinking.

"Your sister will let us out," Nathan said. "We just have to wait."

"I can't wait in here. Not with the… bodies," Lacie said,

also looking out the window.

"I'm sorry, but I don't think you have a choice. I'll keep looking for weak spots in the spell, but I'm not confident."

The three of them sat as close as they could to the open window and Lacie tried not to think about the microscopic blood particles entering her nose and mouth every time she breathed. She tried to imagine what Lacie from two days ago would think if she got a glimpse of her current circumstances. But when she thought it, she realized she did know the answer to that question. She had been seeing bits and pieces of this day for a long time. She had felt the pain from the spells slicing at her skin. She had smelled the blood. She had felt the fear. And her past self had naturally assumed they were nightmares, not prophecies. And now every "nightmare" she had ever had took on new meaning. She had seen more things. More blood. More pain. More fear. The images were all so disorganized she couldn't say exactly what would happen next; she just knew this wasn't over. What a useless gift. All she had was fear and nothing she could do about it.

Everyone seemed to think Lacie hadn't known about magic before they told her. In a way that was true. She had never imagined some people really were considered witches and wizards. She definitely didn't think there were wizard schools or wars against different types of wizards. But of course she knew magic was real. She remembered casting her first spell when she had been around seven years old. Her mother was taking her shopping for new school clothes. Lacie couldn't remember exactly why this had seemed so objectionable at the time, but she remembered feeling as if going shopping was some kind of grave injustice that must not be allowed. She stamped her foot and declared she would not be going shopping, and when she did, she felt something click. She had made the statement true. When her mother dragged her out to her car and snapped her into her booster seat, the car wouldn't start, and they didn't go shopping. She had made it happen, and since then, she had taken for granted it was possible. She had believed anyone could get their way if they really, really wanted it and declared it to be so.

She quickly learned she also had to be careful. Her mother often said, *be careful what you wish for because you just might get it.* The saying was common, but perhaps her mother really meant it as a secret warning about magic. Lacie's older sister Ashlynn was mean. She acted as if life was some sort of game where the goal is to make other people as miserable as possible, and she always won. So, she deserved everything she got, but sometimes it went too far.

Lacie would want Ashlynn to leave her alone and sometimes that meant bad things would happen to her. When she wanted to stop sharing a room with Ashlynn, she fell down the stairs and broke her leg. She had to sleep in the downstairs bedroom for six weeks. Lacie had felt terrible and even tried to be nice to Ashlynn for a while, but it didn't last. The leg had probably been the worst thing, but bad stuff happened to Ashlynn all the time. Ashlynn was bullying one of Lacie's friends in honors geometry class, so Ashlynn failed the first semester and was moved to a regular class. As punishment for various misdeeds, Lacie had given Ashlynn rashes, diarrhea, acne, memory loss during tests, body odor, giant hanging boogers when talking to cute guys, and mono, which shut her down for months. Lacie had not thought of it as magic. It was karma.

And karma bit back. Lacie believed her nightmares were somehow punishment for her ability to bend circumstances in her favor. Nothing good comes free.

After what seemed like hours, but might have been minutes, the boy who had dragged her up here came back with food. He had piled cold hamburgers on a plastic blue tray from a cafeteria. The gray meat also screamed school cafeteria food. No one ate much.

Eventually, Emmy fell asleep with her head on Nathan's shoulder. Nathan had said he would stay up and keep a look out, but eventually he rested his head on the top of Emmy's head and fell asleep too. Lacie's entire body ached and her skin stung from cuts, and she couldn't imagine ever sleeping again.

CHAPTER TWENTY

Xavier slowed as the truck he was following slowed. They seemed unsure where to turn. *Damn.* Xavier could disguise his body well, but his whole car was another matter. They would know he was following him if he slowed down with them. He passed them and turned into the parking lot of a Whataburger so he could watch them from his rearview mirror. They pulled back onto the frontage road. Xavier groaned. Could they have been trying to lose him? Did they know?

As soon as they pulled out of sight, he put the car in reverse and turned back to follow them, causing a honk from someone else pulling out. He drove too fast out of the parking lot and back onto the frontage road. He also braked too quickly when he saw their truck. They must have just driven into the wrong parking lot because he saw the truck parked at a Holiday Inn Express. Xavier turned in quickly, hopping the curb with one of his wheels. So much for being inconspicuous.

But he felt a dark energy building. His anxiety escalated and he felt the need to rush without knowing why. He didn't know why he was following them, but he knew it was about to happen.

Samantha lay in the dark with her hand on Sophie's back, feeling it gently rise and fall in sleep. She nuzzled her nose into Sophie's hair and inhaled the scent of her homemade lavender baby soap. Zander's took his turn as look out, so Samantha pretended to sleep for his benefit. She might never sleep again. Not until that mark was off Sophie's arm. She had tried everything she could think of. Every purifying, cleansing, and healing spell she knew. Nothing worked. Zander didn't know as many spells as Samantha, but he was far more powerful, and he had failed to remove the mark as well. So they ran and they hid.

Zander moved across the room to the window. A sliver of light from the streetlamps cast shadows across the room.

"What is it?" Samantha asked.

He startled at the sound of her voice.

"I thought you were sleeping," he said.

"Why did you look out the window? Is something out there?"

Zander didn't respond.

"Zander?"

"We're safe in here. The door is bolted."

"Zander?" Samantha asked again sternly.

"There are some fall wizards sitting outside."

Samantha sat up quickly. Sophie wiggled at the interruption, but she didn't wake. Samantha got out of bed and reached for the curtain to peek out.

Zander grabbed her arm gently to stop her. "Don't. They might see you."

They stood for a moment in the darkness, his hand cradling her wrist, breathing softly.

"They shouldn't have found us," Samantha said. "The cloaking spell…"

"I don't know. They must know some magic we don't."

"No."

"It could just be two random fall wizards, Samantha."

"No," she said again. "They have a dark energy. Can't you feel it? They are not normal fall wizards. They're out of balance somehow."

Zander said nothing.

Samantha gasped as Sophie clutched her hand.

"What's wrong, Mommy?"

"Nothing, sweetie. Go back to sleep."

"Are there monsters out there?" she asked in a conspiratorial whisper, like they all played a game.

Zander said, "Yes," and Samantha said, "No," simultaneously. She glared at him.

"What?" he asked. "She's not stupid. She knows we're running from something."

"It's okay, Mommy," she said. "I'll protect you from the monsters. I'm not scared."

Samantha felt her eyes get wet. She cradled Sophie's head while she looked up at her, her pale eyes barely visible in the dark.

"No, baby," Samantha said, kneeling down to her eye level. "I protect *you* from monsters. It's what mommies do."

"They don't know where we are," Zander said. "That doesn't make sense. We should be easier to find the closer they get. How could they follow us to the hotel, but not know which room we're in?"

"Maybe they're just waiting," Samantha said. "Like you said. The door is bolted. Maybe they're going to wait until we try to leave."

"They're getting out," Zander said, pulling Samantha and Sophie away from the window.

"We'll be okay, though, right Daddy?" Sophie said, tugging at his shorts. "Because you made our room monster proof."

"Yes, yes, I did," he said.

Sophie suddenly clapped her hands over her ears, as if pained.

"What's wrong?" Samantha asked, her voice high pitched with panic. These hunters were barbarians, killing with Mundane guns. But perhaps those were just the ones who make the news. The better wizards probably used magical methods. With magic, a bolted door wouldn't stop them.

However, before Sophie could respond, the fire alarm suddenly cut into the quiet like shattering glass.

"What is it? I don't like it," Sophie cried.

Samantha held her and clapped her own hands over Sophie to help muffle the sound. "It's okay," Samantha said, even though Sophie certainly couldn't hear her.

"How stupid do they think we are?" Zander said, raising his voice over the incessant siren. Blue lights flashed in the hallway. He laughed darkly. "They pull the fire alarm thinking we'll just scamper out?"

"What if they set a real fire?" Samantha asked.

Zander didn't respond. He peeked out of the peephole in the front door.

"I don't see smoke," he said.

"Either way, we're trapped," Samantha said. With the

cover of the siren, she didn't have to hide the terror in her voice for Sophie's benefit. "We're trapped. We can't stay in this room forever. What do we do?"

"I'll go. My magic burns the brightest. I'm too easy to find. And if I slip out without them seeing me, they won't know you aren't with me. They'll follow me and you can get out. Rent a car or something."

"Don't leave us." Samantha gently peeled Sophie's little hand off of her ear. "Sophie, what is going to happen next?"

"What are you doing?" Zander asked.

"She knew the alarm was going to go off." Sophie was crying now, and Samantha kissed a tear off her cheek. "What is going to happen? If it's bad, we'll stop it. But we need to know."

"I don't know," she said with a trembling lip.

"Don't do that," Zander said. "You're upsetting her."

"She's already upset."

"I love you," Zander said. "Both of you." He had never said those words to Samantha. And she had never said it to him. She didn't know how he felt about it, but she felt like admitting they were happy together meant they were leaving Imogene behind. In any case, she knew he was saying it now because he was worried he might not get another chance.

He kissed Sophie on the head, and when he stood to face Samantha, she shook her head.

"I said no," she said. "Don't leave."

"I won't. I won't do what I said and drive away. I'll be back. It's just… I think we've run out of options. We've tried to run. We've tried to hide. There is only one option left. I can do this. I can take them down."

"With what?" she asked, her voice airy with panic and exasperation.

"Have faith in your season," he said.

Sophie screamed. The shrill sound was preternaturally loud, dwarfing the fire alarm.

"Shh," both Samantha and Zander said. She continued to wail, and Samantha saw the television vibrating on its stand. Samantha tried to cover her mouth. "You have to be quiet," she said.

Sophie bit Samantha's hand. Not hard, but enough to make a mark. Samantha gasped and pulled away instinctively. She had never done anything like that before.

"Sophie, no," Zander said.

She looked him hard in the eye, took a deep breath, and screamed again. Now, Samantha covered her ears. Sophie's scream took on a multi-dimensional quality; both high enough to break glass and low enough to cause a rockslide at the same time. Samantha felt as if the blood vessels in her brain might pop.

Xavier ran through the parking lot of the Holiday Inn Express. He had been waiting, dozing off, then everything happened fast. He closed his eyes for a moment and the cowboy and the hipster had disappeared. He heard a loud pop and smoke billowed from the lobby. People were streaming out of the hotel, but he didn't see Cowboy and Hipster. There was new magical energy in this hotel. He couldn't place it, but the best description of the feeling was *nostalgia*. The familiar scent made him feel happy and sad at once, but he couldn't place it.

He ran into the smoky lobby. A man carrying a child looked directly at Xavier and said, "Fire. Turn around."

The man's words caused his scalp to prickle and he quickly

realized why. The man had seen him. Xavier felt unarmed. Not only did he not have a weapon, he hadn't taken the time to fully cloak himself. He paused long enough to muster a dark cloud to shroud his presence. More people ran by him, and none of them looked his way. None of the people leaving were wizards. The cowboy and hipster and the wizards giving off the nostalgic magic were all inside.

The sound of the fire alarm suddenly changed. Did a second alarm come on? Another sound mixed with the Mundane siren, something dark. Xavier's skin felt clammy and he was afraid he might pass out. The sound made him feel sick. But at the same time, he felt drawn to it, as if it were calling to him specifically.

Xavier ran up the stairs toward the sound. He exited on the fourth floor. There was no smoke here. He stopped suddenly when he saw the cowboy and the hipster both standing in the hallway, cowering and covering their ears. The stairway door slammed shut behind him. Unfortunately, the discordant squealing wasn't enough to completely mask the sound. The cowboy and the hipster swiveled around, still in a cowering position. The cowboy pulled out a gun.

Xavier could see their lips moving, speaking to each other, but he couldn't hear their words. Their gaze swiveled back and forth in his general area, as if they could only lock onto him for a moment before their eyeballs betrayed them. He felt a painful sting in his shoulder. He grabbed his arm and felt nothing but the cotton of his shirt. Then he realized he had felt the phantom pain of a future injury. He flung himself back against the wall, dodging the bullet that would have lodged into his shoulder.

They could see him, if not clearly. He wanted them away from this place, away from the screaming, although he couldn't say why. If he ran, would they chase him?

Xavier held out his hands, in a gesture of "come and get me." The hipster sneered and the cowboy narrowed his eyes. The cowboy raised his gun again and the hipster unsheathed a long, curved knife Xavier hadn't noticed before.

He was about to turn and run when one of the hallway doors opened. With all of the ear-bleeding noise, the cowboy and hipster didn't notice right away. The cowboy fired a shot at Xavier, but the bullet lodged into the wall six feet from him. Either the cowboy was a terrible shot or Xavier's cloaking spell worked well enough to confuse the cowboy. He guessed the latter.

From his ducking position, Xavier saw the person who had entered the hallway. He froze in his crouch, his body paralyzed. But his mind was thrown backwards, catapulting back through time, and falling into a cold, dark pit. He could hear the West Texas winds blowing and could taste the gritty dust in his mouth. A small voice inside him said the sensations weren't real. He hadn't gone anywhere. He could still feel the rough hotel carpet and smell the industrial strength laundry detergent. But pulling himself out of the pit was easier said than done. He had seen his stepfather. The one who had abused him for years. He was here. Somehow, he had lived and tricked him into coming here. He could feel his old scars burn.

Despite all of his instincts to get far away from the horrible sound, Zander had been holding Sophie the entire time she screamed. Samantha had gently rubbed her back. He could tell by her lips she was gently saying "shh," but he couldn't hear her. He worried he might never hear anything again. He was more aware of his eardrums than ever before. He could feel them vibrate and strain.

Sophie stopped screaming suddenly. She continued to whimper into his chest. "I don't want you to die. I don't want you to die," she said.

"I'm not going to die," he whispered into her ear.

"You were," she said. "You were if you went outside."

"He won't go outside," Samantha said soothingly. "We'll all stay right here."

"He can go now," Sophie said. "He won't die anymore. He just had to wait. I had to make you wait."

Zander looked at Samantha and she nodded.

Zander kissed Sophie on the head again and stood up. His legs felt wobbly. He had said he would fight because he had no choice. He would do anything to protect Samantha and Sophie, including fight. Including kill. But he really, really, really didn't want to.

"You can do it," Sophie said. She smiled up at him and he smiled back. "And if you can't, I'll save you."

Zander laughed sadly. He patted her head again.

"I'll save you too," Samantha said quietly. If he had wanted her to say she loved him, that was probably the closest he would get today.

He put his hand on the door and steeled himself. He heard a gunshot and startled, pulling his hand away from the door on instinct. But somehow he also knew it had been his cue. He opened the door quickly and stepped into the hallway. The two fall wizards were facing away from him, aiming their weapons toward what Zander could only describe as a shadow without a body.

He tried not to let the specter distract him. But it had distracted the fall wizards. Zander had only seconds before they redirected their energy on him. Zander didn't know how to fight. He didn't know how to use his magic to harm. But he did know how to manipulate the environment. And the environment knew how to fight.

He tensed his muscles to help him summon his magic. His vision shimmered and he entered what he thought of as "the connection." He could move into another plane where he could see and feel all the energy of life webbed together with streams of light. Some streams were small, some large, but they were all connected. He could tug on one thread and call upon the power of life itself. He called everything he could get his hands on into the hallway.

But he wasn't moving fast enough, the man with the beard turned on him with a giant knife. Zander backed away and winced, knowing he hadn't dodged the hit. But instead of feeling the metal enter his skin, Sophie's scream cut through him again. The man dropped his knife and it shattered on the ground as if it had been made of glass.

Sophie's scream disrupted Zander's spell. The forces of light retreated at the sound, but as if she knew this, she went silent again as soon as the knife shattered. Zander then used his own spell to attack. The man looked naked without his knife. The fool had become so reliant on his Mundane weapon he appeared completely unprepared to engage in a magical battle. So, Zander turned his energy to the man with the gun.

The man in the cowboy hat pulled the trigger, and the bullet swirled through the air in a bizarre pattern, more like a deflating balloon than a bullet. Zander hadn't done that. He saw Samantha standing behind him with her hands raised. *Damn.* He didn't know she could stop bullets.

Zander thrust his waiting magic into the man's lungs. He couldn't use his magic to take away, but he could add. Every particle in the air shot into the man's mouth and into his lungs. Dust, pollen, pollution, the smoke from downstairs. Everything.

The man grasped his throat, wheezing helplessly. He fell to the ground and dropped the gun. It flew in Samantha's direction and she lunged for it, but the man with the beard grabbed it first. He knocked Samantha down and pinned her against the ground with his knee dug into her back and aimed the gun at her head.

No. Zander didn't even have to think of a spell. The force of his anger and fear made it happen. The electricity from the lights above broke from their wire prisons and a lightning bolt broke through the light bulb; the current ran directly into the man's head. He froze, suspended for a moment, and then crumpled, the smell of burning beard hair thick in the air.

The man in the cowboy hat—cowboy hat gone revealing a prematurely balding head—moved toward the stairs, his breath a sickening rattle. Zander considered following him, chasing him down and hitting him with the same spell over and over until his lungs were black and shriveled and he drowned in the middle of a sea of fresh air. But he only watched as he pushed open the heavy door and disappeared behind it.

"Sophie, no!" Samantha cried from behind him.

When cowboy hat left, Zander had thought the battle had ended, but something darker and stranger had materialized in the hallway. He had forgotten about the specter. In the confusion, Sophie had separated from them and moved down the hall toward the elevator. She stood at the edge of what appeared to be a black hole. The end of the hallway had disappeared; the rooms, the carpeting, the lights. Everything had been wiped away as if it had never been there at all. A swirling black mass slowly consumed it. Sophie stood with her toes hanging over the precipice.

Zander felt as if his own lungs had shriveled. Samantha was already halfway down the hallway, running at full sprint toward the abyss. Zander followed her, fearing he was about to lose both of them. Samantha grabbed Sophie's arm, pulling her away. However, her other arm appeared to be stuck in the blackness.

"No," Zander whispered. He felt like he was moving through sand, unable to cross the short space fast enough.

As Zander approached, Samantha did something he couldn't believe. She released Sophie's hand as she stared into the black hole, as if she saw something inside it. Something about the mass had hypnotized Samantha and called to her, as it had for Sophie.

"Stop," he said, his voice sounding far too small against the eternity of blackness.

However, once he reached them, the scene changed in an instant. Sophie was no longer reaching her hand into a black hole, but gripping the hand of an alarmed young man. He didn't shake Sophie off, but he looked at her the same way Zander had been looking at the black hole. Zander knew him from somewhere, but he couldn't place where.

"Xavier," Samantha said, filling in the blanks in Zander's mind.

Xavier's heart hammered and he could still taste West Texas dirt and bile in his mouth, but his rational mind had caught up to his instincts. The man with Samantha wasn't Xavier's stepfather. This could only be his son, the one who inherited the other half of Rachel Colter's wealth. If Xavier had never seen his face, he wouldn't feel sick and humiliated like he did right now. This man's magic was nothing like his father's, and if they didn't look so alike, Xavier would have never guessed they were even distantly related. His aura of spring was so potent Xavier's eyes itched from phantom pollen.

"Your distraction was just enough to throw the balance in our favor," Samantha said. "You saved us."

While Samantha smiled at him brilliantly, she gently pulled the little girl away from him. He had been so distracted by the man; he had barely registered the small hand clutching his. At Samantha's coaxing, she released Xavier's hand and wrapped her arms around Samantha's leg. As Xavier watched the girl with furrowed brows, Samantha tried to push her further behind her and gently pressed her head into her hip to shield her face.

Mundanes might not notice, but the girl's magic was nothing like theirs. A wizard would see two lambs raising a dinosaur. She did not belong to them. For some reason, Xavier felt as if the girl belonged to him instead, even though that wasn't possible. But she was the one who called him here to step in at just the right moment.

"This is Sophie," Samantha said, tousling her hair so blond curls fell over her face. "Our daughter."

Her smile remained ebullient, but her eyes were wide, and she didn't blink often enough. She knew *he knew* she was lying, and her eyes seemed to plead with him to accept the lie. He felt himself nodding as if someone else was running the controls. "Your daughter," he repeated. She had managed to use magic to compel him to nod and agree but her magic wasn't strong enough to actually change his mind.

He shook his head, trying to rid himself of the drugged sensation. "I have to go," he said, without any idea of where he needed to be. He needed to be away from that man. And he already felt sick without Samantha plunging into his mind and trying to move things around.

"Okay," Samantha said.

The man said something too, but Xavier had managed to block him out as well as he could block himself out and all he heard was a muffled murmur, sending vibrations into the air with no sound.

As much as he had the urge to leave, he also had the inexplicable urge to take the little girl with him. Even though he just met her, he felt like if he left her, he'd be leaving something critical behind.

"She's not safe," Xavier said, gesturing toward Sophie.

"We'll keep her safe," Samantha said.

"If I hadn't shown up, she would have died," Xavier said simply. He hadn't done anything special to save her. Samantha and the man had been the ones to truly fight them off, but his distraction had been timed perfectly to give them the edge they needed. Without him, they would have failed, and Sophie would be dead.

Samantha's eyes welled with tears. "I don't know what to do," she said.

"He can take us to the special place," Sophie said.

Xavier was surprised to hear her speak. She looked so small and fragile, but her voice was sure and clear.

"What special place?" Samantha asked.

"The special hiding place by the ocean. He takes us there. That's what happens next," Sophie declared.

"Heartsong Academy?" Xavier asked the tiny person who had somehow asserted herself as their leader.

She shrugged.

"You can get into Heartsong?" Samantha asked.

He nodded. "Evangeline lives there."

"She's right. It's probably the only place with powerful enough magical protection to truly keep out the Los Segadores."

"He can't come," Xavier said. It probably wasn't fair, but he didn't care. He couldn't be around that man.

The man murmured something again, and Xavier blocked out the actual words, but he sensed the assent. Samantha and Sophie faded into his blurry outline while they hugged him goodbye.

CHAPTER TWENTY-ONE

November, The Blood Moon

Patrick woke up before Elena. Although he had never fully fallen asleep. And when he saw the faint blue light of morning seep through the tent, he felt surprised to have made it through the night. Every crack of a twig and rustling of leaves had brought him to full alert. Patrick put on his shoes and jacket. Without having anything to change into, he was still dressed from yesterday. He wished he had a toothbrush.

He crawled out of the tent awkwardly and found the bustling camp remarkably quiet. Gentle plumes of smoke rose from smoldering fires. Patrick had expected more people awake already, making breakfast, brewing up coffee, maybe even packing up camp. But he only saw Abi.

She sat outside the tent closest to theirs and stared at Patrick with alert intensity, as if she had been waiting for him.

"Good morning," Patrick said, wishing he could remember how to say it in Spanish.

She nodded to him. After a pause she raised one knobby finger and pointed in the direction of the street.

"Are you telling me to leave?" Patrick asked.

She shook her head so slightly it might have been an involuntary jerk. "Follow him," Abi said clearly.

"What?" Patrick asked. The command had been clear, but her sudden use of English surprised him.

Abi pointed again. "Follow Carlos," she said.

"Follow Carlos?" Patrick asked, stupidly repeating her.

She cocked a bushy eyebrow at him.

"Okay," Patrick said. "He went that way?"

She didn't nod or point again, clearly deciding Patrick had been given enough instruction.

Patrick considered asking why, but he guessed the question would be ignored. And despite her cool treatment of him, and the showing of the death card, he now had the sense she was somehow on his side.

Patrick nodded. "Okay."

As commanded, he quietly walked through the camp, back toward the road. He saw the Gap ad woman come towards him with a jug of water. Farther along, an older man set up a propane stove. He assumed he had gotten up before most of the other residents of the camp, but actually had had gotten up so much later, many of them had already left—although where to, he didn't know. Once he reached the clearing, he saw Vanessa come out of her trailer carrying a bag of garbage.

"Good morning," Patrick said.

Vanessa didn't reply. She nodded absently.

"Where is Carlos?" Patrick asked.

Vanessa eyed him more closely now. "He went hunting

with some of the others."

Patrick found this information slightly comforting. It meant all the guns lying around the camp actually had a purpose. Patrick had no desire to kill his own dinner, skin it and remove organs, and then cook it over a fire, but he had respect for those who could live without relying on a grocery store to feed them.

"Have they gone far?" Patrick asked.

"I don't know," Vanessa said dismissively.

"Can I take that to the dumpster for you?" Patrick gestured toward the garbage bag in her hand. "I thought I saw one closer to the road."

"Um… sure," she said, eyeing him sideways, as if his kindness confused her. She handed him the bag. "Thanks," she said.

The distance to the road was farther than he had remembered, but he eventually saw the green dumpster sitting behind the tiny gas station he had noticed earlier. He heaved the bag into the dumpster, letting loose a torrent of flies.

Happy to be relieved of his load, he wiped his hands on his jeans and turned back toward the road. Abi had wanted him to follow Carlos, and he presumed she would have only given him that instruction if he had been close enough to follow. Should he have borrowed a car?

However, as he thought it, he caught movement out of the corner of his eye. Paul's truck was inching along the farm road slowly, the engine only gently humming.

Carlos, Pike, and a few other men Patrick hadn't been introduced to, sat in the back of the truck, holding rifles. Carlos pointed down the road in a gesture that reminded Patrick of the same gesture his great-great grandmother had used. He didn't speak, but the group of wizards with him didn't need any further command. Patrick looked down the road and saw what he assumed Carlos had pointed at. A man. He was facing away from them, walking down the side of the highway. He wore a dark gray hoodie with the hood tied tightly around his face and his hands shoved deep in his pockets. Patrick had a brief lurch in his stomach when he thought it might be Xavier. But as soon as the thought came into his mind, he dismissed it. Xavier walked differently, and this man looked shorter.

The pick-up sped up toward him. The man turned around and Patrick saw he wasn't a man, he was a boy. He couldn't have been much older than thirteen. When he saw the approaching car, he ran. They had waited until he was on a bridge, so he couldn't dash into the woods. He could jump to his death or continue along the road. Patrick ran too, unsure why. He would never reach the child before the car. In a sickening flash, he saw what was about to happen, but he didn't believe it. It must have been his sick mind interpreting a vision in the darkest way possible.

But then he saw Pike raise his gun. The boy turned around long enough for Patrick to see his wide, unblinking eyes looking down the barrel of the gun. Patrick saw the gun kick back, and the boy crumpled to the ground. But he didn't hear the shot. The truck made a wide U-Turn and Patrick retreated into the woods, but they weren't going for him, they were heading back to the body. Pike jumped out and went to the boy. From the truck, Patrick actually heard laughter. Like they were smashing mailboxes and not slaughtering children. Pike took something from the body and handed it to Carlos before climbing back in the truck.

White spots popped in Patrick's vision and he keeled over and retched while the men in the truck whooped in celebration. He could smell the metallic tint of blood in the air, and it made him retch again.

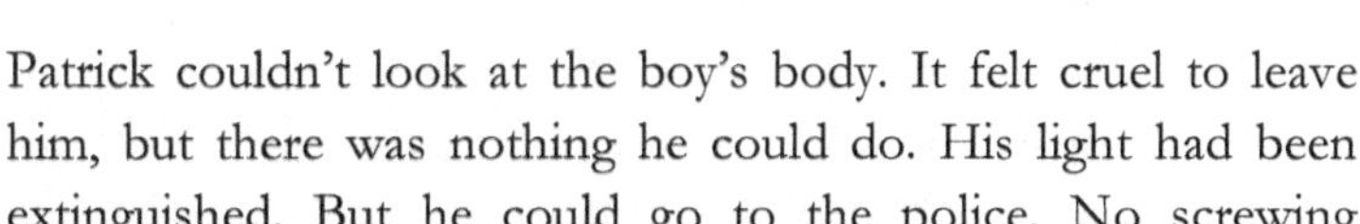

Patrick couldn't look at the boy's body. It felt cruel to leave him, but there was nothing he could do. His light had been extinguished. But he could go to the police. No screwing around with the unspoken wizard tradition of leaving Mundanes out of it. He had witnessed a murder. Even the word murder seemed too tame. He had witnessed a slaughter.

He would go back to the camp. He would get Elena, and try to get Isabella, Vanessa, and Abi too, and then go straight to the police station. But he didn't have his car. He would have to steal someone's keys. Maybe he should go to the police station first. But he couldn't bring himself to leave Elena with that monster for one second longer. Who knows what he would do when he knew Patrick was on to him.

Patrick ran back into the clearing and toward Carlos's trailer. He couldn't remember if Isabella was staying in the trailer or back in the tent with Abi. He poked his head in and didn't see Vanessa. The two small beds in the trailer both appeared empty. He should have left then, and went straight to the tents, but he saw something out of the corner of his eye that bothered him.

A blue Maxwell House coffee can sat on the counter and a red fingerprint was smudged on the lid. Blood. He grabbed the can and pulled off the lid and was assaulted by a powerful flood of magic, an assortment of heat and cold, light and dark, all intermingled. The smudged blood must have been coming from the item on top—a chain carrying a heavy crucifix, fresh blood gleaming on the silver. The smell of blood made his head swim again. He held his breath to stave off another round of dry heaving. His hands shook, so he balled them into fists, squeezing them until they burned. Then he released his breath and continued.

The sight of the crucifix caused another jump in his stomach when he feared it might be Xavier's talisman. But he knew that wasn't Xavier. He had seen the boy's face. And this wasn't Xavier's talisman, the magic felt wrong. But the similarities were too frightening. It *could* have been Xavier. It could be Xavier next time.

The crucifix thrummed with dark magic that felt contrary to the figure of Jesus. But the use of a crucifix as a talisman didn't mean the boy had any connection to Jesus. The cross was a commonly used talisman due to its innate magical properties.

Patrick rifled through the other items in the can. There were probably thirty unique items, and each one screamed with jarring magic. As he ran his hands through, the items took too long to quiet, reshuffling into various positions, angry to be sharing a small space.

There were talismans, and guessing by the recent addition, trophies from kills. Most of the items were jewelry of some kind, many of which were wedding rings. There was also a carved wooden whale figure, a few smooth stones, a conch shell, a large animal tooth, and a lock of stark white hair. Without even thinking about it, he sorted the items into two piles. The items wanted to sort themselves. Summer and winter.

He felt it before he could see it. A glint of silver against his skin made the world sway. He pulled out a man's wedding band. He held it in his hand and squeezed it. He looked again and saw its pair, a woman's wedding band. He held both of them in his fist and closed his eyes to experience their magic again, right there in his hand, his body shaking. He held the wedding rings of his mother and father.

With Patrick's head throbbing, he dropped his parents' wedding rings carefully in his pocket and stood, swaying on the spot. He had to be imagining it. Maybe the rings belonged to some random winter witch and wizard, and they reminded him of his parents, much like the crucifix had done with Xavier. But he knew those rings. He owned them, or he thought he did. The funeral home had given him the rings before his parents were cremated. What had he done with them? When did he have them last? The whole period in his life was a painful haze. He took the rings back to the Oppenheimer's house and put them in a box with other things that had belonged to his parents. Things Jess had thought he would want to keep, but he couldn't bear to look at. And then… what? Was the box still there?

Wait. No. He took the box of his parents' stuff to the unfinished home. When he moved out of the Oppenheimer's house, he moved that stuff to the house. *Shit.* The place didn't even have doors, let alone locks. What had he been thinking? He couldn't look at his parents' things, so he hadn't checked on them.

But Elena had. Elena had touched his parents' stuff.

In October, Patrick had taken Elena to his parents' house, which was technically *his* house. He couldn't tell if she understood how big of a deal this was.

"I like it," Elena had said, standing on the cement slab that would have been the living room. "Minimalist."

"Yeah, I guess you could call it that."

"It's not exactly what I expected."

"No. What were you expecting?"

"More walls. And floors and ceiling and stuff."

"You're so high maintenance," he said with a teasing smirk.

"Thank you for showing me your house," she said. She wrapped her arms around his shoulders and kissed him.

"You're welcome," he said, resting his chin on the top of her head. He loved that she didn't ask him why he didn't just finish the house already. She understood him in a way no one else did. Sitting on the edge of the past, present, and future, and being able to see in all directions made it easy to get to know someone. She knew who he was, what he had been, and what he would be, perhaps even better than he did.

The night was warm, but not too hot, so he set up the air mattress upstairs. In the upstairs bedroom, they were safe from the less nimble animals. They made love in the open air and then lay together and watched the trees sway until they fell asleep in each other's arms.

The next morning, Elena had woken before him. She nibbled at his ear until he laughed. He pulled her back under the covers with him.

"I have a surprise for you," she whispered.

"Yeah?"

"I drove down the street and got us kolaches and coffee."

"You're amazing."

"Come on," she said. She tugged on his arm and he rolled off the air mattress and got dressed.

As he followed her down the stairs, he immediately noticed something out of place. She had removed a box from the coat closet by the front door and placed it on the kitchen counter. Something sparkled on the granite. The tiny objects shone more brightly than what the low morning sun should have allowed, as if they gave off their own light. His stomach seized.

Patrick ignored the bag of kolaches on the counter and moved to the box.

"What did you do?" he asked.

"Oh… I'm sorry. I didn't think you would mind."

He picked up the rings. They felt hot and cold at the same time. But despite the strange uncomfortable energy they gave off, he squeezed them until they dug into his palms. In the box, he found other things that had belonged to his parents. A small gold cross his mother had sometimes worn around her neck. His father's wallet. His mother's keys. Most of these things no longer had any use. The credit cards in the wallet were cancelled. The keys didn't open anything. But he couldn't imagine throwing them away.

"How could you do this?"

She furrowed her brow in confusion. "I'm sorry, Patrick. I don't understand why you're mad. I found it in a closet. Every Dia De Muertos, I made altars with my Abi. I thought I could make one for your parents."

"You didn't know them."

"No, but I'd like to."

"Well, you can't. Because they're dead."

"I know that," she said soothingly. "That's not what I mean. But I could still get to know their spirits."

"No."

"No?"

"No séances, and no gaudy altars."

"Gaudy?" She had a look that could have melted plastic.

"Just don't touch my things without my permission."

"Fine," she said coldly.

After a few hours of awkward walking on eggshells, he had apologized, and so had she. In a relationship with another fall wizard, fights didn't last long. They both tended toward balance and if they swayed too far out of balance, they would find their way back to the middle sooner rather than later. But that wasn't always a good thing. Maybe he subconsciously ignored anything that might alter the balance. Maybe he had missed something important.

He couldn't imagine why Elena would steal his parents' rings and give them to Carlos, but even if she had, why would they be in his box of trophies? Carlos hadn't killed his parents. Perhaps he was a thief, or Elena was. Maybe they grabbed anything valuable when they got the chance, but he doubted it. But Carlos, like many wizards, didn't care much about material things.

With the rings burning in his pocket, he wandered back to camp. He felt disconnected to his body and kept glancing around to remind himself where he was and how he had gotten there. The air had turned cooler since he had left Carlos's trailer, as if the weather had shifted along with his perceptions. Something fundamental had changed.

Patrick found Abi on her hands and knees examining patterns in the fallen leaves. He couldn't imagine such an old woman crawling on the ground in the same way a child might. Her long skirt was muddy, as well as her claw-like hands. With her cloudy eyes, he wondered how well she could see the leaves she examined.

When she saw him, she sat back on her heels in a pose even he would have trouble with. He reached his hand to her to help her stand, and she took it. Her cold hand felt like nothing but bones and skin. When she stood, she took his other hand as well, and the cold made him shiver, but she didn't seem bothered. She was remarkably small. Before her back had become hunched, she might have been five feet and change. Now she barely made it to Patrick's chest. Unwilling or unable to look him in the eye, she spoke to his sternum.

"¿Entiendes ahora?"

"Let me get Elena. She can translate."

"No," she said pointedly. "Elena no puede ayudar." Abi pointed and Patrick followed her finger to see Bella drawing something in the dirt with a stick. She now wore a sock monkey hat and magenta gloves. "Isabella." Abi said the name slowly and loudly so Patrick could understand.

"She's a little girl."

"Se puede confiar en el inocente," Abi said. "Y los niños no son tontos. Ella ve y oye todo."

"Bella," Abi called. She sat on a log and patted the spot next to her. Isabella scampered over, holding her doll. She also still wore the Belle costume, but now had on a clashing lime green hoodie. Her cheeks and nose were pink, and she wiped away a layer of clear snot. Patrick wondered if she should buy her a coat.

Abi spoke to the girl in Spanish and she nodded.

"In four days, the Blood Moon will rise," said the little girl, an odd youthful echo of the old woman. "There are many possible ways the leaves could fall, but all are sprayed with blood."

"What?" Patrick interrupted.

"Those marked with the symbol of the Blood Moon are marked for death. And the great purge will occur."

Abi traced a circle on her forearm to demonstrate.

"The red circle. That was on my brother."

Abi nodded and continued in Spanish. The little girl echoed her in English.

"The old ways have been tarnished and the beliefs I hold most dear have become profane. For centuries, fall wizards have celebrated the harvest, by preventing war, catastrophe, and untold devastation and suffering. We have saved humankind many times over. Prevented nuclear war. Stopped genocide. Saved billions of lives. The harvest refers to the culling of dangerous men whose lives will lead to these atrocities, before they can commit them. Only the most powerful oracles may choose the souls to harvest. As life, even dark lives, can only be snuffed out with the utmost care."

Although he knew Abi was the one speaking to him, Patrick stared at Isabella. This little child speaking such big and terrible words.

"I am afraid my great grandson has perverted the harvest and convinced his followers, and even his sister, of his darker interpretation. He has used his own limited magic to mark many for death, some of which will never have blood on their hands, at least not for a generation or more. Although dangerous men abound in places of power, he leaves them to ravage society, while he goes after easier targets whose path of destruction will be far more contained. He was once a good man, but he has become a demon, overcome by blood lust."

Either Isabella didn't understand the words she spoke, or

they didn't surprise her. Patrick could not believe Abi would ask her to say these things about her own father. Patrick realized the girl must be some sort of conduit. She didn't translate in the traditional way. Abi was funneling her thoughts through the mind of someone who spoke fluent English.

"He not only takes lives he is not meant to take, but he puts the community of wizards in danger with his grievous lack of subtlety. Better wizards have not needed Mundane weapons, they weave fate to cause the deaths they desire. Carlos has drawn attention even from the Mundanes. Even now, they are becoming more aware."

Patrick pulled his parents' wedding rings out of his pocket and held them in his palm, showing them to Abi. He couldn't keep his hands from shaking.

Before he could ask her a question, she took his hand and wrapped his fingers back around the rings; patting his hand in the most nurturing gesture he'd seen her offer so far.

"Why does he have my parents' wedding rings?" he asked when he saw she was not going to offer any explanation.

"A man of autumn does not worry about the past. Most of the paths ahead of you are dark and too short. But there are paths that lead to a fortuitous life. It will not be easy to find those paths. You must focus."

"Tell me what to do."

"No, you are the equinox. The true monarch. And you must complete the true harvest."

"The true harvest?"

"A dark soul must be sacrificed to save the lives of many. You know which dark soul you need to take."

Isabella wiped her nose with her sleeve, oblivious that her great-great grandmother had suggested Patrick kill her father.

"I'm not a killer."

She shook her head. "You are far too good a wizard to get blood on your hands. You only need to lead him on a path that leads to his demise."

Patrick thought that would still put blood on his hands.

Abi put her cold, bony hands on either side of his face and looked at him with her cloudy eyes. He wondered how well she could actually see him, although he doubted she needed her eyes to see. Without them, she probably saw him better.

"Do not react. *Think*." It took Patrick a moment to register that these words were not only spoken in English, but not spoken at all. She had projected a concept into his head he had translated into words. "Draw all your paths until you find the right one. There is not a perfect path, but there *is* a best one. The path marked by love."

Patrick opened his mouth, wanting to say something, but he suddenly felt foolish being limited to human speech.

"Do not react. *Think*," she projected again, louder and clearer than any words she could have spoken with her lips. And then she spoke, "Eres el monarca."

CHAPTER TWENTY-TWO

Patrick found Elena outside their tent. She sat in a camp chair with a flannel blanket wrapped around her shoulders. She clutched a cup of coffee and gave him a tentative smile.

"There is plenty more, if you want some," she said.

"What?"

"Coffee."

Patrick took her suggestion and poured himself a cup. No matter how strange and upsetting life became, there was always coffee. That was why he liked it. Every morning, no matter what, he had smelled coffee in his house. Coffee was one of the most constant things he had ever known. And even now, after his life had been turned inside out… coffee.

He sat across from her and sipped. He could manage the *think, don't react*, advice when it came to Carlos. Abi had been right. With his certain brand of power, Patrick only had the upper hand if he was strategic. If he could wait and have faith, he could bend fate. But with Elena, he couldn't do it. He couldn't think. He had to feel. There was no way around it.

"Something is different," Elena whispered.

He chanced a glance at her. She stared at the smoldering fire. She had one stick in the fire as if she had been stirring it, perhaps looking for her own answers.

"Please say something, Patrick," she said. "I can tell something is out of balance, but I don't know what it is. Just tell me."

Patrick got up abruptly, put his mug down, and dragged his chair closer to hers. He sat down and took her hand. He reached for her hand all the time, but she narrowed her eyes at him.

"What?" she asked. She pulled her hand away slightly, and he clasped it tighter. He needed to feel her reaction.

He reached his hand into his pocket and pulled out his parents' wedding rings. They continued to feel too hot and too cold at the same time, agitating the sensitive skin of his inner palm.

Her reaction wasn't what he expected. A powerful rush of pure joy almost made him drop her hand. But the happiness hit quick and then disappeared again, like a flash of lightning. Replaced with an uneasy mix of confusion, disappointment, and fear.

When he realized what she had thought, he could feel his ears turn red. She had thought he was proposing. But it hadn't taken her long to realize that despite thrusting wedding rings at her, something wasn't right. For one, there were two rings, not one. The reaction had thrown him off but may have given him his answer. If she had stolen these rings from his house and given them to Carlos, she would have recognized them. She would have understood the implied accusation.

"Can you explain these?" he asked, still clutching her hand.

"Are those your parents' wedding rings?" she asked gently.

"How did you know that?"

"I… I saw them before. At your house… " She didn't explain further, probably trying to avoid dredging up the old fight. She managed to free her hand from Patrick's grasp. "You were trying to read my mind. Don't you trust me? What's going on?" After a pause, her cheeks turned red too. She knew he knew what she had been thinking.

"Do you know why I have them?" he asked.

"No," she said.

"They were in Carlos's trailer."

"What?"

Damnit. She had pulled her hand away just in time. He couldn't tell if the surprise had been genuine.

"Are you sure they are the same rings?" she asked.

"Of course I'm sure."

"Why would he have them?"

"That's what I'm asking you."

"I don't know. Are you saying he's some kind of thief? Maybe you dropped them, and he picked them up."

"I don't carry them around in my pocket," he said in a low growl. "The last time I saw them is when you took them out of the box of my parents' stuff."

"Wait… are you saying I stole them? How can you think that?"

"An hour ago, I wouldn't have. Now, I don't know what to think."

"What happened an hour ago?"

"I learned your brother is a serial killer."

Elena's face blanched. "What?"

Patrick's heart raced. His mouth felt fuzzy like he might be sick. He needed to know Elena had nothing to do with this "harvest." He could play a game with the others, but he couldn't do it with her.

"What do you call it then?" he asked, his tone flat. "When someone kills lots of people?"

Elena stared at him with her big eyes. He saw her swallow before responding. "How did you find out?" she asked in a whisper.

His chest suddenly doubled in weight. He strained his shoulders to keep himself from leaning forward and dropping his head into his hands. He kept his gaze steady on her eyes.

She knows.

He took a few deep breaths before he spoke again, working to clear any cracks in his composure.

"I saw him kill a boy on the road. I had heard rumors about the harvest. But I didn't think it was real. Looks like I was wrong." He kept Abi out of it. Not that Abi needed his protection, but he didn't want to give Elena too much information. He wanted to know what she had to say. He held out hope she had some explanation. Or at least some sign she knew what her brother was doing was horrifying.

"Well?" Patrick prompted.

"I'm sorry you had to see that," she said, looking at her hands. "I should have explained it to you before... so you would understand. I knew you grew up without magic. No one has ever explained it to you before."

"So, explain it to me now."

"You probably know more than you think," she said, speaking to the ground. "Sooner or later, every fall wizard realizes what a terrible responsibility they have."

Patrick didn't respond. He waited for her to continue. She finally looked up at him.

"We were given the gift of prophecy," she continued. "If we know something horrible is to happen, we have the responsibility to prevent it." She shrugged awkwardly. "So, during the harvest, that's what we do. We prevent atrocities."

"By killing people?"

She winced slightly. He clung to that wince. She knew something was wrong with the logic even if she didn't say it aloud.

"By killing murderers," she said. "Before they commit their crime."

"How long before?"

"What do you mean?"

"The boy on the road. Was he on his way to kill someone? Or are we talking about something years in the future?"

"I don't know about the boy on the road. You'd have to ask Carlos."

"Okay, then in general. What are the guidelines? Is there a certain probability threshold they have to meet? For example, if the boy on the road was on his way to kill someone, with gun in hand, then the probability of him following through with his plan might be high. But if he were not to commit murder for another thirty years, infinite variables come into play. The probability goes down by quite a bit."

She smiled at him with a touch of pity. "It's not a math problem," she explained. "It's going to happen, or it's not. There is no probability."

Patrick literally bit his tongue to keep himself from arguing with her.

"Okay," he said. "What about severity? Is one murder enough? Or do they have to commit multiple murders? What about manslaughter? Or what if you kill someone by accident? Dead is dead, after all."

Elena furrowed her brow and shook her head.

"And does it have to be murder in the traditional sense? What about an executive who cuts corners on the manufacturing of a car and people die as a result?"

"Yes," she said, her mental block apparently lifting. "You're understanding. The executive is a good example. That's the kind of people targeted in the harvest. People who would be responsible for multiple deaths. My Abi says fall wizards have prevented at least three apocalyptic events, and saved millions of lives by preventing war, genocide, and stopping the spread of disease. We helped stop a nuclear war during the Cuban Missile Crisis."

"How?"

"You'll have to ask Abi about it sometime. It's really interesting. A group of fall wizards formed something called the 1027 Coalition. They worked the situation from several angles. American, Russian, and Cuban wizards were all involved, working together for the good of humanity. At the end, it all came down to making sure a man named Vasili Arkhipov was in the right place at the right time."

"Really?"

She nodded. "There have been plenty of other close calls too."

"So, which one of the marked wizards is going to be responsible for a nuclear war?" Elena opened her mouth but did not reply. "They just don't seem like people with their finger on the button. Shouldn't you guys be tailing Donald Trump and Kim Jong Un?"

"Probably some fall wizards are," she said meekly. "We have different territories."

"Who decides who dies?" Patrick already knew the answer to this.

"Carlos."

"Why?"

She gave him the same pitying smile. "Because he's the oracle," she said simply.

"Right."

She carefully reached her hand out and placed it on Patrick's knee. When he didn't slap it away, she moved closer.

"Carlos can explain it better than me," she said. "I'm sure he can answer all of your questions. Like I said, it's a terrible responsibility. But nothing worth doing comes easy. It's hard. It's scary. You doubt yourself. That's what it takes to do something important. We're the only season that can handle this task. We're the only ones strong enough and smart enough. We can see past the initial discomfort to the end goal."

"So, you sometimes have doubts?" he asked.

"What?"

"You said, 'you doubt yourself.' So, you have doubts."

"Well, sure. Don't you doubt yourself sometimes? It is just part of being human."

She had missed the point of the question. But he clung to it. She had doubts. But he didn't know if he could ever forgive her for not asking the questions he was asking now. Even if Carlos had brainwashed her, she wasn't under a spell. She had free will and an ability to think and question. Either she had asked her questions and been satisfied with this carnage, or she hadn't been smart enough to ask them.

His future crumbled around him. He believed they would end up together. He had seen their life stretch before him, an imperfect, but infinitely beautiful life. He had seen her hair turn gray and her skin turn papery. And he had seen himself loving her until he took his last breath. He had seen himself living his life with Elena at his side. Even when pain and suffering would come, she would keep him standing. Even in the darkness, the deep joy she gave him would burn bright.

Every day they spent together, the probability of that life, and of that love, grew stronger until it became a near certainty. And in the space of a few words between them, it all fell. The grief was excruciating. His heartbreak was more than what was experienced by most. He knew exactly what he'd lost. He'd seen it, *felt* it.

"What are you thinking?" she asked. She had grabbed his hand. Had she seen it all fall too? Maybe. She looked like he felt. She leaned forward as if her chest had become too heavy. Her eyes had turned dull, as if some light he couldn't describe had been snuffed out.

He wanted to hold her. To kiss her. To tell her he loved her, and he always would, and nothing else mattered. Most of all, he wanted to take away her pain. Because he loved her. But he was smart enough to know love wasn't enough.

Her hand fell out of his absently, like she had suddenly lost all of her strength.

Patrick heard voices and the crunch of leaves. The hunting party was returning to camp. Patrick thought he caught the scent of blood carried through the wind along with the voices, but he may have been imagining it. They chatted and laughed as if they had just bagged a prize stag, not murdered a human being.

The rest paid them no notice, but Carlos had his eyes on Patrick, looking pleased but cautious. Did he know what Patrick had seen? The safest choice would be to assume Carlos always knew everything. Or… maybe that was everyone's mistake. Carlos wasn't as powerful as he pretended. Patrick knew better than to underestimate his enemy, but he could exploit weaknesses. Carlos had many, but one of his greatest, and most dangerous, was pride.

The pieces of the puzzle snapped together in his head. He knew what he needed to do. He just wasn't sure if he could.

"I'll be right back," Patrick said.

"Where are you going?" Elena asked.

"I'll just be a minute."

"Patrick—"

He ignored her and followed Carlos back toward his trailer. As he got closer, the smell of blood was no longer in his head. He swallowed hard, trying to subdue the urge to retch.

Carlos had a hose hooked up to the water tank on his trailer, and he was rinsing blood off his boots. He made no attempt to hide it and he gave no explanation.

"Good morning," Carlos said, not looking up. "Sleep well?"

"How can I help?" Patrick asked.

Carlos smiled with only the right side of his mouth. He didn't ask what Patrick what he intended to help with. He didn't need to. Carlos had been waiting for him here. He knew Patrick would choose this moment to visit him, probably before Patrick did.

Carlos turned off the water and examined Patrick, sucking his teeth. Patrick clenched his jaw. He wanted to hit him. He didn't want to play the long game. He wanted to be like all the other seasons and go for the instant gratification.

"You want to help?" he said with a smirk.

Of all the parts of his strategy, this first part was the least certain. Carlos didn't trust him. And even though he wasn't nearly as good of a wizard as he pretended to be, he didn't suck. He could read Patrick. And even if Patrick could cast a strong enough shield around his mind and best Carlos with magic, Carlos was smart and cunning. He had managed to convince a large group of people to murder strangers, and he had convinced them it was a good idea. He should not be underestimated.

Patrick nodded and concentrated on keeping his breath and speech even. To keep his deception from being detected, he had to convince himself he really wanted to help. He tried focusing on part of the philosophy that seemed reasonable, like killing future dictators and terrorists. But he found the best way to convince himself, and in turn convince Carlos, was to think of nothing but Elena. He wanted to be with her, no matter what that meant. Love wouldn't be enough to convince him to kill innocent people, but the story was the closest to the truth.

"I'm not going to pretend I'm completely on board," Patrick said. "I don't agree with your methods. I think you resort to violence too quickly, failing to consider other options. But I think what you're doing is... refreshing. I have seen too many people I care about be hurt by evil wizards. I wish someone had prevented all that suffering. Mundanes have to wait until a crime is committed before they can enact justice. But what good does that do anyone? It doesn't undo the crime. It doesn't take away the trauma. I'd like to prevent it. I want to help."

"You don't want to help me," Carlos said. "I know you're used to being around winter wizards. I'm sure you're always the smartest person in the room, yes? You can talk circles around any of them. Trick them into doing what you want. Read every one of their darkest thoughts while keeping all of yours hidden. You can't do that here. Least of all with me."

"Say what you want about solstice wizards, they get to the point a lot faster. I get really tired of all of this bullshit. So, if you don't mind, I'm just going to skip ahead."

He smirked, but he nodded his head in agreement.

"You need me to get into Heartsong Academy. Don't pretend you don't. You've considered all your options, and I'm your only one. It's the reason you haven't killed me or banished me. If I'm being generous, I might say Elena could play a factor in why you haven't just destroyed me, but I doubt it. You're threatened by me. And you certainly don't like me sharing a tent with your little sister. I'm allowed here for a reason."

"You are clever. Congratulations. But it still doesn't explain why you would want to help me get into Heartsong."

"It's simple. I want something in return."

"All right then. What is your price?"

"My family is off limits. Leave my siblings and cousins alone, and I won't stand in your way. On the other hand, if you hurt any of them, I'll just kill you. Deal?"

Carlos laughed.

"You were wrong about at least one thing," Carlos said. "I'm not threatened by you, Patrick. You're not as dangerous as you might like to think. Don't forget, I *know* you. And you're powerless. You did nothing to stop your brother from raping your girlfriend. You did nothing to stop your little sister from being kidnapped. And you did nothing to stop your parents from dying."

Patrick's stomach clenched and he almost let his defenses break. He wasn't fucking kidding when he said he knew him. And hearing the examples of his powerlessness was exactly as effective as Carlos had hoped it would be.

"Think what you want about me," Patrick said evenly. "You still need me to get into Heartsong. Their magical barriers are too strong to break. Your only way through is to be invited. Agree to stay away from my family, and I'll open the door for you and leave out a welcome mat. You may think me weak, but you know I won't help you do this without getting something in return. I'm too powerful to entrance. I'm too smart to be tricked. And I really doubt your charisma is going to charm me any time soon. So, what will it be? Do you want to walk into Heartsong tomorrow or not?"

"We can negotiate," Carlos said. His tone had changed. Patrick felt like he had broken through some initial barrier. He didn't know if it had been the barrier of a spell or if he had passed through a level of reasoning Carlos found to be sufficient. Suddenly, Carlos sounded sincere. He had lost his smirk and his sneer softened. Patrick no longer felt like Carlos was trying to bore holes into his brain. But he wouldn't allow himself to relax. It could be a trick. He checked his shroud for weak spots.

"But I can't accept your terms, as is," Carlos said.

The meaning behind the statement hit Patrick suddenly, like a kick to the back of the head. His mouth went dry.

"My terms are not negotiable."

"Do you even understand the terms? You are blind. You may see some glimpses of the future, but around the people you care about, it's nothing but darkness. You can't see their crimes because you refuse to. That doesn't mean they don't exist."

Carlos was full of shit. Save for Jude, of course. His siblings were good people. Even Evangeline. She's dangerous, but she would never inflict pain just for the sake of it. And she would never hurt an innocent.

"I don't care," Patrick said. "I'm not going to let you kill her." He said *her* automatically, but Carlos didn't react.

"I can find another way into Heartsong. All you're offering

is a fast track. I'll get to them eventually."

"Before the Blood Moon?"

Carlos laughed. "I don't care about the moon," he said, thrusting his hand up to the sky. "They will bleed just as hot and red during the Cold Moon."

Probably the truest thing he'd said so far.

"Okay. Let *me* do it. Let me kill her."

Carlos laughed again. "Please. You would never go through with it."

"I can kill her without raising a hand to her. I can cause her death. And I can make sure that it's peaceful. I want to give her a good death. That's all I ask. Just give me a chance to end her in my own way. If she doesn't die before the Blood Moon, you can kill her."

Carlos pulled his knife out of his sheath and Patrick stepped back, but Carlos didn't turn the knife on Patrick. He cut a vertical line across his own palm. Before Patrick could react, Carlos grabbed Patrick's hand and made the same cut, and then clasped their hands together.

"I accept your terms," Carlos said.

Patrick felt a shift in fate like the lurch of the floor in an elevator. His nearly infinite choices crumbled. The eternity of paths narrowing into one single line. One single choice. One he never would have made.

Carlos released Patrick's hand and wiped his hand with a towel. "I hope you don't mind me sealing our deal with magic," he said casually. "I don't doubt your honor, *of course*, but you know fall wizards. We're such liars and tricksters. It's always good practice." He winked at Patrick. "We take Heartsong tomorrow."

"Monday."

"Tomorrow."

"Seriously? You can't wait one more day for the true Blood Moon." Patrick pulled out his phone to reference the article he had found earlier. "Monday, November 27th. They call it a Super Blue Blood Moon. I mean, that's clearly why you're doing all this. Right? Should I ask Elena her opinion?"

"Why do you care what day it is?"

"Behind all your bullshit, I believe there is virtue in the harvest. The real harvest. If my sister has to die, then she'll die the right way. On the right day."

Carlos squinted at him. "Buying yourself one day won't change anything."

"Then give me the day. Let your minions continue to believe that all of this bloodshed actually has something to do with the moon."

Carlos nodded. "Monday. Morning."

Patrick walked back toward the camp where he had left Elena. He guessed he wouldn't be making it back to his eight A.M. biology class. He could have used more time to get all his pieces where they needed to be, but even though he learned about all of this fall wizard folklore only hours ago, he felt like the moon was somehow on his side. It would be sacrilege to act on the day before or after the Blood Moon, when he had a chance to use the moon's magic in his favor. It sounded crazy in his head, but it also sounded true.

Elena had gone back to their tent. She must have lost the strength to shroud her emotions, because her pain created a dent in the air.

He wasn't sure how to knock on a tent. "Elena?" he said, standing outside the door.

She didn't respond, so he unzipped the tent. She used a blanket to wipe her face, but no amount of wiping could disguise that she had been crying. The rims of her eyes were red and swollen.

He did what he had wanted to do ever since he saw her heart break. He crawled over to her on the air mattress and took her in his arms. He held her as tight as he could without hurting her, soaking in her warmth and her scent.

"I love you," he said. He couldn't make any promises. He couldn't say he would stay. And he couldn't say it would all be okay. "I love you," he said again, the only thing that didn't feel like a lie.

"I love you too," she said. He could feel the change in her body. She felt warmer, somehow more alive.

"I'm not leaving. I'm just going to walk back to the road to get a better signal. I need to make a phone call."

Patrick rifled through the pockets in his jacket until he found the business card he needed.

CHAPTER TWENTY-THREE

The door flew open, filling the school's main office with cool salty air and the blue light of morning. Emmy blinked at the sunlight. Evangeline stood in the doorway, petite but filling the doorway with her presence. The sun came from behind her and made her appear dark and faceless. Inhuman.

"Go," she said. "Now. Come on."

Emmy didn't know how they were supposed to do that while Evangeline blocked the doorway. She felt as if she couldn't get close to her.

Lacie didn't hesitate though. She rushed toward the fresh air and took the stairs two at a time. She turned around and echoed Evangeline's command. "Emmy, come on. What are you doing?"

Nathan took Emmy's hand and tugged her gently, but Emmy continued staring at Evangeline.

"Did you kill those people?" Emmy asked.

"One of them," Evangeline said. "There were seventeen teachers and administrators who were members of Los Segadores. When we battled, I banished the ones who surrendered, but these three did not. They had planned to kill us in our beds, Emmy. We found gas tanks connected to the air conditioning units to turn our cabins into gas chambers. Even those without the mark. They intended to kill us all at once."

"How did you know it was going to happen?"

Evangeline shook her head in disdain. "They were foolish to think they could kill us so simply. Several students realized what was happening and were able to alert the others. One read the mind of the teacher outside. Another sensed their body heat lurking in the dark and got out to see what was going on. And the little boy you saw at the entrance, he snuck into my cabin and woke me up to tell me before they had made it to our section. He had a premonition."

"I thought only fall wizards could do that."

She scoffed. "That's ridiculous. Any wizard has the ability, some are just more adept than others." Her tone became darker, and had an edge of excitement, or perhaps pride. "But that's exactly why they were so easy to defeat. Even after working with us every day and being fully aware of what each of these students can do, they underestimated us. They thought they could just snuff us out. Thirty-seven of the most powerful and dangerous wizards in the southern U.S. So foolish." She looked out toward the ocean. "Well, there were thirty-seven. Now there are thirty-five. They did manage to kill two of us. They turned on the gas before we could stop them."

Evangeline pointed to the edge of trees facing the waves. Emmy's stomach flipped. What she had previously assumed to be driftwood were actually two small bodies. They hovered in the air, a few feet above the sand. They looked like they were being held in invisible arms. A girl and a boy, both young, maybe eleven or twelve. The girl's brown hair flapped in the breeze and the boy's eyes were open, two pits of black. Both of them had skin so pale it blended with the bland white sky behind them.

Emmy wanted to ask why they hovered there, but she sensed it had been done in honor. Even in death, they wouldn't touch the dirt.

"I understand why you had to do what you did. But Lacie is not one of them."

"I know. That's why you need to take her out of here. These kids are angry and scared, and they're not all… reasonable."

"Do you have the mark?"

"It doesn't matter," Evangeline said. She squeezed Emmy's hand. "Be safe, sister."

Without another word, she jumped from the spot and onto the roof. Emmy scuttled along to follow Evangeline. The wind had increased to match the darkening skies and water now splashed Emmy's face like they were on the hull of a boat even though the sea was hundreds of yards away. The shingles on the roof were heavily battered by wind and sun and salt. Some of them crunched as easily as the leaves on the ground below.

"Evangeline," Emmy said, but the wind grabbed the word out of her mouth immediately.

A shingle cracked under her foot and she slipped, sliding a few feet toward the edge of the roof before she managed to catch herself. Her heart thrummed in her throat.

You're a witch. Be magic. You're a witch. Be magic.

She was so much better at this when she didn't give a shit

about anything. Not giving a shit about anything seemed critical to good witchcraft. She had to be prepared to burn or break or fall or whatever to get what she wanted. Now that she had slid down, she could no longer see Evangeline's dark hair whipping in the breeze.

She imagined herself walking across the roof as easily as if she walked across the ground. There was no wind. No water in her eyes. All she had to do was walk. She found she could conjure the image better with her eyes closed, so despite all her instincts telling her otherwise, she closed her eyes. That had been the one good thing she had learned from Jude. *If you want to see, close your eyes.*

Her imagery worked. She could stand tall, and the wind had muted to a distant hum, like the white noise of an air conditioner. Instead of following Evangeline's dark hair angrily whipping in the wind, she followed her dark energy, which whipped about as wildly, but far greater and stronger than anything she could see with her eyes.

As she got close, she opened her eyes in time to see the tips of Evangeline's hair slide out of view and over the side of the roof.

"No!"

As much as she had feared this, she hadn't really expected it. She had wanted her to come down because it made her nervous to watch her perched on top of the stilted building with the storm coming in. She hadn't expected her to actually jump.

She froze and her legs felt week. She clutched the edge of the roof and peered over. She had so much expected to see Evangeline's broken body below it took her brain a while to fully process what she saw instead. Evangeline stood, perfectly whole and unbroken, in a patch of waist high brown sea grass.

She looked away from Emmy, either unaware or ignoring that she had been followed, and watched grass whipping about in waves as angry as the ocean beyond. Her dark hair and pale skin stood out cleanly against the dull brown grass and gray sky. Evangeline had not only survived the fall—or jump—but had managed to transport herself fifty yards away in the time it took Emmy to crawl the few feet to the edge.

Emmy scuttled back like the crabs on the rocks. Suddenly, she didn't want Evangeline to turn around and see her. Emmy had known Evangeline was powerful, but this was something else. It made Emmy's stomach shift and her heart pummel at discordant rhythms. It felt like when she first saw Evangeline kill a cricket by simply willing it dead. But this was more than that. No matter how creepy, the subtle, quiet magic of snuffing out the life of a bug was within the bounds of her understanding of magic. This was not the magic she knew. This was the real deal. Witches flying around on broomsticks kind of shit. Except Evangeline didn't need a broom.

When Evangeline was sent away, and Emmy stayed behind, their relationship changed forever. It hadn't been Emmy's fault. Not really. She hadn't wanted Evangeline to be sent here. She hadn't supported it. But she hadn't done much to stop it. Honestly, she hadn't done anything to stop it. She had been too afraid. Too afraid of Evangeline. Too afraid of also getting kicked out. Too afraid of the conflict. She had been battered and sore from grief, and unable to muster the strength to do anything but survive. And in that time, she had let Evangeline slip away forever.

Lacie ran into the fresh air, but no matter how far she got down the stairs, she couldn't smell the salt of the sea. Blood continued to overwhelm her senses. The scent hung in her nostrils and she could taste the rust in her throat. She could hear her own blood rushing through her head and even the trees looked as if they had been dipped in blood. She could feel the blood on the soles of her shoes, causing her shoes to stick to the wood on each step.

She would run to the sea. Maybe then she would feel clean. It would be quiet and dark under the waves and the thick salty water would scrub the blood away.

Chapter Twenty-Four

Elena put her hand on Patrick's knee as he drove slowly down Highway 32. They had taken him back to his car, which he took as a subtle sign of trust. He was no longer their prisoner. Instead, they followed him. But if he couldn't find Heartsong, his entire plan would break down.

His aunt and uncle had taken him off the approved contact list—and now he could guess why—but that shouldn't matter now. According to Carlos, Heartsong had fallen. The wizards in charge had either fled or been killed by the students. He had explained this so calmly, as if students murdering teachers was normal and expected. Patrick's stomach suddenly grew heavy. He had walked into a war.

"Are we close?" Elena asked.

"I think so. Let me concentrate."

"Okay."

The trees in the area had been flattened and most of the buildings they passed appeared to have been bombed or abandoned. They were in the hurricane wreckage alley where Heartsong could be found.

He reached his mind out into the salty wind, trying to find Evangeline's magic. Despite being the darkest night, she stood out, at least to him. Her magic felt like a living animal, something dangerous and powerful, but beautiful, like a sleek panther.

However, on the air he caught a hint of something else familiar. He slowed the car and pulled on to the shoulder.

"We're here," Patrick said.

"Where?" Elena looked out at the dunes eagerly.

"You can't see it?"

"No."

"There is a road behind that sign for bait and tackle."

"I still don't see it."

"Well, they're here."

"They?"

"Wizards. Lots of them."

"I don't feel anything."

"They're cloaked, Elena. That's the whole reason Los Segadores couldn't find them."

"I know. I just thought when we got closer… "

"I'm not lying, if that's what you're saying."

"That's *not* what I'm saying," she said exasperatedly. "Why are you being like this?"

"I'm sorry that leading a bloodthirsty army right to my only remaining family members is stressful for me."

Elena didn't say anything.

"I know it's the right thing to do, but that doesn't make it any easier," Patrick added.

"I know. I'm sorry," she said, squeezing his knee again.

Carlos tapped on his window and Patrick startled. He

lowered his window.

"Go in alone," Carlos said. "Get out, Elena."

Elena hesitated, but then she exited the car as commanded.

"When Evangeline lets you in, you'll be able to break the cloak for us too. Do you know how to do that?"

"I think so."

"Keep your phone on so we can track you. Mundane GPS can't beat a cloak on its own, but it helps."

"You have the equipment to do that?"

"How do you think we find our targets so fast? They work so hard to conceal their magic, but they leave their phones on. We've got a tech guy who can find them much faster than any wizard."

Patrick nodded. Most wizards probably would forget about Mundane methods of tracking.

"Be careful," Elena said.

"You too," he said. She moved forward to give him a kiss, but Patrick put the car in drive before she had the chance. She awkwardly stepped back and waved.

Patrick slowly pulled out onto the almost invisible road. He felt confident he had chosen the right spot, but his stomach still felt like lead. He could be about to drive into a sand dune and get stuck in the sand.

However, as he drove, it didn't take long for him to know he was in the right place. The broken trees gave way to a pristine oasis of ancient maples that didn't belong this close to the coast. They were scattered with red and yellow leaves so bright they looked like flowers. Even more leaves littered the sandy road in a rich carpet of color. He cracked his window open and found the temperature had dropped by about twenty degrees.

The last time he had visited, it had been winter and there

had been bizarre misplaced snow on this path. The seasonal change meant he had broken into the cloak, but he wasn't through. He had to make it through the gates.

He pulled up to the large gates emblazoned with a large letter "H." The gates appeared to have been tied together with thick vines, instead of the usual lock. He made a mental note not to touch the vines. Powerful spring wizards, especially ones dangerous enough to land in here, could do sneaky things with plants and were especially good with poisons and potions.

He got out of the car. He could smell the sea air coming in through the gates on the edge of the magical barrier. Droplets of water sprayed his face, coming sideways. Rain fell on the other side of the gate.

Evangeline.

He called for her in his mind. He could feel her presence now and he knew she could feel his. He only hoped she couldn't read his thoughts. Winter wizards couldn't do that nearly as well as fall wizards, but all wizards had some ability, even if only a gut feeling. However, like with Mundanes, love could be blinding. Patrick had certainly learned that firsthand with Elena.

He could sense her coming in the same way he could sense a coming storm. The lights dimmed, the wind increased, and animals and insects began a cacophony of excitement.

Despite sensing her closeness, he wasn't able to react in time. His legs suddenly stiffened, as if the ice in his veins had been flash frozen. The pain made him scream. He knew that pain. He had felt it before. That was a curse from Evangeline Vandergraff.

He had no strength in his frozen legs, and he toppled to the earth. His arms moved too slowly, and he couldn't stop his fall. He fell hard onto his shoulder and grunted in pain again, this time from the more everyday pain of gravity slamming him into the earth.

He winced at the throbbing in his side, but at the same time, the edges of his lips threatened to break into a smile. He was about to see his sister again.

"Was that necessary?" he said, rolling over and tenderly checking his shoulder. It throbbed and felt stiff with swelling.

Evangeline stood over him and couldn't have been further from smiling at the sight of him. She glowered at him. Perhaps her curse caused him to see things, but she appeared to have a faint line of darkness outlining her body, like an anti-halo.

"It's nice to see you," he said. "Will you let me get up?"

"Are you alone?"

"No," he said simply. "My girlfriend is waiting in the car." Lies of omission were much safer. Blatant lies were easier to sniff out; even a winter witch might be able to sense a bold enough lie.

"You idiot," she said, but in contrast to her words, she held her hand out to him to help him stand. Patrick felt the pain gradually leaving his legs. He sighed and took her offered hand.

She continued to glower at him. Standing, he got a better look at her. After not seeing her for a year, she looked so much older. Like a grown woman. She had been frightening enough as a little girl who weighed eighty pounds soaking wet. Her maturity made her even more formidable, but he could sense the vulnerability too. A fire in her eyes still burned young and scared.

"They might have followed you," she said. "I shouldn't have let you in."

His chest tightened. Although she correctly assumed he might have brought the Los Segadores with him, she didn't even consider the possibility it had been anything other than a foolish accident.

"I was worried. I've heard what was happening. I had to know you were safe. And Emmy, she's here too, isn't she?"

"If you want to keep us safe, you have to leave."

"I can help protect you. I know you don't need my help, but Emmy might. If it comes to a fight, a four-season army will do much better than a fall only army. And I'm willing to bet you don't have any other fall wizards coming to your aid."

"Please go."

"There must be something I can do. Can I stand guard at the gate?"

"Just leave. The others will kill fall wizards on sight. You're in danger here, and you put us in danger too."

Patrick sighed. "Promise that you'll call me if there is something I can do. I'll do whatever needs to be done to protect you and Emmy. Anything."

"I've already told you what you need to do."

Patrick nodded and Evangeline took him by surprise by reaching for him suddenly. He readied himself for another attack but then realized she had taken him into her arms for a hug. He couldn't remember if she had ever hugged him, and by the aggressive and sudden way she went about it, it seemed she didn't have much experience with hugging, period. He gently squeezed her back, but apparently that was too much, because she pushed away from him as suddenly.

"I've got this," she said. "I'll take care of Emmy."

"I love you, little sis," he said.

"Go away."

He did as she asked and turned back toward the road. Even though he didn't turn around, he could feel her watching him as he walked. As soon as he got out of her sight, he felt around the air with his magic, searching for a weak place in the barrier he could tear. Once he got a snag, he pulled it down and the maples turned pale and dead as driftwood as he passed.

CHAPTER TWENTY-FIVE

Lacie continued to run toward the ocean. She didn't care if anyone followed her. She needed to be clean. She needed the water. Under the waves she wouldn't be able to see or hear anything. The blood would be gone.

She had recently learned she was a witch—which meant she wasn't alone and wasn't crazy—but she felt more desperate than ever. She was still alone. Everyone hated her here, and her family didn't want her anymore. And the man she loved must not care either, because he was nowhere to be found. And maybe she wasn't crazy, but that was worse. That meant all the horrible things in her head were real. Monsters were real. Demons were real. She might even be one.

She stepped on the edge of a sidewalk and twisted her ankle. Pain shot through her leg, but she wouldn't stop. She *couldn't* stop. She needed the water like an addict needed a fix. She couldn't explain it, but she knew once her head slipped under the waves, everything would be okay. She made it to the sand, and she could no longer feel her legs. Her legs were moving, and she must have been the one moving them, but she felt like a spectator in her own body.

On the edge of the surf, she saw what at first looked like a storm brewing on the horizon, but it only *felt* like a storm. The storm was a person, a girl about her age. The wind seemed to be rushing toward her and her white blond hair swirled around her like she was a mermaid underwater. She was one of the kids from up at the camp, and when Lacie had seen her before, she had thought she was pretty. But now there was something deeply repellant about her. She couldn't describe exactly what had changed, but looking at her made Lacie's stomach churn.

Just get to the water.

She didn't slow when she reached the water and saltwater sprayed her bare arms. The cuts in her flesh burned. She shivered from a mixture of cold and pain. *Just keep going.* Everything would be fine when she was underwater.

She pressed on as the waves tried to push her back. The circle shaped cuts all over her body continued to scream, but after the initial shock, the pain became like white noise. Finally, the waves were high enough to lift her toes off the sandy ocean floor. She swam farther against the waves to make sure she was deep enough even when the waves ebbed.

Once her toes no longer scraped sand, she plunged under the water. She had craved the darkness and quiet of the deep so badly, but she hadn't found the escape she had wanted. Even fully submerged, the ocean was loud and angry. She could still hear the waves and the powerful currents pushed against her while the salt continued to light her wounds on fire. She realized what she craved hadn't been the water, but what the water could give her. She didn't want to hear the blood rushing in her head or see the memory of the bloody bodies burned into her mind. She never wanted to see anything again. She wanted death, and she had never felt so sure about anything.

Lacie loved the fragrance of fall, and no place embodied that fragrance better than the fall festival. Funnel cakes, kettle corn, hot chocolate, and a burning Yule log; all wrapped in the sweet smell of a gentle, honorable death as dead leaves crunched and decayed all around her.

Last year's fall carnival had been the best one yet, because Xavier had been there. She had liked him since the first time she saw him, although she did her best to hide it. Somehow, her father still knew though, which is why he sent him away. And when she complained about how that was unfair, it made her father even more certain of his decision.

Emmy had convinced him to come to the festival and Lacie wanted to use the opportunity to talk to him, but he kept disappearing. She couldn't explain it, but she couldn't keep track of where he was. She would see him sitting at a picnic table looking at his phone, but before she was able to walk over to him, she would lose track of him again, then walk to the wrong side of the food court and then see him again at what seemed to be the exact same place he had been before. It took several circles around the food court before she found herself standing next to him.

"Hey," she said.

He startled as if she had just materialized out of thin air.

"Hi," he said, looking at her quizzically.

"Are you surprised to see me?"

"No. I'm surprised you see me," he replied nonsensically.

"Do you want to share this with me?" She held out a funnel cake that had gotten cold while she circled him inexplicably. She hoped she didn't look as stupid as she felt. "I love them, but I can never eat the whole thing, especially since I've already had two hot chocolates and a candy apple. Also, nachos."

He smiled. He didn't smile often, but when he did, he meant it.

"I'd better help you then," he said.

She sat down next to him and he put his phone back in his pocket and turned to face her. The funnel cake might have gotten his attention, and not her, but she would take it.

"Are you having fun?" she asked.

"Not really," he said. "But this is good," he said, licking powdered sugar off his fingers.

"Where have you been going?"

"What do you mean?"

She didn't want to admit she'd been hunting him down for what seemed like an hour.

"Well, you haven't been sitting here this whole time."

"Most of the time," he said.

"You know, sometimes, when I'm really sick of Ashlynn, and I don't want her to see me, she just doesn't."

Xavier raised an eyebrow slightly.

"She'll be calling my name and walk into my room, look right at me, and not see me."

Xavier nodded, but didn't say anything. Why should he? She probably sounded insane.

"That sounds like it comes in handy," he said finally.

"Can you do that too?" she asked.

Xavier looked at her. He rarely looked directly at her for so long and she almost forgot what she had just asked.

"I don't know," he said finally. "I suppose it's possible. Mind over matter, and all that."

He reached over to wipe powdered sugar off her cheek and her heart hammered. He actually touched her. On purpose and everything.

"I would be careful though," he said. "When invisible people get lost, no one goes looking for them."

Lacie nodded, although she had no idea what he was talking about.

"I think I ate all your funnel cake. Do you want me to buy you another one?"

She couldn't say why she thought that was her opening, but she leaned forward and kissed him. It felt like jumping out of an airplane. Reckless. Sudden. Dangerous. And fun. He didn't push her away. He kissed her back.

When they finished, she said the first thing that came to her mind. "That was easier than I thought it would be."

He didn't say anything and the look on his face was completely unreadable.

"I don't know if it was wrong," she spluttered. "I've never kissed a guy before. I'm not a prude or anything. I just never wanted to. I didn't see why people liked that. I thought maybe something was wrong with me. I'll stop talking now."

He smiled and actually showed teeth.

Ashlynn and Emmy walked by and Lacie froze. "Where is she?" Ashlynn said. "I swear to God, I will just leave her here." Both she and Emmy seemed to look right over their heads, but not at them.

"I think we have plenty of time if you still want that funnel cake," Xavier said.

CHAPTER TWENTY-SIX

Tearing down the magical barrier around the school had been like tearing paper, and for the first time in his life, Patrick understood what it truly meant to be a fall equinox wizard. Despite what he was supposed to be, he never felt truly powerful. He was a good wizard, especially considering he didn't have any formal training, but that was all. Now he felt something new… power. He found himself smiling as the caravan of wizards behind him broke through the trees toward the camp. At the same time, he was outside himself, seeing himself smiling like a maniac and he loathed himself. He was risking everyone he loved because he was certain he had outsmarted everyone.

"Your car is getting scratches on it," Elena said.

Elena's words sounded as if they came from a distance, even though she sat right next to him in the passenger seat. Patrick was driving through a thicket of trees, using his magical senses to avoid large trunks and boulders, but otherwise barreling through any branch that got in his way.

"Since when do you care about my car's paint job?" Patrick asked.

"I don't. But you do."

"It's not important, Elena."

"Are you really going to kill your sister?"

"I don't have a choice."

"But it doesn't have to be you."

"It does now. Your brother bound me to a promise." He shrugged one shoulder.

"The Patrick I know wouldn't be so comfortable with this. Either something has broken in your head, or you're lying."

"Which do you think it is?" he asked placidly as if he was asking her opinion on what to make for dinner.

She continued watching him but didn't respond.

They broke through a clearing and Patrick saw the main administration building of the school, which looked like an old single-wide mobile home on absurdly high stilts. He really did it. He got them in.

He got out of the car, as did Elena. The others had parked as well, and Carlos, along with an army of about twenty fall wizards, walked out into the clearing.

"Stop," Patrick said to the group. "We need to be conscientious. If we just walk in, we'll get ambushed."

Carlos sneered at him. Carlos's voice projected into Patrick's mind. *You're not in charge here.*

Patrick nodded and held his hand out in apology.

"They know we're here," Carlos said. "Their plan is to use sirens to lead us toward the ocean and trap us. If we don't walk into the ocean to drown of our own accord, they'll kill us when we have nowhere else to run. I've sent the sniper team to take down the sirens first. Then we use their own plan against them.

They're waiting for us at the shore. Without help from the sirens, they won't be able to pin us against the waves. We'll do that to them instead, making them back up toward the water. They have some guns, but not many. After the sirens, the next priority will be to shoot down anyone with a real weapon. Don't try to fight anyone using magic. Shoot them in the head before they know what's happening."

Patrick's organs had hardened. Carlos's words made it real now. Had he really considered all the paths this battle could take? What had he missed? Who was going to die because of his plan?

Xavier saw two small figures standing at the shoreline. Even from a distance, he would know Lacie anywhere. He knew the way she stood. He knew the exact color of her hair, matching the brown of the grass among the dunes. And he knew her energy. A perfect October day. With the harsh heat of summer gone, and winter only a promise in the air. That moment that hovered between the seasons, the exact point of change, when winter is a beautiful promise of something different, something fresh and clean and bright. Something to look forward to. He loved being the winter to her fall. The thing worth looking forward to.

To most wizards, Lacie would have been nearly invisible, if not completely blotted out, by the siren standing about thirty feet away. Xavier assumed that's what the monster was. Despite being in the distance, the entire scene sucked towards her like she was middle of a swirling whirlpool. All of it, the sky, the sea, the air, and Xavier himself, would pull closer to her and she would eat it all away before he even knew what had happened.

Fortunately, the intense pull would take him in the right direction. He wouldn't have to fight against it to get to Lacie. At least not until the end.

In his bare feet, he ran down the boardwalk at a preternatural speed. His feet pounded against the hard wood and gritty sand and the vibrations of the boardwalk rippled through his joints and bones. With the assistance of the siren's call, he ran faster than his body was made to run, and he felt like his bones might break and his muscles might tear. He would show up to help Lacie as nothing more than a bag of broken flesh, useless to anyone.

Lacie walked into the water; the waves crashed into her body, causing only a slight push back before she journeyed onward, undeterred. The waves crashed higher than usual with angry white and green heads. Each wave reached toward Lacie like the maw of a beast trying to catch her and swallow her.

He wouldn't make it in time, even at this speed. One big wave would overtake her. And once he got there, what could he do but drown with her? He wasn't a strong swimmer, only learning at all because Patrick made him. Although drowning with her was not the worst alternative. Watching her drown alone and then walking back to his car and continuing to live his life would be far worse. Saying she made life worth living would be an understatement. She made life, *life*. Without her, he had no life.

He continued pounding along the boardwalk until he vaulted into the sand, covering six or seven feet in one leap. He didn't know if the siren's pull aided the superhuman leap or if he had powers he didn't know about. Perhaps the siren made her own gravity and he might leap off the ground and catapult toward her.

Now that he was closer, he had trouble focusing on Lacie. The siren appeared to be a normal girl, a little younger than him. She stood in the waves, wearing cut-off jean shorts and a tank top. Her long pale hair was tangled, nearly into dreadlocks. She looked as if she had stood in that spot for days on end, letting the salt and wind tie her hair in knots. Yet, somehow, her skin remained too pale for someone so beach weathered. It gave her the appearance of a corpse washed onto shore. She looked familiar, but he was sure he would have remembered it if he had seen her before.

He turned away from her to find Lacie in the waves and fell down as if the earth had shifted under his feet. When he hit the sand, he didn't know which way was up. He was stuck to the ground, but the ground was in the wrong place. The sand was a trick and the real earth was the girl standing in the waves and he was about to plummet toward her.

He grunted and rolled away from her in the sand. He had to stop thinking about the siren. He thought about Lacie instead. He tried to conjure up the exact feeling of her magic so he could find it even if he couldn't see her properly, but he felt like he was forgetting her. Despite the month, fall seemed like an impossible place. Something he must have dreamed that had never been real.

"Lacie," he shouted. It wouldn't make a difference. But he liked saying her name. It made her real. As if saying her name had conjured her, he saw her head briefly between two waves before she was sucked under again.

"No." What if she had already drowned and he only saw her body bobbing in the water? "No."

He crawled toward the water, and suddenly the Earth shifted against him, this time throwing him into the water like he had been shoved into the pool from behind. The siren must want him to drown too.

In any case, her pull lessened, and he fought against the waves to get to where he had last seen Lacie. He watched for her head peeking up from the waves, but he couldn't see anything.

He felt dizzy and saw black spots floating in his vision. He could feel himself fading away. He could let it all fall away, like washing the scene away with cool, clean water. He could drift into the water and feel nothing. Want nothing. Love nothing.

Feel everything.

The words jumped into his head. They had been part of the advice his father had left him in his final letter. They had seemed vague and unhelpful at the time. Feeling the grief crushing down on him had not been an option. He could hardly remember a year of his life. A year he had spent in a waking sleep. But the words suddenly surfaced in his mind and sounded relevant and important.

He took a handful of his own hair and yanked on it to keep himself alert. He focused on the sting of the saltwater in his eyes and the bitter taste in his mouth.

"Lacie," he said again.

His instinct told him this wasn't going to work. He could hardly swim in a clear, still swimming pool, and with the waves battering into him and the siren confusing his senses, he could hardly even walk.

He had to use magic. He didn't know what he would do, but he was good with spacial magic. He understood the properties of an object and the forces around it well enough to get it to balance at unbelievable angles. Angles that made it look like magic, but in a way, it really wasn't. He only understood things and how they interacted with their environment.

He imagined Lacie like that—as a thing in her environment. Where would the current take her? How would her volume and mass interact with the saltwater? Where was she as nothing more than a thing in space? The questions answered themselves intuitively. He didn't even need to consider equations or even really ask himself the questions. He saw her. He saw her body floating under the waves. And then he felt her. Her magic, small and flickering, struggling. But there. She was more than an object in space.

He moved toward her with his eyes closed. He wouldn't be able to see anyway in the stinging, murky water. He moved painfully slowly, if he was moving at all. Each wave pushed him back to where he started. But he persisted. He thought about his father and about how he died. He felt like his father might also be floating in the dark water with Lacie, like the waters of death were all one place and one moment. This moment.

He found sand with his feet and pushed off toward Lacie. When he felt her wet slippery skin against his hands, it seemed like a miracle. He grabbed an arm, or a leg, whatever appendage he had found and pulled her to the shore. She felt so heavy, and he imagined her full of water, dragging her down. Far gone.

The terror became harder to fight. He felt dizzy and his vision kept fading in and out like his brain was suffering from a brownout. *Feel everything.* When he thought these words this time, he didn't focus on the salt burning his eyes or the sand squishing under his feet, he felt the terror. An unrelenting wave of fear felt like it might stop his heart. He experienced what it would feel like to lose Lacie in the space of a few breaths. Pure, unmitigated agony, with no hope of ever feeling okay again.

As he gave her one last hard drag out of the waves, he let out a choked sob, now feeling like he couldn't fade away if he tried. The fear radiated through every nerve in his body, humming like a living force. He could taste it like metal in the back of his throat.

"Lacie." He shook her shoulders and then remembered he should probably be doing CPR. He had only seen it in movies. His whole body shaking, he put his mouth to her in what felt like a dark anti-kiss. A last kiss, and a hopeless and useless one. Maybe if he was spring, he could breathe life into her, but he was winter. He blew air into her mouth, but nothing happened. He pressed on her chest, unsure why he was supposed to be doing that.

"Get off." Somebody grabbed Xavier violently and he lost his grip on Lacie's wet body. He turned around ready to fight, but stopped.

"Patrick?" Xavier asked. Xavier felt a rush of relief, like warm water on frostbitten hands. Patrick was a lifeguard.

Patrick kneeled beside her and placed his ear close to her face. He held her wrist to check her pulse. He said nothing and began chest compressions in even, confident motions. He leaned in again to see if she was breathing.

"Come on, Lacie," Patrick said.

He tilted her head back and lifted her chin. He pinched her nose closed and breathed into her mouth two times. Then he began chest compressions again. As more and more time passed without Lacie taking a breath, Xavier seemed to be watching the scene from farther and farther away. His body remained close, but his mind retreated. As he watched Patrick with Lacie, a black fog crept into the edges of the scene, pushing him back. The fog obscured more and more of the world, closing in on Lacie. And then, a sound came from far away. Lacie coughed.

Xavier couldn't find his way back to her quickly. He felt like he moved through the waves again, each movement a fight against the fury of the ocean. But as he found her in the ocean, he found her on dry land. Xavier helped her prop herself up to cough out the seawater, now shaking from relief.

"That's why I became a lifeguard," Patrick muttered, staring at Lacie with blank eyes like he was in a trance. "I thought I was supposed to save Evangeline from drowning, but I got it wrong. It was Lacie. I started having the visions before I even knew Lacie well." He paused and looked at the dunes before he continued. "I should have been here sooner. I should have pulled her from the water. I'm so fucking bad at this. I miss too many things."

Lacie had stopped coughing and wrapped her arms around Xavier's neck like she was still drowning. He clutched her back, afraid if he let go, the siren might suck her out of his arms and into the brown abyss again. He could feel her heavy breathing, rattling from water, and the grit of the sand on her skin, and her nails digging into his back and it was all wonderful.

"Like *that*… I missed," Patrick said, waving his hand in their general direction.

"I don't want to die," Lacie said, still raspy. "I don't understand what happened. I just… wanted to die. I wanted to drown. But… I don't. I don't know why I thought I did."

"You're okay," Xavier said. "It was… " She must now know she was a witch. There was no way she could have made it here without knowing. But he wasn't sure how much he should say. The last thing she needed right now was a seizure.

"It was… a siren," Xavier said to Patrick. "Probably one of the kids from the school."

"Yeah," he said, not sounding surprised. "Lacie, you have

to come with me."

"What?"

"The Heartsong kids are ready to kill fall wizards on sight. You have to join the fall wizards so we can protect you."

"I'm not going anywhere with you."

"I'll get you out of here," Xavier said, gently tugging on Lacie's arm. "Can you walk?"

To Xavier's surprise, she pulled her arm away from him. "You should have told me," she said.

"I didn't have a choice. Your mother put a spell on you."

"You had a choice."

"You were better off without magic."

"You weren't keeping magic away from me. I still had it. I just thought I was crazy. You let me think I was crazy."

"I'm sorry."

She sank down to the sand and put her hands in her face. Xavier carefully sat down next to her, unsure how she would react to an arm around the shoulder.

"And you took way too long to get here," she added.

A gunshot pierced the air. Xavier flinched, and then when he saw neither he nor Lacie had been hit, he turned in the direction of the shot. Patrick was holding a gun and kneeling next to a body.

"Patrick, what are you doing?" Xavier asked. "Patrick?"

Xavier had thought the siren had fled, but she was still on the beach. Patrick appeared to be pressing her head into the sand.

Xavier moved closer to Patrick. He felt Lacie behind him and held out his arm to block her from getting in front of him.

"Patrick?" Xavier said again. Did Patrick shoot her? Xavier wasn't sure how to feel. The siren had tried to kill Lacie, but this still seemed… wrong. Too far.

Patrick ignored him. He had his hand on the girl's head. Now Xavier realized who she was. She was Evangeline's friend, and Nathan's sister, Leona Prescott. *Oh, fuck. Not another Prescott.*

"Drag her off the beach. She can't hurt you now," Patrick said.

"Is she dead?" Lacie asked.

"No, but if the tide comes in, she could drown. Drag her off the beach."

"Did you shoot her?" Xavier asked.

"No."

"I heard the shot."

"Please, just trust me. Move her away from the water. Stay off the beach. And try not to do anything I might not anticipate."

"What?"

"I have to go."

"Patrick?" Xavier asked again as Patrick jogged away.

CHAPTER TWENTY-SEVEN

The wind had picked up and the long stairway from the administration building swayed and shook as they descended. Emmy shivered, wishing she had brought more than her flimsy sweater. They just had to find wherever Lacie had run off to and then get back to Emmy's car. The wind gave everything a sense of urgency. Winter seemed to be racing toward her.

Nathan took her hand. "Where is your cousin?"

"I don't know. But I don't like it."

"Can you follow her presence? You know it better than I do."

She should have been able to. She slept in a room next to Lacie. She knew how her magic felt. But the wind seemed to wipe away everything. Or perhaps that was just an excuse. Emmy was a useless witch.

"I'm concerned," Nathan said. "I don't like the way she just ran off. That wasn't normal behavior. I'm worried she's under the influence of some kind of spell."

"I know, okay," Emmy said aggressively. "Just let me focus."

Emmy's hair whipped around her face, slapping at her eyes. She reached out with her magic, but all she could feel was wind and cold and guilt. Now she had lost Lacie too because she chose to follow Evangeline. Lacie was the one who needed Emmy now.

"It's too late." Evangeline's voice seemed too clear with the wind battering Emmy's ears, and she wondered if the voice had come from inside her head.

"What?" Emmy said. "What did you do to her? What happened?"

Evangeline had seemed to materialize in front of her between whips of hair in her face.

"Too late for you to leave," Evangeline said. "The Los Segadores are blocking the exit. We're trapped."

"I'm sure there must be a way out," Nathan said.

"What about a boat? Is there a boat we can all get on?" Emmy said. "Or maybe we can escape down the beach—"

"Stop talking and do as I say," Evangeline said.

A variety of biting retorts rolled through Emmy's mind, but she said none of them.

"I'm sorry, we just have limited time," Evangeline said. "We can beat them. They underestimate our intelligence and we can use that to our advantage. But you have to follow my instructions. Leona will help draw them to the beach. Once there, we'll have the high ground in the dunes. They've become lazy with their Mundane weapons, and we should be able to easily beat them using magic, with only minimum casualties."

"Minimum casualties?" Emmy asked. Evangeline sounded like a military general. And since they appeared to be heading into battle, Emmy guessed that was exactly what she was.

"You'll be fine. No one cares about you and Nathan."

Emmy knew she meant 'no one cares to kill you and Nathan,' but that's not what she said. She said no one cared about them, and at that moment, her words felt very true.

"Evangeline," Nathan said. "That might not—"

"Please, just trust me," Evangeline said, cutting him off. "Emmy, promise me something. Promise me you won't try to fight. You'll just get yourself killed. Please, just hide. Can you promise me that?"

"No," Emmy said without needing to consider the question. "If Nathan or I, or anyone else I love is threatened, I will fight. How dare you ask me to do otherwise?"

Evangeline did not reply. She was clearly in charge at this school and probably wasn't used to being told no. Emmy relished the tiny bit of power she had left.

"Go hide in the dunes. Find a low spot where you can't see the boardwalk," Evangeline said.

"I need to find Lacie."

"She is already there. Just go. Now."

Emmy and Nathan did as Evangeline instructed. She rested her head against Nathan's chest, and he had his arms around her. Blocked from the wind in the dunes and surrounded by the warmth of Nathan's body, she finally felt warm. If she closed her eyes and inhaled Nathan's scent intermingled with the salty air, she could imagine they were on a beach vacation, resting together in the sand and listening to waves crash. This might be the closest they would ever get to that moment, so why not enjoy it? She nuzzled herself closer and he tightened his grip around her.

Her brief moment of comfort was shattered with the sound of a gunshot. She dug her nails into Nathan's arm. Her heart hammered against her chest.

"Wha—"

"Shh," Nathan interrupted. "Stay here."

"Where are you going?"

"I need to see."

"See what?"

"I don't know. Something's not right."

"No," Emmy whispered.

Staying crouched down, he moved up the dune. They had to stay out of view of the boardwalk. That's where the fall wizards were supposed to come. Then they could pin them against the ocean, but not until after they were clear of the boardwalk.

"Nathan," she hissed. As he moved over the top of the dune, she saw him suddenly break into a run.

"No," she said, and followed him, trying to stay low, but more concerned with getting to Nathan. She would curse him if she had to, anything to get him to hide.

She slid down the final dune to the beach, scratching her leg on broken seashells. Emmy was surprised to see Xavier. She wanted to punch him and hug him at once. Lacie was there too, and okay. Thank God. But someone wasn't okay. They were carrying a body. Xavier had her hands and Lacie had her legs. Emmy felt like she had been hit with a wrecking ball. *No. No. No. Not Leona.*

Nathan shoved Xavier away and gathered Leona into his arms. Emmy slid toward him, holding him as he held his sister. Emmy looked imploringly up at Xavier.

"She's not dead," Xavier said. "I don't think she's dead."

"Leona?" Nathan asked, wiping sand off her face with his hands. He took her wrist and felt for her pulse.

"Is she alive?" Emmy asked.

Nathan nodded.

"Oh, thank God."

"She tried to *kill* Lacie," Xavier said.

"Did you do this?" Nathan asked, his voice dark.

"No," Xavier said. "But I would have."

Nathan moved to get up as if he was ready to attack Xavier. Emmy pressed him back down. "Don't, please."

"Who was shot?" Nathan asked, not looking at Xavier.

"No one. I think Patrick shot the gun into the sand."

"What?" Emmy asked. "Patrick is here?"

"He did something to knock her out," Xavier said, gesturing at Leona. "And he asked us to move her off the beach."

"Where have you been?" Emmy asked.

"Oh God," Xavier said, looking past Emmy. "They're here."

CHAPTER TWENTY-EIGHT

The winter solstice witch, Patrick's sister, met them at the end of the boardwalk. She was flanked by three of the other older kids at the school. Two boys and a girl. Only one of them had a weapon, the tallest one, and a boy with wild black hair held a knife. Elena wished they had weapons. It seemed unfair otherwise.

Although, perhaps she underestimated them. Elena heard something like a clap of thunder. The sound came from all directions and her body was thrown forward. Fortunately, she landed in the sand, but her cheek and arms burned. She turned over quickly, pulling out her gun, ready to fight. The gun fell from her hand immediately. Her hand became paralyzed, every nerve squeezing and pulling. She cried out in agony. Patrick's sister walked toward her.

"Leave her. Find the marked ones," Carlos shouted. Paul had been coming at Evangeline from behind, coming to Elena's rescue. Carlos's words distracted Evangeline. She watched the others run down the beach, turning away long enough for Elena to stand and face her. The gun was gone. The sea had come to snatch it with one well-placed wave that reached too far up the shore to be natural. But Elena didn't like the gun anyway. Evangeline may not have been the one to call the sea to take it away. She had wished it away.

Elena used magic to put up a shield. Evangeline wasn't marked, so Elena didn't have to kill her. And she knew Evangeline would not kill her either. She only needed to distract her so the army could find the marked ones.

Despite the shield, Elena could feel magic building around her. The tide was coming in too quickly. Elena's entire calf burned from the hot salt water. Evangeline called the ocean to her. Elena was awestruck. This girl had the same power to pull the seas as the moon itself. And there was the moon, pale in the twilight, but full and majestic, looming above Evangeline like a friend who had sided with the enemy.

Elena's legs felt weak and rubbery. She crumbled into the surf and tried to crabwalk away from her. Her shield had already fallen and she didn't have the strength to bring it back. The wind whipped Evangeline's hair nearly vertical, like gravity had shifted. Despite the wind, Evangeline had no trouble moving toward Elena. She had been sure Evangeline wouldn't kill her. A marked person would never kill anyone... otherwise they would have been marked. But Elena continued to weaken. Evangeline was doing something to drain her. Maybe this was what a killing spell felt like. And even if the spell didn't kill her, she didn't know how long she would be able to keep herself propped up above the water. Her arms shook under her weight.

"The winter solstice is not the height of darkness, it is the beginning of light," Elena said.

Elena hadn't expected Evangeline to really hear her over the wind and surf, but something had changed. Everything became still. The winds quieted. The sea went flat like a massive lake. Dark flecks hung in the air around Evangeline, shimmering like pieces of black glass. Elena hadn't been able to see the darkness around Evangeline before, but something about the suspension of time had made it real.

Evangeline stared at Elena, her eyes glowing green. Her hair hung suspended around her, whipped by the now still wind. The glowing eyes and the wild tendrils of hair made her look like Medusa. The spell that had weakened her had stopped too, and Elena crawled out of the water. She was shaky, but able to stand.

The wind picked up again, taking the suspended darkness with it in tiny flakes, once again invisible to the naked eye.

"What did you say?" Evangeline asked, turning toward her.

"Nothing."

"Who are you?"

"Elena Vega."

The literal response didn't satisfy Evangeline. She moved even closer to Elena. She had an eerie grace about her, able to move completely silently, slipping her toes into the sand as if walking were a choice and she could have hovered over the ground if she preferred.

"Where did you hear those words before?"

"What words?"

Evangeline's eyes narrowed and Elena could feel her building her energy up again, ready to strike. Elena put up her shield, but it did nothing. Evangeline hit her with a curse. Elena felt a massive pain in her chest, like a heart attack might feel. It felt like tiny needles were shooting through her veins instead of blood, and she had the insane fear Evangeline had frozen her heart and turned her blood to ice.

Elena crumbled to the ground again, unable to stifle her scream. With the pain cleaving her chest apart, she didn't understand how she wasn't dead already. She tasted blood. She had bitten down hard on her own tongue. The torment had grown so intense she could no longer scream. And she couldn't think or feel anything but agony. Life and love suddenly had no value. She would let them wash away without a second thought, only to end the pain.

The torture slowly receded. Finally, she was dying. But she wasn't. She felt her blood warming again, and moving quickly, she vomited into the sand, hardly aware she was doing it until she tasted the bile in her mouth. But she didn't care. The pain was leaving, and nothing else mattered.

She saw what had stopped the curse. Evangeline had fallen to her knees and Patrick stood over her. He had his hand on the back of her head gently pressing it down, although clearly there was a much greater magical force in play. Evangeline trembled with wide eyes, staring at the sea retreating around her. She looked completely different now. Wet and cold, long strings of dark hair plastered against her thin, pale arms. Patrick had somehow made her human again, with just a touch.

The Los Segadores soldiers moved toward them. Emmy pulled on Nathan's arm, wanting him to run, but he held his ground. So did Xavier. Seven people moved toward them. They ranged in age from teenager to grandparent. Some of them appeared to be wearing brand new clothes while others appeared to have not changed in several months. However, all of them—young or old or dirty—they took wide steps and held their heads high. They also all carried guns.

Emmy felt certain they were going to die. After all, they had no weapons. And they may be okay wizards, but none of them were special.

"Stay behind me," Xavier said.

Emmy began to protest, but then she realized Xavier was doing something. The air around him blurred like someone had smeared Crisco on the scene. The sound of the Los Segadores voices sounded muted. She clasped Nathan's hand. When she touched him, her arm hurt like a spider had bitten her.

A gunshot shattered the blurry air and every muscle in Emmy's body seized. Nathan wrapped his entire body around her. She tried to wriggle free. She didn't want him to be her shield. He felt less like a shield and more like an extension of herself, a more valuable part of herself. Xavier and Lacie had also cowered instinctively, but no one went down. The shot had sounded close and far away at once. Her arm continued to burn, and she wondered if the bullet grazed her, but it had hurt before the gunshot.

Another shot rang out. This time, Emmy saw the shooter. One of the younger ones, who wore pink camo, had shot her gun in the wrong direction. One of the other men—the one who seemed to be in charge—shouted at her. His voice sounded distorted, but she could thought she caught the words, "stop," and "down," and "girl."

"Run," Nathan whispered in Emmy's ear. "They can't see us, but I don't know how long it will last."

"No."

"Please."

Another hand suddenly clutched Emmy's wrist. The world

had become so blurry and disorienting, she had forgotten Xavier and Lacie were with them too. Xavier had been the one to grab her. His nostrils flared and he dug his thumb into her skin painfully. She tried to pull away.

She looked down at the arm he had grabbed and saw an angry red mark had blossomed on the soft skin of her inner arm. A red circle.

"You're the one they want," Xavier said, his voice fuzzy and distant.

"No," Nathan said. He was close enough to her that she could hear his voice clearly. "No."

Emmy touched the mark, feeling the tender, raised flesh, as if the skin wasn't her own.

Nathan released her suddenly. She felt a painful tightness in her throat. Something was wrong with her. Something dark and twisted. And now everyone could see it right there on her arm. Now Nathan could see it. Nathan pushed her into Xavier. Even though the push had been gentle, she felt like the wind had been knocked out of her. Despite the crazy people with guns and the mark of death emblazoned on her skin, his rejection eclipsed everything.

"Hide her," he said. Then he took off his jacket and left it in the sand. He turned his arm outward to display a red circle on his own arm, darker and scabbed as if it had been there for a while. Emmy's turmoil turned on a dime. He wasn't rejecting her. He intended to sacrifice himself for her.

He ran at full sprint away from Xavier, and he became blurred and distorted like the others. Emmy tried to follow him, but Xavier had wrapped his arms around her. A gunshot pierced the air again, and Emmy screamed.

CHAPTER TWENTY-NINE

Emmy tasted sand. Had she passed out? Xavier did something to her. Knocked her out or wiped her memory or something. She wouldn't have fainted like a woman in an old movie.

"No," Emmy said, spitting out the salty grit in her mouth. She felt completely off balance. Her body was so cold she could barely feel her own skin, and her face burned as if it might melt. She blinked more sand out of her eyelashes.

"Shh," Lacie said.

They were under the boardwalk. Lacie may not have known how futile that was. Wizards couldn't hide from each other, at least not without magic.

"Nathan," Emmy said.

"They didn't kill him. They took him. Xavier told me to hide here… and now I can't get out."

"What do you mean?"

"I don't know. I try to crawl out and I feel sick. The

farther I get, the worse I feel."

"Shit. That asshole. I have just as much right to fight as he does."

"I just want to go home," Lacie said.

"I can beat the spell."

Emmy had broken through other repulsion and confinement spells. The trick was just to keep going, no matter how strongly her instinct told her to turn back. In many ways, magic was just an illusion. Nothing truly kept Lacie and Emmy under the boardwalk. They were not bound and nothing blocked their path. The impediment was in their heads.

"Just stay here. This will be over soon. I promise. Stay here."

Emmy put her head down and army crawled out from under the boardwalk. As expected, she felt an overwhelming urge to turn around. Her heart raced, and she felt as if she couldn't get enough oxygen. Lights popped in her eyes. Damn. Xavier could cast a good repulsion spell.

She backed up without realizing she had done so.

"Are you okay?" Lacie asked. "Your nose is bleeding."

Emmy wiped her face and saw the blood on her hands.

"Screw you, Xavier. Seriously?"

When she saw the blood on her hands she also saw the red circle on her forearm. She had almost forgotten the circle was there. It pulsed with a nagging pain. And Nathan had one too? She had to be remembering that wrong. Nathan was the best person she knew. If he had the mark, then it only meant one thing. This was all bullshit. Bullshit they might all die for. And then she remembered the gunshot.

"Before I passed out, there was a gunshot," Emmy said. "Who was hit?" Her throat was still constricted by the crushing of her throat in the repulsion spell. Or perhaps she just didn't want to answer the question.

"Nathan. But just his leg," Lacie added quickly. "When Xavier lifted his spell they were all gone, and they took Nathan with them."

"I have to find him."

"Let me help you," Lacie said.

"You can't. You don't know anything about magic."

"I know you're going to live. You'll survive this day. And you'll definitely survive crawling out from under this boardwalk."

Emmy nodded. She wanted to ask Lacie what else she knew. But she resisted. If Nathan was going to die today, she didn't want to know. She wanted to spend every last second they had believing they would be together. She had already spent enough time in grief, and she never wanted to grieve a moment longer than she had to.

"Get out, Emmy."

"I will. I'm going," she said, but she didn't move.

"Get. Out." Lacie's voice changed. It echoed through Emmy's mind, cutting like a piece of glass stuck in her brain.

"What are you doing?"

"Remember Ashlynn's trick? If I ever complained about being hurt or sick or having any kind of pain, she would pinch me or punch me or elbow me in the ribs. And then she would laugh and say 'you're welcome. Now you have real pain to worry about, so you can stop bitching,' or something to that effect."

Emmy nodded.

"I'm going to try it."

"Wait."

The red circle on Emmy's arm burned as if stinging insects were trying to eat their way out. The circle went from red to black and she could see her veins turning black all around it until it looked more like a tarantula than a circle.

"Get out," Lacie said again. Her voice sounded normal this time, but as she moved slowly toward Emmy, she seemed to hiss. Her blue eyes appeared to be turning black.

"Okay, okay, okay."

Emmy scuttled backwards, deep into the repulsion spell before she even felt it. But when it hit, it hit hard. Her arms and legs went limp and she fell on her back, staring at the gray white sky. She felt as if the sky pressed down on her. Under the pressure, she couldn't get enough air into her lungs. She felt the warmth of blood around her nose again. The sky slowly crushed her whole body.

"Emmy. Go get Nathan." Lacie's voice trickled into her brain. "Nathan. Nathan," the voice repeated several times. Or perhaps that had been an illusion.

The sky is not crushing you. That's not possible. There is plenty of oxygen. You're fine. You're safe. All of her mantras felt like lies, but she was able to flip over onto her stomach and army crawl forward with the sand digging into her pulsing forearm like shards of glass. But she kept moving. All she had to do was move forward. She didn't think about why or how long it would take. *Just move.*

Suddenly, she gasped as if she had made it to the surface of water. She breathed in the salty air greedily. She had made it. She made a mental note to punch Xavier in the arm the next time she saw him.

When Emmy stood, she fell again, her knee digging into the sand. She pulled herself back up and looked around. A familiar figure stood near the waterline. No, two familiar figures. She moved toward them. As she got closer, she wondered if her mind was still altered from the repulsion spell.

The image didn't add up correctly.

Evangeline shook as Patrick held her head. Tears spilled down her cheeks. He was hurting her. She had never believed Jess's warnings. She had never lost faith in her brother. And she had been wrong.

Patrick turned and looked at Emmy. He didn't look surprised to see her, but he said nothing. He gently released his hand from Evangeline's head and mumbled something to her that might have been 'get up.' Emmy didn't know who was more powerful—Patrick or Evangeline. They were both the most powerful of their season, the solstice and the equinox, so they were probably evenly matched. It depended on the magic that needed to be done. In battle, she was shocked to see anyone bring Evangeline to her knees, even Patrick. He probably had used her trust to his advantage. She would have hesitated.

The realization made her even more furious. Patrick was probably the person Evangeline respected and looked up to more than anyone else in the world. And he had used that against her.

"Don't touch her," Emmy screeched. "Get away from her."

Patrick froze, and Emmy wondered if Evangeline had managed to do something to him. He furrowed his brow and grabbed Evangeline's arm. He held her arm by the wrist and examined the unblemished underside of her forearm.

"Go back to campus," Patrick said. "Now."

"Fuck you," Emmy said.

"Now," he shouted at her with such sudden fierceness Emmy turned her face away, instinctively shutting her eyes like she might be hit.

His eyes maintained the same level of command that had

been in his voice. Not the same magical command Nathan had, something far more human, but in this case, just as effective. He should have been apologetic or ashamed. Possibly begging her for forgiveness for his devastating betrayal. But instead, he was unabashed. Unafraid to look her right in the eye and shout at her.

CHAPTER THIRTY

Patrick ran down the beach until he came to an inlet where Carlos was waiting for him.

"What's the story?" Carlos asked.

"This isn't worth the risk," Patrick said. "You won't be able to take them on like this. There are at least thirty powerful wizards at the school, all dangerous as hell, and working together like an army. We should retreat."

He smirked. "That is exactly what I expected you to say."

"Isn't patience the mark of a good fall wizard? Wait for your moment. Wait until you can get each one alone, in a vulnerable position. This is uncalculated and rash. You're as bad as they are."

"The Blood Moon is tomorrow. I owe it to my descendants to follow through on the promise and cull the next three generations of killers before the Blood Moon rises."

You are so full of shit.

"I really don't see why a few more days, or even weeks,

months, or years is going to make a difference. For some of these people, the danger lies in their *grandchildren*. It could be thirty years or more before these people are even born, let alone become killers.

"You don't understand the synergy of it all." He held up his hand as if he was clutching an invisible ball of fire. "It's not about taking down one killer, it's about cleansing the Earth. The cleansing power of blood. The rise of the Blood Moon is necessary for the cleansing to take effect."

Bullshit.

"These people trust you. Are you ready to lead them to their deaths?"

"I almost forgot," he said, ignoring Patrick's last statement. "I have a present for you."

Patrick felt a lurch in his stomach. There was nothing this man could give him he would want, and the light lilt to his voice, like a phantom in the air, gave Patrick a chill down his spine.

"I'll show you," Carlos said. "Follow me."

Carlos gestured for a heavily armed Pike to come with them. As they walked through the thick, gray brush, Patrick felt like he was floating. None of this seemed real. He thought he could shake his head or dig his nails into his forearms and he would wake up. Carlos had caught one of them. Someone Patrick cared about. Maybe even killed them. And the terror of the possibility was making him break from reality.

Around the corner, with his heart thrumming in his chest, he saw Nathan kneeling on the ground in a small clearing, his hands tied behind his back. Patrick felt relieved it wasn't one of his siblings, but only slightly. Nathan was a good man. And Patrick knew Emmy loved him, or she would. He hadn't spoken to her recently enough to know if they were together, if she would even tell him. Emmy and Nathan falling in love, getting married, and having children was a prediction so crystal clear, everyone should be able to see it. Their pairing was unlikely, but inevitable at the same time. Of all the reasons they might not work together, all the paths, even the darkest ones, led them to each other… except for the ones in which one or both of them died. Only death could thwart them.

Nathan raised his head and his eyes appeared to glow. Maybe they did. They had a yellow sheen, like a cat caught in headlights. Nathan's lips curled into a snarl, and blood was smudged on his cheek from a cut near his eye. He looked more animal than Patrick had seen him before.

"Do you understand why I've brought him to you?" Carlos asked, eyeing Patrick closely.

Patrick didn't want to answer. He didn't like being toyed with. Carlos acted as if everything was a game, and he had no poker face. He had the smirk of someone with a royal flush clutched in his hands.

"I assume he's been marked," Patrick said. "Because, of course, you wouldn't hurt someone just for fun."

"I know you think I'm a monster, and maybe I am. But I'm more than that. I'm a father. I'm a brother. I understand what it means to love someone. And I can't imagine how painful it would be to have someone you love marked for sacrifice. I can't imagine having to choose between the life of one dangerous person you care about and the innocent lives of strangers. The logical choice may be clear, but we are all human, after all. It's normal to love the people you know more than the people you don't. It's normal to care more about the people who are like you, than the people who are different… normal to want to save a neighbor over someone on foreign shores. We would be lying if we said otherwise."

Where the Hell was he going with this?

"I'm straying from the point, aren't I?" Carlos said. "I do that. I can always tell because Elena will start staring off into space with this bored look." He chuckled at the image.

"What are you trying to say?"

Nathan shook. His shoulders jerked unevenly. He watched them like a predator, waiting for a moment to strike.

"Emmy doesn't have to die," Carlos said. "I thought she wouldn't be marked at all, but time is an ever moving stream, isn't it? Things changed somewhere along the way and her future shifted, and it shifted to include this man. That's when she was marked."

Patrick literally bit his tongue. Carlos was wrong. All of Emmy's living paths led to Nathan. And every time Carlos was wrong, it ached. Carlos was killing people based on flawed and incomplete predictions.

"Why does being with Nathan lead Emmy to be a killer?"

Carlos shook his head and snickered. "Oh, come on. You know your sister. She can certainly do some damage if threatened, but she's not a killer. Honestly, it shocks me that this isn't obvious to you."

Carlos pointed to Nathan who let out a shaky breath. "They are one generation removed from the target," Carlos continued. "I mean, let's be frank here, that shouldn't be a surprise. Emmy and Nathan may be decent people, but they're playing some real Russian roulette with their genetics. There are some really nasty monsters lurking in the depths of that gene pool. Do you really think that out of the four children they are going to have, not one of them will fall to the darkness? You know as well as I do that's unlikely."

"This isn't about odds," Patrick said. "You're supposed to be preventing future atrocities that you know will happen, not just taking a guess."

"Please, Patrick. I am not guessing. I know which of his children will be dangerous and exactly what they will do."

"What?" Nathan asked. Patrick was actually surprised to hear him speak and not growl or grunt.

Carlos leaned in toward Patrick and lowered his voice, cupping his hand over his mouth, perhaps to stop Nathan from reading his lips. "You know what," Carlos said in a quiet, but clear voice. "You know what his child will do you to your child."

Patrick felt a rush of nausea and adrenaline as his head was populated by all the most horrible, unthinkable possibilities. No. He wasn't going to let Carlos put thoughts in his head. Patrick didn't know if the thoughts were his own, triggered by the suggestion, or if Carlos had literally flushed his mind with disturbing ideas, but he wouldn't let it get to him. Patrick had the secret weapon of belief. In the past, thoughts like this might have concerned him more. But now he knew what he believed. The future isn't written. No child is damned to be evil before they are even conceived.

"It takes two to make a baby," Carlos said. "If Nathan dies, Emmy's mark will fade. And *that*, my friend, is my present to you. If you kill Nathan, Emmy will be spared."

At this suggestion, Nathan stopped fighting against his binding. He looked down at the ground and was still.

"Since you're new to this, I would recommend the 9mm," Carlos said. "It's easy to shoot. Not much kickback. But if you'd rather do it another way, I understand. I know some wizards think killing with guns is the Mundane way. I say, whatever gets the job done. Dead is dead."

Carlos held out his hand to Pike and he put the gun in Carlos's hand, and then Carlos held it out for Patrick.

Patrick spun all the possibilities through his head. Carlos would consider any refusal to be proof Patrick wasn't really on his side. And it might even be reason enough to kill him. If Patrick shot Nathan, he would like a live of darkness. He would never recover. Never be happy. That wasn't an option.

He could shoot Nathan, but not kill him. Shoot him in the arm or something. But when he watched this option play out, Carlos simply laughed at him and asked him to try again. It would gain nothing and only cause Nathan more pain.

He could shoot Carlos, but in the vast majority of scenarios, Pike then shot Patrick *and* Nathan. He could shoot Pike first, and then Carlos, since Carlos wasn't armed. But in most of the scenarios, Carlos saw it coming and knocked the gun away from Patrick before he figures out how to cock the gun for another shot. Patrick could shoot himself, but that wasn't choosing a path, it meant snuffing them all out. He couldn't see the future in scenarios where he no longer existed, and that scared him almost as much as death itself. He would not be able to protect the people he loved.

He did his best to flip through his options at rapid speed so Carlos would have trouble determining which one was his choice.

"Do it," Nathan said. "If one of us has to die, please let it be me."

"If it helps," Carlos said. "Emmy will still get married and have children. She'll still find love in the end. I've always thought the idea that there was only one person with whom you could be happy was more bleak than romantic. She'll find her way without him."

Nathan closed his eyes and took a shaky breath.

"I would like privacy," Patrick said. "He's a friend of mine. Let me do this quietly and humanely… without spectators."

"You didn't really think that would work, did you?"

"I can't do this," Patrick said.

"If you're with us, it's time to own up to what that means."

"You don't understand," Patrick said. "There is something you've missed."

"Oh, really?"

"He no longer meets the criteria for having the mark. You just haven't seen it."

"What do you mean?"

Patrick didn't have to fake his distress; he just had to redirect it toward a lie. He let a tear spill down his cheek and made a show of trying to hide it. "I wish I could kill him and save Emmy. But it won't work. It's too late. And if I kill Nathan knowing that, I'll just be a murderer."

"And… what did I miss?"

"Emmy is already pregnant," Patrick said.

"What?" Nathan said.

"The dark child has already been conceived. I understand how you missed it. It happened very recently. Fate has only just started to shift. I only think I saw it before you because I'm so attuned to her magical presence. I sensed the imposter. I am sure she doesn't even know herself."

Patrick couldn't read Carlos's reaction, but he wasn't smirking. His face had turned serious, like he was considering a new piece of evidence in an investigation.

"I—" Patrick let his voice break in manufactured sobs. "You're right that only one of them has to die. But it has to be… Emmy."

"No," Nathan said.

"I can't pretend I don't know. And it won't help. You'll realize it soon, and then Emmy will have to die too. Nathan will do good in his life, he'll have other, better children. I can't wipe all that away for nothing."

"No. You're lying," Nathan said. "She can't be pregnant. We're… careful."

Patrick felt a sudden lurch in his gut. The correct response would have been, *No, she can't be pregnant, because I would never defile her virtue.*

"Shut up, Nathan," Patrick said with rage he didn't have to feign. "I can still kill you just for the hell of it."

Carlos grabbed Patrick so suddenly he almost dropped the gun. He grabbed him by the head and pressed his own forehead into Patrick's. If it hadn't been so abrupt and aggressive, it might have been mistaken for tenderness. But Patrick knew what he was doing. He needed skin contact to best determine if Patrick was lying. And it's easier to read thoughts if the subject has no time to prepare.

However, Patrick was already ready. He had flooded his mind with images and thoughts of Emmy's pregnancy until he himself might have been convinced of its truth. He was more powerful than Carlos. He could throw these manufactured thoughts at him and he wouldn't have the skills to look deeper. Carlos kept his forehead pressed up against Patrick's long enough for it to be truly uncomfortable. He could smell his sweat intermingled with tobacco, and his skin felt unnaturally hot as his magic invaded Patrick. Finally, he released Patrick as violently as he had grabbed him.

Patrick waited for the verdict, his heart thrumming. It could still go wrong. But he had turned Carlos's trap on its head. Now, if Nathan died, Carlos must be the one to admit he didn't believe the dogma he spouted to his followers. The strategy wouldn't have worked if they were alone, but Pike, Carlos's most loyal disciple, listened intently. If Pike's faith was shaken, he would tell the others. Carlos would lose the illusion.

"I'm sorry," Carlos said solemnly. "I'm truly sorry."

Patrick drew in a deep breath through his nose. He believed him. Patrick nodded solemnly, keeping his eyes down in grief.

"It was good of you to spare him," Carlos said. "He's responsible for your sister's death. So perhaps he is a killer in a way."

"Patrick, what are you doing?" Nathan asked, his voice scratchy as if he had been screaming for days.

Please, shut up. Nathan knew something wasn't right. Solstice wizards were likely to say whatever they had on their minds. He might be good enough and stupid enough to call Patrick out. Especially if it might save Emmy.

"I'm so sorry, Nathan," Patrick said.

"Please, don't hurt Emmy. Kill me. I really don't think—"

"There is no point in that, Nathan. Emmy would have to die anyway. You still have a purpose on this Earth. You may not have much left, but you have a mother and a little sister who need you."

"Patrick, please," Nathan said.

"Carlos," Patrick looked him squarely in his dark eyes, so much like Elena's. "Please, just let me do this my way. I know she has to die. But she's my sister. I love her. I know you understand."

Carlos nodded.

"It needs to be merciful. Poison, like you do for the children. Let her just die peacefully in her sleep. And I want to be there. I don't want her to die alone."

Carlos considered him. "I am there too. I'll provide the poison."

"I understand."

"We'll do it now," Carlos said.

"Now?"

"The Blood Moon will rise in only a few hours' time. There is no more fortuitous moment. If her blood is shed under the Blood Moon, you will know it was not shed in vain. The power of the act will be at its most potent. You'll know your children will be protected."

Carlos said the words with no concealed smirk or melodramatic flair. A bad actor had stopped reading his lines and the performance had ended. Patrick's calculations had all been based on the idea that Carlos was simply spouting lies because he enjoyed the power and because he had a taste for blood. But Patrick wasn't sure anymore. Part of Carlos believed his lies. Or even more frightening, perhaps they weren't all lies.

"Of course," Patrick stammered after a pause that had gone on too long. "Tonight."

"He will stay with us until it is done," Carlos said, gesturing toward Nathan.

"Patrick," Nathan said, the word dripping with a mixture of pleading and horror.

Without thinking, Patrick glanced toward the trees behind him. Someone familiar was close. Carlos followed his eyes to the trees, but didn't react.

"Elena," Patrick said. "She's calling me."

Carlos appeared to believe his lie. He made a sort of shrugging motion.

"Two hours until the moon rises," Carlos said.

"I haven't forgotten," Patrick said.

CHAPTER THIRTY-ONE

As soon as Patrick made it out of Carlos's sight, he broke into a run. He had felt Samantha had some part to play, but he hadn't understood it. He still didn't understand it. He just knew she had arrived to play that part, and he needed to see her. Perhaps, in some cases, spring witches did bring luck. In any case, he sensed she had something he needed, something that would make everything clear. Because, as Carlos had reminded him, he was running out of time.

Patrick knew nothing of magical promises, or binding spells, or whatever Carlos had done when he got him to agree to kill his sister… which apparently had been Emmy all along. But this all reminded him of the killing spell that had been let loose two and a half years ago. As the saying went, he could run but he couldn't hide. They had done everything they could to evade the killing spell, but it had to hit somewhere. And he feared he had done it again. Perhaps he could delay his promise, or even redirect it, but the spell would be completed.

He saw Samantha's shining blonde hair clearly against the bleakness of everything else. Gray sky. Brown grass. Murky ocean. Even the sand appeared gray. She moved slowly and appeared to be carrying something heavy. She must have sensed, or heard, him coming toward her. She turned around and faced him, shielding her load with her body.

"Oh my God," Patrick said, as he approached her. No matter how she tried to position her body, he could now see she carried a child. A girl. All he could see was her blonde curls under Samantha's hand. The child appeared to be squirming and wiggling, but Samantha worked hard to keep her face shielded.

"Oh no," Samantha said. "Okay, um."

"She's the baby the lawyer was talking about. And that Jude was talking about. She's Jude and Caroline's daughter. My *niece*."

Samantha parted her lips to speak but said nothing. Her eyes glistened in the waning light.

"Why do you have her?" Patrick asked.

"Don't take her from me." Tears spilled down her cheeks and Sophie buried her face in Samantha's chest.

"I don't understand. Did you just take her from their house?"

"She needed me."

"You kidnapped her."

Samantha placed her hand over Sophie's ear, gently pressing her head into her chest so she couldn't hear.

"They would have put her in foster care."

"Her parents may have been dead, but she had family... "

"Sophie is meant to be with me. She's my daughter."

"Why in the hell would you want to take care of Jude's

daughter?"

"She's *my* daughter."

"No, you're her abductor."

"I just knew, okay. As a fall wizard, you must understand that. I know I don't have powers like you, but in that moment, I saw all the paths leading from that moment, and I knew the best one—the only right one—was for me to take her right then and there."

"*As a fall wizard,* I know that even fall wizards can't know things like that for certain. So you certainly can't."

"I know the difference between the path to life and the path to death."

"And I'm the path to death?"

"More than I knew. Death is all over you."

"Can I see her?"

Sophie, who seemed to be aware of the conversation, despite Samantha's attempts to cover her ears, turned and looked at Patrick.

All the phantom pain from Caroline's torture swelled suddenly, cracking like electricity in his nerves. Patrick gasped and looked away. The pain passed as quickly as it came.

"She has her father's eyes and her mother's face," Patrick said. "How can you stand to look at her?"

Samantha put her hand over Sophie's ear again. "She can hear you," she said through gritted teeth. "What is the matter with you?"

"You're right. I'm sorry. It just took me off guard." He moved closer to them and Samantha leaned away, keeping her eyes on him.

"I'm not going to hurt her."

"I don't believe you."

"I would never harm a child."

"I don't know that. I don't know you anymore."

"I haven't changed."

Samantha scoffed.

"Please." He gently took her hand to pry it off of Sophie's face and she let him. "Hi, Sophie," he said.

She ignored him and buried her face even further in Samantha's chest.

"It's nice to meet you. I'm your uncle."

"What's uncle?" she asked.

"That means I'm your daddy's brother."

"You're Daddy's brother?"

"You know your daddy?" he asked, surprised by her response.

"Of course she does," Samantha said. "Zander is her father."

"Zander," Patrick repeated. "I guess that's better than the alternative."

"Yes," Samantha said.

"Can I hold your hand?" Patrick asked, reaching for the little hand clutching Samantha's shirt.

"Don't you touch her," Samantha said. "She is an innocent child and that's all you need to know."

"I know what she is," Patrick said.

"She's a child. By definition, a child is a person who still has hope for the future. That's what childhood is about. Nothing is written. The whole world is open to her."

"I know."

"No, you don't. You think you know, but you're not God. You don't know what she will do."

"I never said I did," Patrick said. "But others of my kind might not see it the same way," he said quietly. "I just want to know what I'm dealing with."

Samantha gently uncurled Sophie's fingers from her shirt. "It's okay, sweetie."

He gently pulled up her pink sleeve and saw the ugly red mark on her otherwise unblemished, new skin.

"It's a mistake," Samantha said. Her voice shook with suppressed tears. "It's a mistake. Give her a chance. She deserves a chance. I'll make sure she never hurts anyone."

"Do you know what this circle means?" he asked Sophie.

"It means I'm bad," she replied.

Samantha gasped. Patrick could tell she hadn't expected that insight.

"Can I tell you a secret about that mark?" Patrick asked. Sophie nodded. "Some of the nicest people I know have a mark like that. And some of the meanest people I know have a mark like that too. Do you know what that means?"

Sophie shook her head.

"It means the mark doesn't mean anything. It's just like any other scrape or scratch. All you need is a Band-Aid."

Sophie's eyes grew wide. "I want a Band-Aid," she said, as if Patrick had said she could have her own unicorn. She leaned into Samantha's ear and whispered loudly, "I told you, Mommy."

"Are you sure?" Samantha asked quietly.

"I'm sure," he said. Samantha shouldn't have taken her like that, but she was right. Samantha was Sophie's mother. Patrick couldn't quite explain it, but he knew it to be true.

"Evangeline is hiding the younger kids from the school in the mess hall. It's got every kind of magical protection possible. Take Sophie there. This will all be over soon."

"Thank you," she whispered.

Patrick watched Samantha and Sophie disappear through the brush. He exhaled deeply. Sophie. She had been the missing piece of the puzzle. Now he knew what to do. But all would be lost if his most important puzzle piece didn't show up.

He looked at his phone. No messages. "Come on," he whispered under his breath.

CHAPTER THIRTY-TWO

As the sun slipped behind the horizon, cold air followed it. Wind coursed through his thin jacket as he waited just outside the school's main gate. He knew where everyone was supposed to be. Carlos, Elena, and the Los Segadores were near the beach in the inlet. Emmy, Evangeline, Xavier, Lacie, Samantha, Sophie, and the kids from Heartsong had moved back inland to the school. For now, the fighting had stopped. Although he didn't think that wind could blow a magical presence like an odor, it seemed to. He would be sure he felt everyone in their proper place, then a hard gust would come through and he'd lose them. Patrick looked at his phone again. Still no messages and the minutes ticked by. He couldn't stall for much longer.

As he was considering what he might select as plans B, C, and D, he saw headlights moving through the brush. A yellow taxi pulled up. Patrick knew who would step out, but that still didn't prepare him for the rush of hatred and fear. Jude stepped out of the back of the taxi. Patrick expected the driver to come out to open the truck and give Jude luggage of some kind, but he didn't. Jude shut the door and the taxi headed back out the way it came. Jude appeared to have brought nothing with him. Or perhaps he simply had nothing to bring. He wore heavily wrinkled clothes that looked like they had been stored in a box for several years. He had his hands in his pockets and shivered in his thin track jacket, just like an actual human.

"Where is she?"

Thank God. The message he had left on Carrie Ann Carr's office voicemail had found its way to Jude after the appeal.

Jude walked closer to Patrick. Patrick thought he looked shorter than he remembered him, but then he realized he had just gotten taller. And Jude's shoulders were hunched against the wind. His clothes also smelled as if they had been stored in a box in a prison for several years.

"Where is she?" He asked again. "My lawyer said you had her."

Patrick had to put on the performance of his life, and he was worried he wouldn't be able to pull it off, but it turned out to be much easier than he expected. He raked his fingers through his hair in what he hoped looked like a gesture of desperation. "I tried to protect her. But… Jude. You're too late."

"What? What happened to my daughter?"

"She had the mark too." He pointed to Jude's arm. "I'm so sorry."

"She's… no."

"Carlos came here at the end of the harvest. He, well… he went for the low hanging fruit first. He got the young ones over with quickly. I think Sophie was one of the first."

Jude's face had contorted into an agony so thoroughly human Patrick thought he wouldn't be able to continue. Jude clutched the sides of his face with his hands and made a strange grunting sound. No matter what the circumstance, telling someone their child is dead is a devastating act.

"She didn't suffer. He has some compassion. The children were killed with carbon monoxide poisoning. She just hugged her little doll and fell asleep."

Patrick tried to mimic Jude's grief on his own face, and it worked. Jude's tears were as contagious as a yawn, and with a few blinks, he was able to bring them to his own cheeks. "I'm so sorry," he said, his voice now laced with tears. "I loved her too. Like my own daughter. I would have died to save her if I had been given a chance."

"You fucking liar," Jude shouted with the ferocity of an animal.

Patrick's teeth clenched and he tried not to panic. Jude had believed him in all the scenarios that could come from this conversation, but he could have missed some hidden roll. "I wish I was."

"You say you would have died to save her, but now you follow her killer like his little dog. You do his bidding. You happily kill others for him. If you had really loved her, if you had really cared, you would have killed him. *Tortured* him. For what he did to Sophie."

Patrick felt like the die was teetering on its edge. Jude did believe him about Sophie's death, but that wasn't the relief Patrick had been hoping for. The question was all in where he would direct his anger.

"Carlos has a daughter, doesn't he?"

No. No. No. Please God, no. That one unlikely, but darkest roll of the dice. The one where he would direct his anger at

Isabella. An eye for an eye.

"No, he doesn't." The words came out of his mouth before he could properly consider the consequences. Jude wouldn't have even mentioned it if he didn't already know about Isabella. If he was just guessing, he would have said, "Does she have a daughter?" or something less certain. Less final.

Jude narrowed his eyes at Patrick, his grief overtaken by a more dangerous emotion: suspicion.

"He doesn't have a daughter," Patrick said again firmly. He cast the spell on instinct, before the plan even fully formed in his mind. He had sent a memory once before, but he had never taken one. And when he sent his own memory into his mother's head—the memory that had led to her death—she had been unconscious and easy to manipulate.

Isabella was hard to grasp in Jude's mind because she had no face and no name. Jude didn't seem to have any information other than the fact that Carlos had a daughter, and the tiny wisp of knowledge was too small to find and grasp. Instead, he quickly inserted a new image of Carlos into Jude's mind. This Carlos was exactly like the real one, but with no family. No Isabella, Elena, Vanessa, or Abi. Just Carlos and his crew of assassins. However, this only meant that two Carlos's now existed in Jude's mind. Hopefully, the fabricated one would be more powerful, but both memories would exist.

For a few seconds, Jude stared through Patrick and not at him and his eyes appeared blank and unfocused. Then he blinked hard and looked back at Patrick.

"What did you do?" Jude asked.

"You have the mark," Patrick said, trying to distract Jude's confused mind. "If you stay here, Carlos will kill you, just like he killed Sophie."

"Sophie," Jude repeated. "Where is he? Where is Carlos?"

"Just leave, Jude."

As expected, Jude flung himself into Patrick's mind roughly and began metaphorically rifling through things and flipping over furniture. Jude's revolting presence made Patrick's neck stiffen and seize with pain. He could push him out, but he stopped himself, and instead manufactured an image of Carlos's exact location at the right time. Then he jettisoned Jude out of his mind. Patrick thought he could still taste him and he spit on the ground, trying to rid himself of the last of Jude's magic inside him.

Jude's jutting chin and crossed arms told Patrick he had received the message.

"Stay out of the way," Jude said. He turned and walked back toward the road. Patrick had no idea why he retreated and he didn't like it. He could be on his way to find Isabella.

As soon as Jude turned away, Patrick ran back to camp. He hadn't expected to need to manipulate Jude's brain, and now he had changed the variables. Who knows what he might have accidentally messed with while he was in there. Or he might have left himself vulnerable and bled his own thoughts into Jude. He could have shown him the exact locations of everyone he cared about.

He should have let the damn conversation progress. The chances had been so small that he would have hurt Isabella. Despite how dark and broken Jude already was, he needed to have the right extra part of him break in order for him to be willing to murder a child. He was capable, but only in the darkest of scenarios. In most scenarios, Jude had some level of perverse conscious left that Patrick could count on to direct his actions. He should have trusted that and not bet on the worst possible, most unlikely, result. Now he'd probably fucked everything up.

As Patrick got closer to the camp, he wondered exactly where his feeling of unease was coming from. Behind him… or in front of him? Suddenly, the unease became pain. He felt like some of his skin had been ripped off and he fell to his knees, in too much pain to scream properly, and he only let out an agonized wheeze.

He thought someone had struck him with a curse from behind, but the pain faded and turned into thoughts. He had experienced a prophecy, a flash of a future so terrible it caused physical pain. A lifetime of grief, regret, and fear, all bundled into one moment. The paths before him crumbled, all the ones with any light at all were about to fall, leaving only the darkest options. Ones where he took Carlos's place and became a killer, his soul darkening through the years until unrecognizable. Lifetimes marked by loneliness and depression that ended in alcoholism or suicide. And other lifetimes that were alarmingly short—paths that ended in a pool of blood over the next hill.

All the paths that crumbled had one thing in common— Elena. Very soon, she would be irrevocably gone from all possible futures, which could only mean her death.

The paths were crumbling and fading, but they had yet to fall away completely. He still had time. He ran, trying to sift through the sudden painful prophecy to get the details of her death. But he struggled to think while his legs burned from the run and he could barely keep his breath. All he could surmise was that her death would be sudden. Everything to nothing in one breath. So, something decisive, like a bullet.

He came up to the camp and saw everyone faced away from him, watching something. He knocked his way through the onlookers without stopping to apologize.

As he feared, a gun was in the air, waiting to be fired, but Elena was the one holding it. Carlos was on his knees and Elena had one arm wrapped around his neck, and in the other hand, she held a gun to his temple. Tears were streaming down her face, and her hands shook.

"Elena," Patrick said.

"Stand back, mate," Paul said, moving his gun to Patrick. Elena was alone against an army. Five other guns held by Carlos's minions were trained at her head.

Patrick froze on the spot as Paul had commanded and held up his hands.

"Elena," Patrick said in the calmest voice he could muster. "Just put down the gun, and the others will put down their guns. Isn't that right? No one needs to get hurt."

"Listen to him, Elena," Carlos said. He had managed a more genuinely soothing tone than Patrick had.

However, Carlos's voice didn't soothe Elena. Her face grew redder and her bottom lip quivered so much she had to bite it. Seeing her agony made Patrick's chest feel heavy.

"Elena," Patrick said. "It's going to be okay. Just put the gun down and come with me. We'll walk right out of here." He held out his hand to her, trying to will her to come to him. It seemed so simple in that moment. He could even see the path. They might lose both their families, but they would have each other. They could just walk away.

"He... he made me kill someone. There wasn't even a good reason. He's just slaughtering people. And he made me..."

"I didn't make you do anything," Carlos said.

"Shut up," Elena said. "Just shut up."

"If you hadn't killed Lucas Prescott, he would have gone on to kill Patrick. Is that what you want? To become widowed before you turn thirty?"

Dear God. Elena killed Lucas Prescott?

"You're *lying*. I realize that now. Patrick hasn't had any visions of Lucas killing him, or any visions that show Lucas playing any important part in his life at all. And Patrick would know better than you. It's his life. His death. And he's a fall equinox wizard. He's so much more powerful than you are."

"You're so ungrateful," Carlos said. "I can't stand Patrick, but since you love him, I gave you the information you needed to save him. I gave you a gift."

Patrick was unnerved by how unconcerned Carlos was. Sure, Carlos was less powerful than him, but he was an accomplished oracle. And by the way he acted, he knew that he wasn't the one about to die.

"No, you knew if I killed Lucas, Patrick would always see me as a killer. He would never be able to really love me."

"Elena," Patrick said, his hand reaching for her. "I still love you. I know Carlos has been manipulating you. It's okay." Patrick wasn't sure if that was true. He feared Elena's description was more accurate. But right now, he just needed to get the guns down.

Elena's eyes remained too wide and wild. Patrick's words didn't reassure her. She pressed the barrel of the gun harder into Carlos's temple and he cringed.

"Boss?" Pike asked.

"Do not shoot her," Carlos growled back. "She won't shoot me."

"I will," Elena said. "I've killed someone once. I'm sure it will be much easier the second time. And this time, I really will be saving Patrick. Once the curtain lifted, and I saw you for what you were, I could see everything. I could see *you* killing Patrick. I have to kill *you* if I want him to live. And not just

Patrick. If I kill you, I'll save all the other people you are going to kill. This is the right thing to do."

"It's not the only way, Elena," Patrick said. "Trust me. Getting over killing Lucas will be hard enough for you, but you'll do it. It will always mark your soul, but it won't end you. Killing Carlos will be much harder to survive. You won't ever be the same."

She had her jaw clenched and her finger twitched on the trigger.

"Please, Elena. I can't live without you," Patrick said. "And I'm not just saying that. I've seen my future without you, and it's a dark place. Losing you is what would really kill me. I've seen myself die in a thousand different ways without you. The paths with you are not all perfect. Some of them are even kind of terrible, but it's just completely different with you. There is joy and meaning in the lives with you, even the short and terrible ones."

Elena slowly moved the gun away from Carlos's temple. Patrick was afraid to move.

"Yes," Patrick said. "Just come to me." He looked at the men around them. "Lower your guns too. She lowered hers."

Although that wasn't exactly true. She had removed the gun from Carlos's temple, but the gun remained raised. Carlos scuttled away like the spider he was. She held the gun in both hands, her eyes almost crossed as she stared it.

"What are you doing, Elena?" Patrick asked. "Just put it down."

She slowly turned the barrel of the gun towards her own face, her hands trembling violently as if her muscles and brain were not in agreement.

"What are you doing?" he asked again, now with an increased edge of panic.

"You're wrong, Patrick. I'll never be okay." Her voice was oddly calm. "Once you've taken a life, your soul is forever tainted. The only way to avoid the suffering is just to sleep."

Her gaze stopped bouncing from Carlos to Patrick and she went still. Her shoulders softened and she looked longingly at the sky.

"No," Patrick said. He walked toward her slowly. "No, please."

"Suddenly, it's all so clear," she said dreamily. "I'm going be at peace." Elena looked behind Patrick for a moment and he followed her gaze.

Leona Prescott stood about ten yards away. One of the fall wizards had found her and tied her to a fence post like a dog. Perhaps they needed another "lucky charm." Her eyes had turned black and she had her gaze fixed on Elena. Her jaw was jutted out slightly and every muscle in her body appeared tensed.

No. It all came together. Leona had been right there the whole time and had heard Elena confess to murdering her brother. And apparently, she believed Elena should die for her crime, right here and now.

The shot echoed in the shadow brain where he sensed things yet to come. He had less than a second to act. He lunged at Elena and grabbed her arm as the gun went off.

CHAPTER THIRTY-THREE

Carlos crawled away from the gun and didn't stop moving. The group kept their eyes on Elena. Once he had made it to the edge of the group, he heard a gunshot and he flinched as if the bullet had hit him. But he couldn't stop now. Elena had burned through the time he had needed to flee. Now, he only had moments remaining. His death was coming for him. The dark tide had turned toward him suddenly.

He had his life planned so carefully, and he hated surprises. And as much as he hated to flee, he had found that in the few times life had thrown him a curveball, the best thing to do was run until the tide passed.

Sensing that attention was not on him, he broke into a sprint. However, as he ran, he didn't feel as if the looming death retreated. No matter which way he turned, death grew closer. His heart rate picked up. The only thing he hated more than being surprised was being afraid. He reminded himself that if he were about to die, he would have seen it coming for years. Small things might surprise him, but nothing that big could have caught him off guard.

"Carlos Vega?"

Carlos turned around to see Jude Vandergraff. What the holy fuck was he doing here? He was supposed to be in prison. Patrick put him there and he would have made sure he stayed there. The Vandergraffs and Prescotts had always been fun to play with. Predictable and surprising at once. And always ready and eager to destroy themselves.

He had been playing chess against Paul for four years. Paul's district had been five counties around Austin, and Carlos had been working the Houston area. The rules were simple. Cause the death of as many solstice wizards in your area as possible without interacting with your targets. The game was for intelligent, patient wizards who could spin fate to cause death without ever getting anywhere near a crime scene. And after the deaths of Julie Prescott, Caroline Prescott, David Vandergraff, and Amanda Vandergraff, he had a wide lead over Paul. Over time, he had managed to find trophies from all of them, including the object talismans of the Vandergraffs, which Patrick had left so callously unguarded.

He didn't always play by the rules, but the deaths were what mattered, and he didn't actually kill any of them. Not with his own hands. And here was one of his stubborn pieces. He had hoped he might get stabbed in prison. No such luck.

"Tienes al hombre equivocado. Mi nombre es Ramon."

Jude smirked and shook his head. "I know who you are. You've got the stink of death all over you."

On Carlos's next blink, his eyes stayed shut. He froze, unable to breathe. He was able to shake the sensation, but when he opened his eyes again, Jude was only inches from his face, as if he had materialized there.

Carlos jumped back so quickly he stumbled. When on the ground, he found that, once again, he couldn't move. His spine had become as straight and stiff as a metal rod and every move was agony.

His face was in the dirt and he couldn't move his neck. He had no choice but to suck dirt into his lungs and he coughed. Carlos felt pressure on the back of his neck. He thought Jude was stepping on his neck, ready to crack his frozen spine, but the weight only came from Jude's lightly placed hand. A painfully cold sensation seeped into the back of his neck and into his brain. It reminded him of an ice cream headache, but immeasurably more painful. As his brain burned, his vision blurred, and darkness encroached on the edges of his sight. His recently speeding heart slowed and he felt more exhausted than he ever had in his life. He wanted nothing more than to go to sleep.

This was it. This winter son of a bitch could kill him with his bare hands. No one with that power should be allowed to live. If he was going out, he was making one final sacrifice.

Carlos used his remaining strength to confuse Jude's mind. He did what he did best—and what he'd been enjoying doing to Patrick for months now—he filled Jude's mind with terrible visions. He projected an image of Jude killing Sophie. He didn't have the energy for nuance, so he made it as violent and simple as possible. Jude beat her and beat her until her face was nothing but a mass of flesh and brain matter.

It worked. Jude took his hand off Carlos for a second, and he felt his hand warm enough to move it again. He reached for the knife he had attached to his belt. In one swift motion, he pulled the knife out of the sheath and slashed in Jude's direction. He couldn't move his head, but he felt the exhilarating rush of cutting deep into flesh. Jude made a gurgling sound and warmth pooled on Carlos's back.

He laughed in triumph, but it came out like a hiss. He had got the demon in the neck. Jude would die in seconds, minutes at the most, and he wouldn't have the strength to finish his killing spell. Carlos couldn't conduct killing spells himself, but he knew they took a lot of concentration and energy.

Carlos's spine felt like it had been dipped in liquid nitrogen, but his legs and arms had warmed, and he was able to flip himself over. He groaned as he did so. The nerves in his spine felt like they had ripped as he pulled himself over.

As he had expected, Jude leaned over him, clutching his neck, blood rushing down his arm. Carlos had won. He should have known better than to fear death. He would have known if it had been coming.

As soon as the thought tumbled through his fuzzy and aching mind, Jude clutched his throat. Carlos took a rattling gasp. Instead of being weakened by the blow, somehow, Jude had become more powerful. He had little life left in him, but that wasn't the kind of power he wielded. And he now held hands with Death.

Carlos's last thought was of his daughter, and how warm she felt when she curled herself into his lap. And then Jude took Carlos with him into death.

CHAPTER THIRTY-FOUR

Elena went down and Patrick fell on top of her. Her big, brown eyes found his and she seemed surprised to see him there.

"It hurts," she said in a strained whisper.

Patrick pulled himself off of her to see a round hole in her stomach and a growing red stain on her blouse.

"No," he said. He pulled up her shirt to see blood pouring out of a wound in her abdomen. He had managed to pull the gun away from her head, but not far enough to miss her.

"I don't want to die," she said, her eyes wide and glassy.

"I know," Patrick said, taking her hand. "And you're not going to. You're going to a hospital, and you're going to be fine."

He tried to find the path. The glimpse at the future that confirmed his promise. But in this moment, there was no future, no past for that matter, only Elena—bleeding to death. A shadow fell over Elena's face and Patrick saw Paul hovering over them. He had forgotten they weren't alone.

"Call 9-1-1," Patrick said. "And someone take that siren away from here. You fucking idiots."

"The protective spells on this place block cell phone service," Paul said, kneeling next to Elena. Paul took off his shirt and pressed it firmly against her wound.

"I'll take her to the hospital. Help me carry her."

Paul stared at him, his face pale. "There isn't time for that, mate."

"Just help me. Take her legs. I'll grab her arms."

"Stay with her. I'll go get help," Paul said. He ran toward his truck.

Patrick pressed his hands against the makeshift bandage, trying to staunch the bleeding. Elena's eyelids fluttered and closed, her mouth agape.

"No." Patrick grabbed her jaw and tried to shake her awake. "Stay with me, Elena. Paul is going for help. Just hang on a little while longer. Why is everyone just staring at her?" Patrick shouted to the assembled group. "Can't someone help her?

The only one who might be able to keep her alive until help came would have been a powerful spring witch. Leona was out of the question. Vanessa was back at camp with Isabella. Maybe Samantha.

"Don't leave me, Elena," Patrick whispered. He kissed her pale lips and ran.

He sprinted up the hill, with large leaps between steps, nearly flying. A part of him was in awe of what he was capable of. This bounding was far beyond human. He made it to the outskirts of the camp in a few minutes, but it felt like longer. Far too long. They were at war and he was bounding into the enemy camp.

He held up his hands. "Please, I need help. My girlfriend is hurt."

The cabins appeared deserted. He kept running. He made it to the main lodge and mess hall. "Hello? Is someone there? I'm not going to hurt you. I'm looking for Samantha Carthage. Or another spring witch or wizard. You know I won't kill spring. Please."

Nothing.

He didn't know if the clan was ignoring him or if they had fled. Either would make sense. They had no reason to help save the life of one of the killers of the Los Segadores. And they had no reason not to run at the first chance they got. He had never felt so alone. Elena was dying and he had no power to save her. And everyone he loved had left.

"Hello? Please help me."

He had wasted the last minutes of Elena's life running up this hill in vain. He should have stayed with her, so she could die in his arms. By now, she had probably died alone. The weight of his hopelessness made it difficult to move as quickly on the way back down the hill. His only hope was Paul, a killer he barely knew.

He ran back to Elena, his legs heavy, feeling that no matter how fast he tried to run, he was moving through thick syrup. When he returned, he was surprised to see the group of Los Segadores who had been uselessly watching Elena die had moved back even farther, forming a circle around her. Maybe they were performing a spell he didn't know about. Maybe fall wizards could do something.

He saw a kneeling dark-haired figure and his heart leapt, thinking Elena had gotten up. But the long curtain of dark hair belonged to Evangeline. As he got closer, he heard shouting from the circle and a saw a ring of reddened faces and jerky hand gestures. They weren't doing a spell; they had been pushed back by a strong repulsion spell.

If he hadn't recognized the dark-haired girl as his sister, he might have assumed she was the angel of death, there to take Elena's soul. Perhaps that was the truth. The winter solstice witch wielded the darkest of powers. She was the angel of death.

"What are you doing?" Patrick added to the shouts as he got closer. "Evangeline! Stop!"

He braced himself and pushed into the repulsion shoulder first as if he was pushing against a strong wind. The air inside the circle felt painfully icy. His lungs hurt to breathe in the cold and empty air. He felt suddenly tired, as if he might be freezing to death. He couldn't stand anymore and fell to the ground, crawling slowly toward the pair in the center of the circle.

Stay back, Patrick. He heard Evangeline's voice in his mind.

"Don't kill her. Please." He didn't know if he had successfully projected his response into her mind or not. "If you love me at all, don't kill her. She's dying anyway."

"Shh… " Evangeline purred into his mind. Or perhaps the sound was only the wind.

Patrick used the last of his strength heave his body one more foot, then he could no longer see. His eyes were shrouded in black. The oxygen had gone, and he uselessly gasped at the empty, dead air. His head throbbed painfully and then he collapsed.

Patrick woke to a piercing headache and something on his face. He swatted at the obstruction and found he was wearing an oxygen mask. A paramedic was taking his blood pressure. Patrick ripped off the mask completely.

"I'm fine," he said in a wheezing voice that suggested otherwise. "Where is Elena?"

Patrick pushed past the paramedic to find two more hovering over Elena. One had a stethoscope on Elena's chest and she listened with a face devoid of expression. Another was holding a larger mask on her face and pumping air into her lungs.

Without losing a step, they moved her onto a stretcher and carried her away.

"Wait," he gasped. "I'm coming with her."

Patrick stumbled and the paramedic caught him on one side and Paul caught him on the other and they helped him follow to the road where the ambulance was parked. Everyone else had fled. The remaining Los Segadores were gone, as was Evangeline.

When Patrick crawled into the ambulance, Paul nodded to him and ran off as well. The paramedic put the oxygen mask back on Patrick's face. Elena looked dead. Her skin was pale with a light yellow tinge and her lips were bloodless. But they wouldn't be moving this quickly if she were dead.

The female paramedic attached a heart rate monitor to her finger and the screen showed slow, but even, heart beats. Her heart paused for a dangerously long time between beats and Patrick stared at the flat line, panicking until the next beep flashed.

CHAPTER THIRTY-FIVE

Patrick waited alone in the ICU waiting room while Elena was in surgery for six hours. His head ached from lack of food, sleep, and a dive into a repulsion spell, but he didn't rest. He focused every ounce of remaining energy on watching the fates. They spun so quickly. Elena on the edge of life and death, but hope was not lost. The paths spread out like an infinite web. They had no one fate, but an infinity of possibilities. But he had to watch. He had to keep the paths with Elena from crumbling.

"Mr. Vandergraff?"

Patrick's head shot up, causing lights to pop behind his eyes. He had been expecting an update from a doctor, and he squinted to make sure he wasn't seeing things. Jude's lawyer, Carrie Anne Carr, sat in the chair next to him.

"What? What are you doing here?"

She squinted at him, as if she couldn't see him clearly either. "Your brother Jude is dead," she said.

Patrick nodded.

"You don't seem surprised."

"Why don't you just leave me alone? I didn't kill him. I helped him get his appeal."

"Which was a strange thing to do. Perhaps you just wanted him free so you could kill him."

"Leave me alone."

Carrie Anne Carr sat down next to Patrick. He wanted to shove her away, but he was too tired. She wore too much floral perfume and it made his eyes water.

"I will," she said. "If you tell me the truth. I just want to know. Are you really a wizard?"

The Mundane woman had given up her nose scrunch and stared at him intently.

"What?"

"You don't remember. But you've seen me before… or perhaps you didn't see me. I'm not very remarkable."

"Where?"

"At your uncle's funeral three years ago."

Patrick searched his memory and came up with nothing. "You knew him?"

"Yes. He was my brother-in-law. Well, not officially. But his partner, Justin, is my brother."

"Oh my God. Why didn't you just tell me? Are you really a lawyer?"

"Of course I'm a lawyer," she said indignantly. "How do you think I won Jude's appeal? Magic?"

"Funny."

"I gather it's against the rules… but James had told Justin he was a wizard. He showed him what he could do. But Justin never believed him, even when Justin conjured amazing things right in front of his face. He always found a rational way to explain it away. But then when James died, Justin was never satisfied with how it happened. And all our attempts at legal recourse fell flat. We couldn't even get that far, as the assigned detective's IQ seemed to drop about fifty points every time he thought about this case. I can't tell you how frustrating it was for him."

"I'm sorry."

She nodded absently. "Rational explanations failed him, and he started thinking about what James had told him in a new way. And then when your parents died, he wanted to know more about that too. Since there was actually an indictment and conviction for your mother's death, I had more to work with. I may not understand magic, but I understand the legal process. Jude's arrest, trial, and conviction defied all logic. And I can't understand how all the other lawyers, judges, and jury members didn't notice it. It didn't take me as long as my brother to accept that something supernatural was in play. Everything just felt wrong. Jude feels wrong. *You* feel wrong. And I always thought there was something a little off about James, but I thought I was just being an over-protective big sister. Now I see he's the same as you."

She stopped talking and stared at him, waiting.

"I didn't kill anyone," Patrick said finally. "But I knew that if Jude won his appeal and was pointed in the right direction, Carlos and Jude would kill each other. And that's what happened, isn't it?"

"It seems so, although the cause of Carlos's death wasn't immediately apparent. There will be an autopsy, of course."

"If I said I was a wizard, you would think I was more powerful than I really am. I'm a human man, who is better than most at manipulating situations to my advantage. Think of it as magic if you want. But if I were really a wizard, my girlfriend wouldn't be in that room on the edge of death. I would have been able to save my parents, and all the other people I've seen be hurt and killed. I can't be a wizard. I'm just a man."

Carrie Anne smirked as she nodded.

"If Justin wants more explanation of James's death, I'll tell him whatever he wants to know. But I won't be able to explain why terrible things happen for no reason."

"He would like that." She handed Patrick her card for the second time. "Well, whatever you are, I find you fascinating. If you or any of your siblings ever need a lawyer whose magic is limited to excellent legal research, give me a call."

She patted him on the shoulder awkwardly and walked away, her squat heels clicking. Patrick slipped the card in his wallet, still unsure if Carrie Anne was friend or foe.

An hour later, Patrick had expended all his energy and was about to pass out whether he wanted to or not. Then the doctor finally came in and called his name.

With his heart beating in his throat, Patrick stood to meet him.

"I'm Dr. Elliot Chang," he said, holding out a cold hand.

"Is she alive?"

He nodded. "She is a lucky girl."

Tears streamed down Patrick's face. He was far too tired to stop himself from crying.

The doctor patted his shoulder. "She's still in a critical condition, and we'll watch her carefully, but I don't have any reason to believe she won't make a full recovery."

Someone watching them might have assumed Patrick had

gotten the opposite news. But the relief felt like melting.

"It's been a strange one, I have to say."

"What do you mean?"

"What happened after she was shot?"

"I… I don't know. I went to go get help."

"Well, her body temperature dropped dramatically. Her heart rate slowed to a crawl. It's the only reason she survived. If her heart hadn't slowed to almost nothing, she would have bled out long before help arrived."

"Really?"

"Do you know how that happened? I've never seen anything like it, although I've heard of it happening in extreme low temperatures. But unless she was moved into a walk-in freezer, that wouldn't have happened here."

"I don't know," Patrick said, although he thought he did. He couldn't have imagined how a winter solstice witch could have been doing anything but making sure she was dead. The kindest thought he had considered was Evangeline was performing a mercy killing, like shooting a deer hit by a car so they wouldn't suffer. He hadn't considered even for a moment that Evangeline would or could use her powers to save a life, least of all Elena's life.

"I've yet to see a miracle in my career," Dr. Chang said. "But maybe that was the first."

Patrick followed the doctor back to the post-op room where Elena lay attached to copious tubes and machines. He kissed an exposed patch of skin on her cheek, relishing her renewed warmth.

Chapter Thirty-Six

Once Elena was conscious and moved out of intensive care to regular long-term care, Patrick felt comfortable leaving her side for an afternoon. The only person who had a cell phone at the camp was Paul, so Patrick had called. Paul had been thrilled to hear from him and picked him up at the hospital.

When Patrick crawled into the over-large truck with antlers on the grill, he was once again surprised to hear the South African accent coming from Paul, even though he expected it this time. He had never met another redneck "convert." One was born a redneck, they didn't move across an ocean to become one.

"Thank you," Patrick said.

"No problem, mate. I'm glad you called. Everyone has been worried."

Sure they have. The only one of them that bothered to help had been Paul.

"Not just for picking me up. Thank you for calling an ambulance. I passed out, so if you hadn't gone for help, she would have died."

"Yeah, I heard you ran right into that winter witch's spell. Not a good idea."

"Elena wants to see her Abi. So if it's okay with you, we'll just pick her up and go back to the hospital."

"Oh… " The hesitance in his voice made Patrick worry. Had Abi died? It could happen any moment.

"What? Is her Abi okay?"

"Yeah, she's fine. Always seemed convinced Elena would pull through. But she's been casting protection spells for her non-stop anyways." Paul paused. "It's just that… are you coming back after? Maybe after Elena gets out of the hospital?"

"Back where?"

"To the clan. We assumed you would take over since you took down Carlos. And, if it's true you're a fall equinox wizard, then it should have been you all along."

"I didn't take down Carlos."

"Aw, come on, mate. You did something."

"Well, whatever I did, I didn't do it to take Carlos's place. If you haven't noticed, I'm not one of you. I don't believe what you believe."

"So, what? You're just going to do nothing?"

"If by 'nothing,' you mean 'not kill people,' then yes."

"The truth is, I've been wanting to take Carlos down for a while. I was looking for my move. But you beat me to it. You're right. He's a killer. He has no discipline, no planning. He's used our sacred rites as an excuse to kill people."

"And you helped him."

"You're right. I should have spoken up sooner. But it was

one of those frog in the boiling water things. He made changes so gradually, I didn't notice until we were already deep in it. But just because he went too far, doesn't mean Los Segadores isn't doing a good thing. For centuries, our clan has been preventing war, genocide, and all manners of atrocities. Without us, the world would have ended several times over."

"And what about the atrocities you didn't stop? You don't know as much as you think you do. The future is an infinite web of possibilities. A human mind might be able to follow each path along a few turns, but we're far too limited to see the ultimate result of the paths we choose."

"So, because we can't prevent all atrocities, we should just not try at all? You're right, we aren't powerful enough to predict and prevent every bad thing that ever happens, but we can do some good."

Patrick paused to consider his next words. "If I took over the Los Segadores, I would make a lot of changes."

"That would be your call, mate."

"Our focus would be on preventing terrorist attacks and wars—preventing the death and suffering of hundreds of people. Nothing less. Even then, everything would be calculated and planned carefully. We'd avoid killing at all costs, and only kill when one death could prevent hundreds."

Paul took his hand off the wheel and held it out to Patrick, who shook it. "I'm with you, mate," Paul said.

Crap. What did he just do?

"Actually, before we go to the camp, can we make a stop?"

Paul waited in his truck, rifle at the ready, as Patrick walked up to the school. He had the nagging feeling he was being called.

Sure enough, it appeared he was expected. Evangeline waited for him beyond the gate. Without hesitation, he went to her and hugged her, and she hugged him back.

"You saved her life," Patrick said.

"So, she'll be okay?"

"Yes."

"Before you are too grateful, I want you to know I didn't send Leona away. Elena killed her brother. But I know it was all more complicated than that. And I know you love Elena."

"I do."

Evangeline nodded, as if it were an expected but unfortunate prognosis.

"Where are Emmy and Xavier?"

"They went home to Houston with Nathan and Lacie." Evangeline paused, never one who was comfortable with delicate conversations. "I believe you were only with the killer clan because you loved Elena and because you wanted to stop Carlos, not help him."

"You're right. I should have realized what was happening sooner. But yes, that's why I stayed. I knew the fastest way to stop the killing was to do so from the inside."

"I think they'll accept that eventually, but they're still angry at you now. They don't trust you anymore."

Patrick nodded.

"I want them in my life," he said, his voice cracking. "Will you tell them that? You and Emmy and Xavier are my family, and I'll do whatever I need to do to get them to forgive me."

"I'll tell them."

"There is one thing though. I promised Carlos I would kill Emmy. Well, actually, I promised I would kill you."

Evangeline raised an eyebrow.

"Obviously, I never intended to kill either of you. Well, it might not seem obvious to you, I admit. But I would have died before I raised a hand to either of you. And for a while, that's what I thought would happen. But we all lived. And I'm worried that means this isn't over. When you cast the killing spell… " he trailed off, not wanting to complete the thought.

"It wasn't over until someone died," Evangeline finished. "Are you saying you cast a killing spell against me?"

"No. I'm not explaining it right. I made a promise to Carlos and he cut my hand and clasped our hands together. It was some kind of magical promise. I felt like I would *have* to kill you. The spell would push me in that direction until it happened. Maybe since he died, it will void the promise, but that seems too good to be true."

"You're right about that," Evangeline said. "Magical promises outlast death."

"Then what do I do? Do I have to stay away from both of you for the rest of my life?"

"Please don't," she said, sounding uncharacteristically vulnerable.

"I… I won't."

"You said that when you made the promise, Carlos thought it referred to Emmy, and you thought it referred to me?"

"Yeah."

"That's really messy magic. I honestly don't know what that would do. But I'm not worried."

"Why not?"

"Because, Patrick, you're the most powerful wizard I've ever met. More powerful than me. And you know I hate to admit that. But you broke through my protection spells like they were nothing. And you managed to keep everyone alive during a battle against two groups hell bent on killing each other. That's too impossible to be an accident. I know *you* did that. Carlos was dwarfed by you from the beginning. If you didn't really mean the promise you were making, then it was no promise. And I don't believe Carlos would be able to coerce you to do anything. I'm sure he tried and failed lots of times. *You're* in charge."

"I don't know. I don't know all the details, but I'm pretty sure Carlos has been fucking with our lives for a long time. Playing us like pieces in a game. *He* has been in charge."

Evangeline shook her head. "I'm sure he thought that. And maybe he was once. But not when you made that promise. And certainly not now."

"You're really not worried?"

"You could kill me without lifting a finger. But if you don't want to, then you won't. *No one* is powerful enough to make you do something you don't want to do."

Patrick wanted to believe her. And perhaps, in time, he could. He felt different than he had even a few weeks ago. He couldn't imagine that he, or really anyone, ever felt completely in control. The harder one tried to control the people around them, the looser their grasp became. But he felt in control of himself. He knew how to use his power, and how not to use it. He was no killer.

"Are you staying here even though the teachers are… gone?"

"For now. The other students look to me as their leader, and most of them have nowhere to go. None of us belong anywhere except for here."

"Are they still here?" Patrick looked around at the abandoned school. They appeared to be alone.

"Yes. We're good hiders when we need to be."

"Can I give you something?" Patrick asked. Evangeline

cocked her eyebrow at him. "I've been keeping it with me for a long time, because I thought you might want it someday." He pulled an old piece of paper out of a fold in his wallet. "Two and a half years ago, you threw this away without reading it. But I took it out of the trash."

Evangeline stared at the paper with her lips pursed, but she reached for it.

"Why didn't you keep it?" Patrick asked.

"I don't know," she said, running her finger across the folds. "It hurt. And I guess I figured if I didn't have it, it wouldn't hurt me anymore." She opened it with trembling hands. "I did read it though."

"You should know, I read it too. I'm sorry."

"I know you did. And that doesn't bother me. It bothers me that you let *her* read it."

"I didn't. But it wouldn't surprise me if she did. I was never very forthcoming about my past. And she had a bad habit of nosing into my things, and my brain, without my permission."

"I see."

"I'm glad I got to read it. He's right. It makes me wonder if we've been thinking about everything wrong this whole time."

Evangeline looked at the paper to read the words again. And Patrick knew what she read.

The winter solstice is not the height of darkness; it is the beginning of the light. Let them see you shine. Love you always, Dad.

Epilogue

The winter solstice, four years later

Emmy looked into the floor-length mirror and did her best to bottle the memory the way her mother had once taught her. She would have lots of memories to bottle today. Perhaps she should skip this one to make sure she had plenty of mental room, but the moment meant so much to her. She had never felt more beautiful or content. The gown was the blue-white color of moonlight and it shimmered when she moved, making it even harder to stay still.

But what she loved about this moment even more than how freaking awesome she looked was the three women weaving flowers into her hair and into the cascading folds of her gown. Apparently, this was a wizard tradition. The women in your life offer blessings in the form of flowers.

"Quit wiggling," Evangeline said as she attempted to affix a black hellebore to Emmy's hair. They had all chosen flowers that can bloom in the winter.

Samantha wrapped a strand of fragrant lavender around the hellebore and then moved on to continue arranging a spectacular evergreen bouquet of holly, rosemary, and gardenias. Samantha had the stern mask of a surgeon. As the spring witch among them, she took flowers very, very seriously. And apparently, wedding flowers were the most serious flowers of all.

Lacie was kneeled on the ground, tying witch hazel and winter honeysuckle around the hem of her dress. "I'm bad at this," she announced. Although Emmy thought the lacy tips of petals adding a small burst of color to her train looked amazing. But hey, Emmy was in a pretty good mood. Everything in this room and surrounding gardens was the best thing ever.

After everything they had been through, these three women wanted to adorn her with flowers and stand by her. Emmy had felt like she had lost her family, all of them had. But somehow, here they stood—a family. And that was the memory worth bottling.

The company of three witches from three different seasons made the energy of the room like a chord of three notes harmonizing perfectly together. However, it also made the absence of the fourth season more palpable.

"Don't forget the bracelet," Emmy said to Samantha.

"I haven't forgotten. It goes on last."

If Nathan's sister, Julie, had lived, she would have likely been Emmy's fourth bridesmaid, creating a perfect and rare balance of all four seasons. In her honor, Emmy would walk down the aisle with Julie's talisman, a charm bracelet Emmy had found almost eight years ago, and that had ultimately led her to Nathan. And, of course, summer also waited for her at the altar where all four seasons would stand together.

"Wow, you look amazing, Emmy."

Emmy was startled by the sound of a male voice. She saw Zander poking his head into the room, careful not to open it too wide and give the whole hallway a preview.

"Are you ready for your flower girl?"

Sophie ran in before any of them could reply. She careened toward Emmy and grabbed her dress.

Samantha gasped. "Sophie, no. Be careful."

"It's okay," Emmy said, smiling. Because everything was okay. Everything was perfect.

Sophie looked like a miniature Emmy in a dress of the same blue white and a crown of flowers in her hair.

"You are a princess!" Sophie declared.

"Thank you," Emmy said. "You look like a princess too."

"I've been practicing outside. I know exactly where to walk. And I know I'm supposed to walk slowly. And then I have to stand still during the ceremony."

"That will be the real challenge," Samantha said, smiling.

"You don't have to stay too still," Emmy said. "I probably won't be able to stand still."

"Are you ready?" Evangeline asked, smoothing her dress in the mirror. It seemed wrong to make her bridesmaids dress the same since they were all of different seasons, so everyone got to choose their own. Evangeline wore a simple, elegant black dress. The backless dress clearly showed the line of hatch mark scars on her back. They had faded to be nearly invisible, but the strange pattern was still apparent. However, she didn't try to hide them anymore. If anything, she seemed to choose clothes that displayed them as prominently as possible. And, of course, she had to show skin to display the tattoo by her shoulder blade. The design was something between a moth and a butterfly with large black wings and red eyes. Emmy liked to think of it as the badass butterfly.

"It is really time?" Emmy asked.

"Yes," Evangeline said. "But I'm sure you could stall if you wanted to. It's not like they can start without you."

"No, I'm good. I already feel like I've been waiting for several lifetimes."

Her sister, cousin, and friend smiled at her. Sophie literally bounced up and down. "Yay, yay, yay," she chanted.

"You look how I feel, Sophie."

Emmy followed her bridesmaids down a back hallway, and she tried to drink in every moment. Every tile on the floor. Every lamp. And the harmonious scent of flowers and herbs.

They went into an atrium and Evangeline pointed to the place where her escort was waiting for her.

"Wow," Patrick said. "You clean up nice."

"Thank you," Emmy said. "You don't look terrible either." What she was really thinking, but didn't say, was that in his suit and tie he looked almost exactly like their dad. But if she said it, she would start crying too early.

"No one will be looking at me. I know people often say brides are glowing, but I think you actually *are*. You look almost... radioactive. Are you doing that on purpose?"

"I look radioactive?"

"I meant that in the nicest possible way."

"I'm really glad you're here," Emmy said.

"Me too."

"Is she with you?"

"No. She stayed in D.C."

Emmy nodded. "That's too bad. She should have come."

"No," Patrick said. "It would upset Nathan. I don't want anything to complicate your day."

Understandably, Nathan could not forgive Elena for murdering his brother. And he would not forgive Patrick for using his magic to keep her from getting convicted or being punished in any way.

"I would like to know her. I mean, ideally, she wouldn't have murdered my soon to be husband's brother."

"Ideally," Patrick agreed.

"Our family is now a hodgepodge of seasons with all kinds of crazy baggage and strange shit. Look at Zander, Samantha, and Sophie. I mean, what? They are the weirdest, but most adorable family I've ever seen. Elena fits in with all this madness perfectly."

"I'll tell her you said that. She'd like that."

"Give it one more year," Emmy said. "Next year, you'll come down for Christmas. That gives me a year to convince Nathan it's a good idea. I'm sure I can. He might actually be the nicest guy in the world. And I mean that literally."

"I'd like that," Patrick said. "I want to know what the house looks like inside. You know, I drove by when I came into town. It looks great."

"Thank you for being okay with us finishing it."

"No, it's great. It's what Mom and Dad would have wanted." He paused, swallowing heavily. "It's time."

"So what are you guys up to in D.C.? I imagine it's something very secret and important. Saving the world and all that."

"Occasionally. But most of the time, we're pretty normal and boring."

"That's great."

"It is."

She offered him her arm and he took it.

"Are you ready?" she asked him.

"No," he said.

She laughed and patted his hand. "Your job is easy. Just one foot in front of the other."

"It shouldn't be me," he said, looking down. Grief hung off every word.

Emmy was quiet for a moment. "Yes, it should," she finally said in a whisper.

The two of them stood together arm in arm and silently shed tears for the glaring absence.

Emmy couldn't see her bridesmaids walk out ahead of her, but she couldn't wait to watch the video later. She imagined how beautiful and perfect they all looked in their different dresses with bouquets of different flowers.

When Emmy and Patrick's turn came, they walked outside the atrium and out into the crisp, fragrant air. She had seen the courtyard set for the wedding before the sunset, but nothing could have prepared her for what she saw now. The garden had been decorated with thousands of twinkling white lights. She might have been stepping out into the starry night sky.

Clutching Patrick's arm probably more firmly than she needed to, they walked out onto stone walkway to the sound of the Trans-Siberian Orchestra's Christmas Canon. There must have been a speaker somewhere, but the music seemed to be coming from the air. Or, more specifically, the music came from the lights. The trees were wrapped in lights from their roots to the towering branches above. The wind made the branches sway to the rhythm of the music, as if the lights were the bow and the darkness the violin.

As she moved through the lit hedges, more lights came on as she passed and she left a trail of sparks as if she were a comet. She didn't know if was simply a Mundane special effect, or if one of her bridesmaids had enchanted her gown somehow. But it was magic either way.

They reached the end of the hedge and she prepared to walk down the aisle. Sophie began carefully walking down the aisle with measured steps, clearly working hard to walk slowly. Emmy noticed she didn't have a flower basket. Samantha had been in charge of all of the flowers, so she had taken it for granted she would have remembered to give her daughter, the flower girl, some flowers. But in a moment, Emmy realized Sophie didn't need a basket. Emmy gasped in awe as she saw Sophie fling sparkling light from her fingertips into the aisle. The light drifted and fell just as petals might and swirled in glowing eddies behind Sophie.

They say your wedding is the happiest day of your life, but Emmy had always assumed that wouldn't be true for her. All a dark witch could ask for would be a pretty dress, a nice cake, and an event that would look good in pictures. But no real joy. The closest thing she would get to happiness would be brief reprieves when she was distracted from the pain. She had been dead wrong. When she came into the courtyard and saw Nathan waiting for her under the archway, her chest filled with warmth. Her happiness was clean and pure and unafraid. Tears streamed down her face and she didn't attempt to hide them or wipe them away.

The two of them walked down the aisle to the traditional bridal march. The archway ahead of her was decorated with hundreds of bright white glowing butterflies that fluttered with life. More clever magic. She loved her girls. They had created a moment more perfect for her than she could have ever imagined herself. Seeing Nathan's face light up as he watched her approach made more happy tears slide down her cheeks. Now this was a moment to remember. She thought she probably didn't even need magic for this one. No one would forget this.

When she reached the altar, she hugged Patrick and he squeezed her back so hard she almost grunted. She saw he was crying too, but he was trying to hide it, nonchalantly wiping away tears.

"Thank you for walking with me," Emmy said.

"Yep," he said. His reply might have seemed glib, but Emmy could tell he kept it short to hide his barely restrained tears.

Emmy hadn't been expecting the second hug. As soon as Patrick released her, Nathan's mother, Thea, stepped forward and embraced Emmy. She smelled like freshly cut grass and peaches. She held Emmy's cheek to her own for a moment, and said nothing. Emmy felt a sudden rush of warmth that reminded her of how it felt as a little girl to curl up in bed next to her mother after she had a nightmare. More tears spilled from her eyes. Thea kissed her on the cheek and then gently pressed her back to lead her toward her son.

Nathan held his hands out to her and she took them. The sparks she left in her wake swirled in the air around them, twinkling as stars she could touch. Some of the floating lights landed in Nathan's hair and he held out his hands to catch them, and laughed like a child first seeing snow. And then he looked at Emmy, and the joy in his eyes nearly made her stagger.

Thea stepped onto the altar as well to perform the wedding ceremony, which was often performed by the matriarch in wizard families. In the absence of her own mother, Emmy couldn't think of anyone better. Thea had quit drinking and her skin once again glowed with almost the same golden light as her daughter Julie's had. She held her hands out to their small audience. Despite a rocky relationship over the past few years, Carson and Jess and all of the Oppenheimer cousins were in attendance. She had worried this might lead to drama, but if Lacie and Ashlynn had entered into any death matches, they had at least had the courtesy to hide it from Emmy. Some other friends, mostly Nathan's, and a variety of Prescott cousins also smiled up at them. Even though the group was small, Emmy could still hardly believe so many people would come here just for them.

"This is the winter solstice, the most joyful day of the year. On this, the darkest night, we celebrate the promise of light. From this day forward, the days will grow longer, and although the nights will come, they will be warmed by the light of long days. We all know, of course, the seasons cycle through every year. The light of the days will return, but again retreat, again and again, until the end of all things.

However, tonight we celebrate a light even more enduring than the sun. The light of love does not fade. The light of love endures through all the seasons of life and death. Although the skin can still grow cold and light can be shielded from the eyes, this light continues to burn untouched by cold or dark. It is my great honor to lead this celebration of the light between this man and woman, which will burn brightly for them in all the seasons of their lives."

She gestured again toward the group and Xavier stepped forward, holding an unlit black candle. As he approached the altar, he took Emmy's hand and squeezed it.

"Summer wizards often call this candle the memory candle, but it can also serve as a tribute to darkness. This candle honors the darkness of the past season. When we light this candle, we show respect for all the dark parts of our lives. It's a forgiveness of the hidden parts of us that bring us shame. It is a tribute to our hardships that have given us strength. And it is a light to honor everyone we've lost." Thea paused for a moment, and then collected herself again. "This light honors the love that lives in grief."

Xavier placed the candle into the holder on the altar. He held his hand up to the wick and when he took his hand away again, a light had been left behind. He had lit the candle with magic as easily as breathing. Emmy thought something seemed strange about the light perched on the candle. It didn't flicker, but it still seemed alive. Iridescent bursts of color danced within the white light.

Xavier smiled at her again as he walked back to his seat. The light was so beautiful, she didn't want to look away, but tears blurred the image so much, she could hardly see. She wanted to believe her parents were here, dancing in that light somewhere.

"And now, the solstice candle," continued Thea. She gestured toward the group again, and the tone of her voice and the look on her face had changed. She now dripped with warmth. She reserved that look for her granddaughter alone. One day, Thea would look at Emmy's own children like that.

Sophie bounced back up to the front holding a white candle. "This candle represents the light of the future. It represents hope and faith and—well, it looks like she's already lighting it."

A murmur of good-natured laughter ran through the crowd. Sophie's candlelight was the opposite of Xavier's. It jumped and sparked and twisted, but fortunately appeared to remain contained to the wick. The candle reminded Emmy of how Sophie danced and twirled with infinite energy, with perhaps too much energy, as if she'd also just had a cupcake. Sophie proudly held her light up to the crowd and beamed as she received applause.

"Right here, honey," Thea said, pointing to the altar. She helped Sophie carefully place her candle in the holder. Then she led her back toward Samantha.

"Now, everyone will have the opportunity to provide their blessing of light. Please bring your offering to the fire pit. There are also votive candles and matchbooks in the pockets behind the chairs for those who require them."

One by one, lights sparkled to life around Emmy, of all colors and intensities. Everyone, including Emmy and Nathan, conjured light in their own hands and brought it to the fire pit at the front of the aisle. As far as Emmy knew, the only Mundanes in the audience were her Uncle James's partner, Justin, and his weird sister. Neither of them used a votive, and just stayed at their seats. They both looked as if they had stumbled upon a unicorn. However, Justin appeared alarmed, while Carrie Anne looked like a kid in Disneyland.

The mere presence of her cousins meant Carson and Jess had finally told them about magic. Emmy saw Ashlynn spray a web of light from her wrist, much like Spiderman. She smiled as she did it, still thrilled by the novelty.

Patrick approached near the end and added a fully formed golden rose to the otherwise messy mixture of light. Other than the fact he had crafted something out of light that looked like she could touch and hold, the light reminded her of the golden stream of light he had created on their first winter solstice as wizards, nine years ago. Even then, he had power none of them could have comprehended.

The light danced and sparked and spit in the pit. The offering of light was common in wizard wedding ceremonies, but she wondered how often wizards of all four seasons were in attendance and mixing their magic. It probably happened far less often than it should.

"Are you ready for the vows?" Thea asked.

However, Emmy had her eyes on Patrick, who had stood back up and approached the altar. Before Patrick could reach her, Lacie suddenly grabbed Emmy from behind and shoved her.

"What are you doing?" Nathan asked, as fiercely as he could manage, which still sounded quite pleasant.

To answer Nathan's question, the light from the fire pit jumped out of its confines and lapped at the spot where Emmy's train had recently been.

"Oh. Thank you," Emmy said to Lacie. Patrick moved back to his seat.

Evangeline held out her hands and did something to the fire. The flames appeared to relax, transitioning into a gentle sway. Evangeline had an on again off again relationship with the fire starter boy from Heartsong, whose name was Isaac. Since he had a habit of starting fires, usually accidentally, but sometimes on purpose, she was probably very skilled at extinguishing. They must have been dating again because Emmy had glimpsed him in the crowd. Patrick must not have been pleased as he strongly disapproved of Isaac. However, Emmy disagreed. She thought he was nice enough, other than the fire thing, and nobody was perfect. And as long as Evangeline dated him, she couldn't throw any shade at Emmy for being with a summer wizard.

"Yes, thank you," Thea said. However, her tone implied she thought occasionally catching fire was preferable to comingling with fall wizards.

Emmy doubted catching fire would have upset her much at this moment; she turned back to Nathan and took his hands. She began her vows without being prompted.

"Before my dad died, he wrote all of us letters. He gave

each of us advice," Emmy said. "I want to share part of the letter with you now."

Nathan squeezed her hands back and his eyes sparkled. She released his hands and Evangeline handed Emmy a piece of paper. Emmy had her father's words memorized, but she felt like it would be easier if she could hold something as she spoke. The paper shook in her hands as she read.

"I don't know if there is a Heaven or Hell after death, but I do know Heaven and Hell can be found here on Earth. I've experienced both. So, a long time ago, I stopped waiting for Heaven after death. Instead, I started looking for it in life. It's hard to explain the feeling, but you'll know it when you experience it. You can't live in Heaven for weeks or days, it comes in a moment, where the world glows and you feel so much love you can barely stand it. Those moments have come at different times in different places, but they always had one thing in common—you. My kids and my wife. In those moments, I felt like I wanted for nothing, in this life or the next. I learned that love, and God, and Heaven, are all part of the same force, and the best way to experience God was to experience love. Don't wait for Heaven. Find it."

Emmy looked back up at Nathan. "I did," she concluded.

At the end of the reception, Emmy and Nathan walked hand in hand through a line of magic created to look like sparklers. Even after the music had faded, Emmy thought she could hear Auld Lang Syne playing in the breeze, and she thought of her parents. *For auld lang syne, my dear. For auld lang syne. We'll take a cup of kindness, for auld lang syne.*

The whole night, she had felt her parents with her, almost as if they had stood next to her in flesh and bone. She had felt their presence many times, but never in the way she had tonight. She realized that although she could always find them in dark places when she needed them, they didn't live there anymore. All their darkness died when they did, and all that was left was the light.

ACKNOWLEDGEMENTS

First and foremost, I thank my readers. You waited far too long for this last book. I hope it was worth the wait and it means the world to me that you've stuck with me through to the end. It still thrills and amazes me that strangers would want to spend their time reading my words. I feel an unexpected and intimate connection to all you whom I've never met but shared so much.

There are so many wonderful people who I've never met in person, many of whom live across oceans, who have reached across the miles to support me and my stories. The first person I name is Clare Dugmore. She has supported me through most of my publishing journey, but most importantly, she has supported me here at the end, lifting me up and showing me the right path toward publishing this final December People book. I believe I would have eventually managed to get Harvest published (because I'm stubborn like that), but I don't know when it would have happened without Clare pushing me forward at the right moment.

I also thank the other fantastic authors and publishing professionals at Animus Ferrum, especially Tracy Korn and Lyssa Chiavari who had faith in my work and helped me publish, while asking for nothing in return. I thank Kimberley Marsot of Kim G Designs for re-imagining my December People covers in a beautiful and intriguing way, Kyra Lennon for her careful examination and editing of my words, and Dorothy Dreyer who brought everything together with skillful formatting.

And finally, my family, especially my husband and my mother. I've been lucky enough to have nothing but unwavering support throughout my journey. I know that is rare and special and it means so much to me.

And like the winter solstice, this is not is not the end, but the beginning. It only gets brighter from here.

ABOUT THE AUTHOR

Sharon Bayliss lives in Austin, Texas with her husband and children. She hates wearing shoes and loves jogging in the rain. She only practices magic in emergencies.

She is also the author of the young adult science fiction novel, *The Charge*.

You can connect with her at www.sharonbayliss.com, www.facebook.com/authorsharonbayliss, and @SharonBayliss on Twitter.

www.ingramcontent.com/pod-product-compliance
Lightning Source LLC
Chambersburg PA
CBHW051648180726

48284CB00006B/1916